A WINDOW TO THE SUN

A WINDOW TO THE SUN

By

Lisa Whatley

Whatley Publishing

Denver, Colorado

This is a work of fiction and is not intended to refer to any actual persons, other than famous historical individuals mentioned in passing.

Copyright © 1999 by Lisa Whatley

Library of Congress Catalog Card Number: 99-94080

Whatley, Lisa
A Window to the Sun
324 p. 22.7 cm.

ISBN   0-9669868-0-6

Book Jacket Design by Carl A. Fisher
Proactive Syndicate, Inc. (PASI)

Printed in the United States of America
By BookCrafters USA

First U.S. edition

To my son, Lee Adhemar G. Feldshon

Acknowledgments

This book could not have happened without the help of my editor, Jan Beattie, an extraordinary human being, educator, wife, mother, and dear friend who never ceased to enliven, support, shape and motivate me in my desire to write. She has become a very dear friend whom I respect and love very much.

To my son, Lee Adhemar G. Feldshon, who believes in me and went through the whole book during his Christmas vacation to ensure accuracy and uniformity in my novel. His support and encouragement have been unsurpassed by anyone I know. His ideas and suggestions emphasized the symbolism and spirituality in my novel. For his friendship and love my most heartfelt thanks and my unconditional love.

To my husband, William J. Whatley, my gratitude for placing the manuscript within the specifications required by the printers.

Also, my everlasting gratefulness, admiration and deep love goes to the extraordinary souls whose lives inspired me to write this story.

1

It was a somber day. The funeral parlor had picked up the coffin at 8:00 a.m. at the tiny shack, which had been built for Arizle to spend the last days of her life. Just the day before, she had talked softly to the flowers in bloom through the picture window in front of her bed, and they seemed to respond by swaying with the cool breeze. She had enjoyed that window so much and had named it her window to the sun. She had loved light, flowers, the blue sky and the powerful sun.

A nurse had been called to assist Arizle with her last days. The nurse's name was Beatriz, but Arizle nicknamed her Bea. Bea was delicate, patient, soft-spoken, tender, and she seemed to have been sent by heaven. Bea had worked all day and she was asked to spend the night with Arizle. Arizle had been the one to ask Bea if she could work a double shift that day, and Bea had agreed with the sweet smile of a kind angel. Arizle felt as if that night would be her last among her loved ones, and with Bea at her side, she thought, her loved ones would not be able to sit near her and would not touch her and feel her skin losing its warmth. She wanted her loved ones to be spared the sensory reality of death's proximity. Arizle passed away at 11:30 that night.

A week earlier Arizle had been experiencing a deep conflict with death. She asked Bea to raise her head by placing extra cushions underneath her pillows, and she requested paper and pen to write a letter to her doctor. As she found a more comfortable position to write, she tried to control the shaking of her hands, fighting against the intimidation of mortality. She wrote:

> Dr. Hermogênes,
>
> There is an illness that is killing me, Doctor, and only you can help me—it is fear! Fear of contracting tetanus made me rip the intravenous needle from my arm. I was very sorry, because I lost a lot of blood that I cannot afford to lose. I did not take my homeopathic pills because I was afraid. I am afraid that I will go to sleep and die. I fear eating and not being able to digest it. I fear being poisoned so that I will die faster. I fear taking baths and I fear any medication. My blood pressure, my cancer, my pains—everything consumes my energies. Come to see me, for the love of God! An oncologist prescribed these pills of which I am sending you a sample. I am not going to take them, for I know the effect is like that of morphine. Please prescribe some medica-

tion that is not so strong. Come to see me; forgive me for my depression and state of mind.

Your devoted patient and friend,
Arizle Somar

When she finished writing, she asked Bea to place the letter in an envelope, stamp it and mail it. Her head was lowered once again by the removal of the extra cushions and she became lost in thought.

For the past week, Arizle had become very calm; she complained of neither pain nor discomfort. She seemed to have developed the patience of an angel and the forbearance of a martyr. Nevertheless, it seemed as if the nearness of death had bleached out much of her vividness.

Two hours before her death, Arizle had asked for Dr. Hermogenes. He agreed to come, and arrived in her room in twenty minutes. Arizle was bleeding from her nose, her ears and her mouth. She asked him not to give her anything to prolong her life, for she was tired and wanted to rest. Instead, Arizle asked him to give the men in her life, Ricardo, Rameda and Leumas, an injection for them to remain calm.

"Will you please help them, Dr. Hermogenes?" Arizle asked softly, and the doctor prepared the syringes and gave them each sedative injections. Rameda and Leumas embraced each other with a suffocating sob between them. Their Arizle was about to extinguish herself like the fragile candle that burned in the room. Ricardo was so benumbed that he could not think, talk or hear. Bea and Dr. Hermogenes both sat by Arizle's side.

Everyone seemed to have been stricken by the inertia of the soundless, lifeless atmosphere in the room. Suddenly, there was a weak cry.

"*Papai*," gasped Arizle, almost inaudibly, her lungs pleading for air but finding none. Her body fell still and her voice was silenced. Her heart had stopped and life had slipped away. Arizle's family knew that her last thoughts had been involved with the love and memories of her *papai*, her father. Bea waited silently for a few minutes, tears rolling down her face. After Dr. Hermogênes sadly pronounced her dead, fifteen minutes went by. Everyone in the room was still silent.

Bea broke the stillness and asked Rameda if she could prepare his Arizle to be buried. Rameda nodded his head numbly and lowered it in his hands, his teardrops continuing to fall on he dusty floor below. Bea moved Arizle delicately as she dressed the motionless body, gently tying her arms and legs in a straight position. The rain fell copiously outside, as if wanting to wash away all memory of Arizle. In a few hours the shack was deserted. Only a few pieces of humble furnishings were left behind, along with the white bedding soaked with her blood.

Arizle's casket was modest. It sat on a rustic table, almost flagrant in its simplicity. Her body was dressed in a blue chiffon sari, one of the garments she had enjoyed wearing when she entertained at one of her magnificent homes. Her face was stony and lifeless. The colorless lips were slightly distorted as if she had wanted to say something, but rigor mortis had set in mercilessly. Even after death, it seemed the suffering had not left her cold body.

The rain continued, warm and steady, very unlike the rain that had fallen near the beginning of summer. Inhaúma Cemetery was the poorest one, located in the suburbs of Rio de Janeiro. That is where she had wanted her funeral to take place, since she could not be cremated. She had requested that the money that would have been used for an elaborate funeral be instead donated to the orphanage for girls that she had started many years before.

Arizle wished to die poor, in the manner in which she had been brought into this world. She knew very well that the power of money could not prolong anyone's life. She gave away all that she had and professed a vow of poverty. Her funeral was reassuring to the few present that her last wishes were being respected by the executor of her will, her first husband Leumas. She was a woman of contrasts, a woman of spirit, a woman not ever to be forgotten by the four men who loved her, each in his own way.

The only sound in the shabby funeral room was that of the train, moving north on the railroad track. The high-pitched whistle sounded sad and senseless. The world fell still and noiseless. For the ones in that room, nothing mattered except that she had left them. Her husband Rameda's gaunt face was pale and wet with tears. Leumas, on the other hand, showed an almost spiritual serenity and composure. Though devastated by the loss of his former wife–the love of his life, his first cousin and best friend–he seemed to be at peace, for he knew that she suffered no longer. He was the only one present who seemed convinced that the body is only a temporary house for the soul. Rameda, desperate, anguished and desolate, was lost in a sadness so intense that he nearly cried out with the pain. The train's whistle sang to him over and over the meaninglessness of death.

Ricardo's thoughts revolved around his need for her. He could not conceive of not having her arms around him any longer; not kissing her cheeks while smelling the fragrance of her perfume; not hearing her laughter ever again; not turning to her for support; not depending on her to always tell him the truth in such a way that even the most unappealing truths sounded wonderful. It could not be—she was just sleeping. How would he survive without his mother?

Only a few attended the burial. Her culinary chef of twelve years wept silently; João, her butler, who had often sought her advice and guidance, had red and swollen eyes. Her sister and brother, faces seemed hard and scared of their own destinies, wondered at the prospect of life slipping from one's grasp so quickly.

Four pallbearers came into the room; one whispered something into Leumas's ears. Leumas nodded his head in approval. Ricardo stood, laid on her feet a bouquet of forget-me-nots, and kissed her cold cheek another time. They gently closed the coffin and lifted it from the table to carry it to the gravesite. The few in attendance followed the coffin in silence. The train's shrill whistle continued to play its melancholic farewell.

The small crowd stopped at a concrete crypt in a high place, just like she had wanted. The low-lying cemetery's graves filled with water during the rainy season. The thought of going below ground had always been distasteful to Arizle, and the possibility of submersion added to her dislike of being buried.

Arizle's coffin rested on the ground nearby while the men removed the concrete lid from the tomb. All kinds of insects crawled out. Several centipedes ran in frenzy. The light had awakened them all from their morbid sleep. The men slowly lowered the coffin inside the cold and desolate soon-to-be darkness. People stood a short distance away, some sobbing and others consoling. Once again, the locomotive's shrill note echoed the anguish of the mourners.

The sound of the stone rasping against the rough concrete edges of the crypt drowned out the sobs as the lid was replaced. The outside world continued still and soundless, until once again a train passed, leaving the smell of burned coal in the air. The engine noise was a sharp pain. She was gone.

The mourners retraced their steps through the stillness that surrounded them. Only the low prattle of the ones stricken by grief was heard. At the main gate, the tiny crowd dispersed, and, in groups of three and four, got into their cars and left Inhaúma Cemetery.

No one returned for the next ten years. Arizle could not be there for that place was cold and dark. Arizle loved the sun, lights, people, music and warmth. Her tenderness and passion for life would never be forgotten. Years later, a green marble stone with an inscription was placed atop the grave, replacing the colorless concrete one. The inscription contained Wordsworth's lines: "Though nothing can bring back the hour of splendor in the grass, of glory in the flower.... We will grieve not, rather find strength in what remains behind." Nothing could replace her splendor, her soft and tender touch, her elegant and refined manners, her kind hands, her brilliant mind, and her green eyes with all the softness of a loving kitten.

Thirty-eight years had passed since that mournful day in November. Inhaúma Cemetery is still there. Its modest graves and dirt roads still look as they did years before. The train continues to rumble and whistle as it passes, but the rain stopped long ago, and Arizle's body is no longer there–only dust remains inside the crypt. The bones had long since been removed and deposited by Ricardo in a vault in the city's cathedral.

2

A fair, little girl with beautiful green eyes came into the world on September 23, 1912, on the first day of the Brazilian spring. The little girl's father was neither an aristocrat nor a person of wealth like the Rapôsos, her maternal grandparents, and the grandparents had not really approved of his marriage to their daughter. Even though Arizle's mother's actions had not pleased her parents, they had invited their daughter to come home to give birth to their first grandchild.

The little girl was born in Sabará, a historic and wealthy colonial mining town near Belo Horizonte, capital of the state of Minas Gerais. Sabará was a charming town perched on the side of colorful mountains full of all kinds of semi-precious stones, silver, gold and other minerals. The little town had more churches than houses or businesses. Seen from the highway, it resembled one of Bruegel's paintings of little villages. Its streets were paved with river rock, making walking difficult and slippery. The churches, though plain and simple on the outside, were real treasures inside. The Rio das Velhas meandered through the town among the churches and other buildings, and the murmur of the water cascading on the pebbles created a tranquil and soothing atmosphere for the town residents.

The house where the little girl had been brought into the world with the help of a skilled midwife was built in Portuguese Colonial style. All the window covers and lovely second floor veranda railings were made of wrought iron, patterned after English lace. The façade of the house was covered with white stucco, and just below the eave was centered a magnificent rosette, surrounded by garlands of flowers in high relief. This design was so imposing and artistic that tourists stopped in front of the house to admire the workmanship.

Inside, the house was decorated in all the splendor of the Victorian style. Through a tall window the sun's rays penetrated, brightening the furniture and washing out the colors of Chinese and Persian rugs on the polished wood floors. Everyone inside the house had prayed for the child to be born healthy. The prayers were answered, for in the midst of lace of Cantú and white linens embroidered with the initials of her grandparents, slept the little girl, side by side with her mother. She had just begun her life journey into a world created by others. Her parents had decided to give up luxury for love, so although the little girl had been born amidst wealth, she was to live an impecunious childhood.

On the evening she gave birth to Arizle, her mother had asked God for the baby to be born before September 24, day of the Holy Lady of Mercês, an occasion of enormous celebration in Sabará. She wanted to be able to attend mass, and the date of the baby's birth seemed an answer to her prayers.

The infant was born with absolutely no hair, which concerned her mother, who for two years feared that her daughter would be bald forever. When the little girl turned two, she began to grow a head full of lustrous, ebony black hair so profuse that everyone was astounded.

The baby was named Arizle Somar, and she was baptized in a little eighteenth century church called Igreja de Nossa Senhora do Ó, an enchanting and magnificent little building. It housed some of Aleijad-inho's sculptures, which were considered prizes of Brazil's eighteenth century, and it was also home to a beautiful, refined altar carved of golden wood. Even though Arizle knew nothing of the location of her baptism, as the years passed and she grew older, she loved going back to the little church. For her baptism, she looked radiant in her angelic white gown, a present from her grandmother. When the brief ceremony concluded, everyone was invited for English tea and biscuits.

After a week of rest and chicken soup, Arizle's mother, Amélia Somar, took her back to their simple and poor home in Baiapendí, where her husband worked for the railroad. Baiapendí was a tiny town in the middle of nowhere with freight and passenger trains passing through several times per day. Amélia's home was modest, but spotless. She swept the house with herbs from the field and the sweet fragrance of balm mint lingered on the concrete floor long after the hand-made broom was left idle behind the kitchen door. The mournful whistles of passing trains often interrupted the chirping of small birds in her sunlit

11

garden. Amélia had grown accustomed to the constant noise of the trains, and she came to associate it with life passing her by.

Arizle's mother was a slim, gentle being with a lovely light soprano voice. The church's choir where she went to mass every Sunday was enhanced by her beautiful and educated voice. People came from far away to hear her sing Schubert's "Ave Maria." She was tender and soft-spoken and her husband claimed he had married her because he had fallen in love with her pigeon-like walk.

From an early age, Arizle presented a nature full of contrasts. She could be a little princess and a little devil all in the same day. Her father had to spank Arizle often, for she was a naughty, challenging girl, who asked questions constantly about everything she saw. Everyone but her mother was tired of answering Arizle's questions. Hers was a patience to be found only among the sweet angels in children's storybooks. When she did not have the answer, she suggested that Arizle look it up in an old encyclopedia that had belonged to her as a child, and Arizle would look up the answer, handling the encyclopedia with great care.

Amélia knew that her daughter possessed an enormous amount of curiosity to learn, and she supported Arizle's quest for knowledge. Amélia obtained new books for Arizle whenever she could. Whenever relatives came to visit and asked her what they should bring, she asked them to bring books for Arizle. Growing up among books was like having a magic carpet to fly away to endless lands of wisdom. Amélia often asked herself whether knowledge gave one real power, or whether the wisdom gained through experience was the more powerful force, and she wondered which would serve Arizle better to make wise choices in life.

3

rizle grew up surrounded by the affection and tenderness of her mother, her grandmother and her former wet nurse, babá Emilinha, who came to visit whenever she could stay for prolonged periods of time. The years passed by, for time has neither a port nor an anchor to stop it from its swift destination, and Arizle developed into an extremely intelligent girl, precocious and perceptive, sensitive and caring.

Emilinha, the former Rapôso family slave who became Arizle's nanny, developed a strong bond with the little girl, and it was obvious to anyone's eye that they cared deeply about each other. Emilinha had come to Baiapendí when Arizle needed a wet nurse, but once Arizle started to walk, she went back to Sabará, making trips to Baiapendí only when she could not stand to be away from Arizle any longer. As a girl of three, Arizle had run and hidden herself underneath Emilinha's skirts as she always did whenever her father pursued her, anxious to punish her. The multiple skirts that women wore in that era were the best hiding places for unruly, little girls.

Arizle loved to hear Emilinha tell stories. She moved her body and made funny faces while emulating the voices of the different characters in the stories. The fable of the Saci Pererê was one of little Arizle's favorite tales. The Saci Pererê, a Brazilian folklore figure, played pranks on anyone who came near the forests. He was described as being pitch black, having one leg, a red, pointed cap on his head and a clay pipe in his mouth. When telling this story, Emilinha managed to hide one leg under one of her long skirts, and she jumped like the Saci, making Arizle giggle with enjoyment. Saci Pererê was a persuasive figure for adults to bring up when they wanted their children to obey them. Emilinha, however, had given away the big secret to Arizle by letting her know that the Saci Pererê did not do any harm to anyone, especially little girls who were pretty like Arizle. Emilinha confided to Arizle that the Saci Pererê was a playful, harmless, joyful lad, just like any other child.

Whenever Emilinha was sewing or mending socks, she would sing a melody that described the cobalt blue butterflies in the forests of Minas Gerais. The metallic blue described by the former slave stayed in Arizle's mind long after Emilinha had finished singing the folksong. Emilinha talked to herself from time to time, and this habit led people to believe that she was simple-minded, but for Arizle, she was nothing less than a good woman, a loyal friend and a playful companion.

Emilinha had worked all her life for the Rapôsos, first at the spacious ranch house built in 1802 by their parents. Their emerald mines were famous in the region and their precious stones were marketed all over the world. After the liberation of the slaves in 1889, Emilinha's mother had decided, together with the other family slaves, to remain under the Comendador Rapôso's care. Comendador was a title given by the Portuguese emperor to citizens who were extremely philanthropic. A few years later, Comendador Rapôso received the title of Baron do Espírito Santo from the Emperor as well.

The Rapôso family was also nicknamed the Piabas, for whenever the Comendador was asked how he was, he would answer, "Vái-se piabando," an expression meaning, "We are getting along." The Baron did not change his manners or the way he treated others upon receiving his noble title. He believed in being down-to-earth and generous with everyone, and he also wanted to help his community preserve its history and traditions.

His wife started a once a year tradition of offering her servants a dinner once a year based upon a popular custom that had begun with landowners offering food to the poor annually. They believed that in return, they would receive God's protection against illness. She offered the servants a sumptuous Christmas dinner in the formal ballroom of the mansion. At these dinners, she set a long table with her best china, Portuguese silver and Baccarat crystal, and she served gourmet food.

Another ritual observed by the Baroness was that every night, in the gatehouse, a hot plate of food was placed on a small table for a homeless individual to come and eat a good meal. This unusual concern for the poor was known for a hundred-mile radius. Each night a different person had a good meal, slept on a clean cot, and left early in the morning before the sun rose.

Arizle's father's name was Cantarini Somar. He was of Italian descent and was a tall man for his generation. His green eyes, sculptured nose and bronzed skin made him a very handsome man. However, his personality was not as attractive as his physical appearance. He always seemed to be angry at the world, and he constantly demanded that chores be done here and now and not a minute later. His dutiful wife performed them all expeditiously, and he claimed he adored her for her fast reactions to his demands. She possessed a conciliatory nature, and whenever he asked that something be done, she abided by his orders. He never seemed to know how to request anything from anyone. Instead, he ordered his family members around constantly. Cantarini did not allow Arizle to go to the movies if she did not take her brother and sister. Whenever she wanted to go to the movies, she had to work hard selling eggs to make enough money to pay for tickets for herself and for her siblings.

Cantarini was a difficult man at home, but at his job, he was extremely responsible; hard working and honest. Whenever his boss asked him to perform a task contrary to his moral values, he would ask his boss for a written order, which he then executed expeditiously upon receiving it. Cantarini enjoyed hunting, and his yard contained large pens of dogs that he took on his hunting expeditions. Hunting was his passion. He spent his free time cleaning and polishing his Saint-Etienne rifles. Sometimes his relatives commented that he seemed to love them better than his own family.

Cantarini fathered five children. Two girls had died from whooping cough in a time when antibiotics did not exist in Brazil. A fourth girl and a boy grew up alongside Arizle and eventually married and had their own families. Arizle, being the oldest of the three children, was responsible for watching her sister and brother.

Arizle's father could be violent when one of the children displeased him. He lost control and spanked the children brutally, often leaving bruises and marks on their hands, legs and torsos. Sometimes he even beat them with his belt. His children were terrified of him, except Arizle. Several times he spanked her, telling her to cry, and Arizle's eyes remained dry. Nevertheless, it did not take much for Arizle to show her tears at the smallest reprimand from her mother. When Arizle misbehaved, all Amélia needed to say was, "Oh, little Arizle, how could you have done this deed?" and Arizle's eyes would shed tears of distress for having caused her mother such grief. Often sobs of repentance were heard and visible, until Arizle found that she had been forgiven.

Amélia suffered from a heart condition, and Arizle was aware of her mother's illness. Many nights Arizle lay awake, afraid that if she went to sleep, her mother would die, and she would never see her again. Arizle lived with the fear of death in her heart. She was careful not to upset her mother, whom she revered, but with others she liked playing pranks like the Saci Pererê in Emilinha's stories.

One day while Cantarini slept in the garden' hammock, Arizle went to the chicken coop, picked up some chicken excrement on a stick, and gently wiped it on her father's mustache. He woke up a few minutes later, incensed with all the females in the family,

19

claiming that they did not clean the house, for it smelled like feces! Even though Arizle enjoyed playing the prank, she was saddened by her father's insults to her mother about her house cleaning.

Her mother made Arizle's clothes with great attention to detail. Material for clothes was sent from time to time by the Baroness, and Amélia sewed for weeks at a time until every child was clothed. Arizle liked to dress in frilly, feminine fashions, and she was coquettish and flirtatious.

Arizle had an active mind that needed constant mental stimulation. In addition to being a voracious reader, she took great pleasure in collecting interesting pieces of broken crystal or porcelain that she found on the ground. Arizle kept the beautiful pieces of china and glass she found in soapboxes. The soapboxes in the early twenties were simply gorgeous. Frequently they displayed Limoges figurines on their lids, and Arizle loved her collection and was very protective of her boxes. Cantarini knew Arizle's weakness regarding the boxes, and he often took advantage of it by throwing the boxes out as part of a punishment. Arizle never cried in front of her father, but she hated him because of the way he treated her mother, sister, and brother.

Arizle loved life, loved to laugh, to climb trees, and to pretend that she was someone famous like Tarzan, Isadora Duncan, Madame Curie, or Helen Keller. However, she was hardly all tomboy. Since her early years, Arizle could change quickly from being Tarzan to behaving like a delicate little princess. By the age of ten she had read many good books written about great men and women. At grade school, Arizle marveled her teachers with her culture and knowledge of literature. She wrote beautifully and her handwriting was that of an well-educated upper class girl. Arizle never finished high school, because she was given too many other responsibilities, the weight of which children are not usually asked to bear.

Despite her lack of formal education, later on in her life, Arizle shaped herself into an erudite woman with a self-taught knowledge of chemistry, physics, biology, philosophy, medicine, religion and the literature of several different countries. She also taught herself piano. She played beautifully by ear and sang the songs of the past with her unforgettably sensual and sweet voice.

Arizle's most memorable trait was her tenderness and simplicity with ordinary people. No one who crossed paths with her could forget her. She always had words of incentive and praise for everyone. She was a passionate being: a young girl hungry to be loved, needed and wanted. She had many dreams for her life, but many of them were delayed or never happened, because her father was a self-centered man who placed his personal pleasure and desire to control others above the happiness of his children.

Amélia died at the age of thirty-three from a massive heart attack, and Arizle, age fourteen, was left without a mother. Arizle was devastated by her mother's death, never forgetting the woman who had been her best friend. She had revered her mother as a true biblical example of the model wife. She cried whenever she saw or heard something her mother had loved, and she always shared her mother's beliefs and wisdom with others as if they were the gospel.

4

Upon Amélia's death, Arizle's sister was placed in Catholic school and her brother sent to a seminary. At the time, Arizle was attending a commercial/technical school. Arizle had made some friends there, but was not allowed to invite them to the house. Cantarini saw his remaining daughter as a nuisance, and he decided to marry her off to one of his nephews. Arizle was told to marry her much older, first cousin Leumas. For Leumas, it was a dream come true, for he had loved Arizle all his life. He adored the young girl, but Arizle only loved him as a cousin, nothing more.

Cantarini wanted freedom from his duties and responsibilities as a parent. He frequently brought prostitutes to the house. The well-read Arizle, though a child in many ways, knew about sexually transmitted diseases, and she was very concerned for her siblings. She washed the bathtub and the toilet bowl thoroughly, but her sister caught a venereal disease from one of her father's call girls, despite her efforts to disinfect the tub and bowl with alcohol. Arizle sensed that her father wanted everyone out of the house so that he could lead the life of a young bachelor. He definitely did not want children interfering with his plans.

Arizle did not want to marry Leumas and told her father just that. Cantarini was furious with Arizle's audacity and refusal. He and Arizle had a terrible argument one day when Cantarini returned from one of his hunting expeditions. After lunch he had sat down at a small table and was cleaning his rifle. He called Arizle to keep him company. As she sat down near him, he told her that she would have no say whatsoever in the matter of her marriage, and that she was going to marry her cousin Leumas, and soon. Arizle replied that she could not marry him, because she was not in love with him. Cantarini explained that love would come later. Again Arizle refused and said, "No, I will not marry him!"

At that, Cantarini became enraged, and as he threw his rifle on the tabletop, it discharged, and the bullet struck Arizle in the thigh. Blood was everywhere. Arizle was terrified of her father's temper and his actions. After her wound healed, she abided by her father's wishes and married Leumas a few months later. She was short of fifteen by a few weeks on the day the wedding took place, and Leumas was thirty.

Arizle met with her cousin prior to their marriage and told him that she did not love him in a romantic, sexual manner. She pleaded with him not to marry her, but Leumas thought that by marrying her, he could protect her from her father's violent temperament. Arizle then asked Leumas whether, if she ever fell in love with someone, he would give her the freedom to marry the other party. Leumas assented, and gave Arizle his word of honor on the matter.

Leumas was one of six children. His father, like Leumas, was a graduate civil engineer and his mother a homemaker. Leumas had been a good child, well-behaved and thoughtful. He was slim and tall by Brazilian standards. His hazel eyes, fair skin and prematurely gray hair bespoke the countenance of a man with ethics and solid moral values.

Leumas was a self-made man who had often walked the twelve miles from his house to the center of the city, where the Escola Politécnica de Engenharia was situated, so that he could save carfare and buy lunch. He had to get up at four in the morning to get to class on time, yet he never thought that this schedule was a big sacrifice on his part. Instead, he thought that it was his responsibility to do anything and everything he could to achieve his goal of becoming a civil engineer. Leumas finished his doctorate in Civil Engineering at the age of thirty. His first job was measuring lands in the interior of Brazil, in the remote hinterland where the only visible lights at night besides the stars were the flickering ones from the kerosene lamps in the small shacks scattered in the wilderness. These tiny lights were the only signs of life in the darkness of the plains.

Leumas jumped at the opportunity to use his skills as an engineer, and he considered himself privileged to have found his first job so quickly, mainly because he was about to marry the girl of his dreams, his cousin Arizle. The wilderness of the interior of Brazil seemed like a good beginning for his professional career, and measuring remote lands seemed like an ideal first assignment.

Married life was a joy for Leumas, because he had married the girl he had loved as a child and he had work he loved to do. For Arizle, those early married years were hard work and no play. All the ranch workers had their meals at the large house of the owner of the ranch. Even though Arizle and Leumas were given a small house to live in, Arizle spent long hours at the main ranch house, where she had to cook for thirty men at a time. To do their laundry, she walked to the river, carrying heavy bundles of clothes. At the riverbank, she scrubbed the clothes until her hands were red and chafed from rubbing the shirt collars and cuffs. Her youthful hands were developing calluses as her skin toughed from the hard work. After three months, her hands did not hurt as much when she washed the heavy trousers the workers wore.

Arizle's life was very lonely, and often she was in total despair. She wished she had books, but they were hard to come by, and when she found one to read at night, the kerosene lamplight was hard on her eyes. Life was difficult and boring, and the routine was getting on her nerves. Her only escape was to write about her anguished feelings. She wrote after her morning chores were done, lunch for the ranch workers had finished, and all the dishes were washed. Arizle longed for those afternoons in which all her secret thoughts and feelings could surface on paper. She wrote and wrote, absorbed in her thoughts, consumed by her need to love.

One rainy afternoon, while locked in the outhouse, Arizle wrote on an old yellowish pad on her lap while tears rolled down her young face:

Fifteen Years Old!

If at fifteen years in this dark bed
I allow my curse to sleep
Today, tired of my bitterness
My soul opens up like a volcano

And in a gush of rage and madness
On your head my feelings will boil.
Fifteen years and only silence and torture,
Fifteen years and only agony and loneliness.

Damn you for the lost ideal!
For the harm you caused me by wanting
The love that died without having been born!

For the hours lived without pleasure!
For the sadness of all I have seen,
For the splendor of what I have not become!

Arizle was in turmoil because of her marriage.
She liked her cousin as a friend, but she had no romantic love for him. Sometimes she hated him for
having married her, for believing that a woman's love
for a man could be developed. She hated herself at
these moments of hopelessness, for she knew Leumas
was a good man and deserved to be loved by her. Yet,
she could never love him in the manner he needed.
Intercourse was a difficult and painful time for her.
She tightened her lips when Leumas kissed her, and
she had to control her feelings of nausea.

"Only God knows," she thought, "how much I
want to love this man, who is more like a father to me
than a husband," she repeated to herself. Lovemaking
was an ordeal for Arizle. While Leumas made love to

27

her young body, she tried to get her thoughts as far way from that moment as possible. She imagined herself as a princess in a castle with a beautiful garden in bloom. She imagined herself being Madame Bovary, young and in love with a man other than her husband. She imagined herself making love to a man whom she loved, feeling like a woman being seduced by desire, at the mercy of being enraptured with passion, admired and wanted. She longed to feel passion, and she dreamed to feel the climax that was described many times by the heroines in the books she read. Instead, the smell after sex was disgusting, and she detested it.

Arizle frequently sat by the river to write down the feelings that would not stay suppressed. In a book with pages yellowed by the sun, she wrote down her thoughts, her feelings, her desires and her dreams. One afternoon, after she had finished her chores, she wrote in her journal:

> My steps ran, delicately and swiftly on the road. My eyes fixed on the horizon, my lips half-opened in a smile, I was not running, I was flying! Hunger, cold, poverty, sadness, pain–nothing detained me, for I searched, looked for something beautiful, yet concealed. I wanted the future–I was fifteen years old. Why do I have to wait for love? In my search, I was about to find it. Then, no longer was I running as much, but I was in love—I yearn to find love. I want to feel it. In my restless desire, I say, "Where will my soul find your soul? My heart wants you, but I can not discern you. At thirty years of age what will I find? I will find pain. I lost you, oh,

my present! I lost you as I partially closed my eyes; with you, I lost faith, hope and often charity. I no longer believe in love from anyone or anybody. I feel lonely and tired of walking alone. My life seems dark; nothing attracts me or cradles my being. Nevertheless, I search for something to warm my heart. I move faster now. I search for the unknown. I seem to have found something. I stop and say to a lost silhouette, "Come into my mind, my dreams! Come in; do not wait in ceremony. Come in and stay within me. Do not abandon me, I want you, I need you. Oh, I want to be with you–you are not my past. I will not run; I will fly. I seize you and you envelop me in tenderness and feeling! Come in, present, and stay, before death takes over my soul."

Arizle found strength and consolation in her writing. She wrote almost every day, for it seemed to help heal her pain. Whenever despair haunted her, she turned to her writing.

One afternoon, sitting below a giant tree, she wrote to her mother:

Mother, dearest,
You are so close in my thoughts and so distant from my tired body, anxious for your understanding and tender arms. I want your arms to hug me against your warm bosom; I want you to love me, ugly, old, sick or unhappy. Only you, sweet Mother, can be my safe port which life

took away from me mercilessly while I was so young. Only you would receive me with real love, kindness and a true desire to make me happy. Through the tears that now drown my eyes, I see you, a wonderful woman and loving mother. I see your smile, always eager to share and give, to forgive and forget! You accept all just as they are, giving them your love without reservation. I see you doing your house chores, sacrificing your rest that is necessary for your fragile health.

How many wonderful examples you gave as all! How it has been difficult to follow them! I lack your fiber, your patience and above all, your humility. I see you during your visits to the doctors, when without tact, they would tell you that with a weak heart like yours, you would not live long and could die suddenly. I heard their statements and I experienced fear that consumed my days and my nights as a child, fearing to lose you. Not even the doctors with their diagnosis could change your facial expression, which always contained a sweet smile, your eyes full of the golden light that enveloped your being, your strength and your endless reserve of love.

I remember how you covered the defects and faults of others, persuading us to change our negative prejudice and our childish judgement. Today, Mother dearest, I turn my eyes to the past and I feel devastated for having lost you on the threshold of my youth and in the complete ignorance of my fifteen and a half years of life.

I ask myself, where did you find so much sweetness? Where? In your husband, my father? No, he was not like you. Not even in your children, for we gave you very little. I want you, Mother dearest. I need your patience, your strength, and your humility. I will have them, Mother, whether the world wants me to or not. I will have them, for I know that if I display these traits, they will be your crown of glory for all that you suffered and for all the love that you gave us! Little woman, how tall you stood in love to us all!

She felt calmer after expressing her thoughts to her mother. Warmth enveloped her, giving her courage and strength to continue the life of a married woman who wanted to love her husband, a good man, but could not. Although she had no prospects to find happiness or to make her life change, she felt she could endure.

Arizle also frequently wrote poetry. Her poems told of her fear of not ever having a happy future:

Fear

Do you by chance know
What is to be afraid?
Afraid of everything that we do,
Afraid of life, of death,
Afraid of your own destiny?
Afraid to look back?

To be afraid is to have a tortured spirit
By the sorrow and memories of the past.
Afraid to remember,
Afraid to be forgotten,
And of not to be loved,
Of living handcuffed in darkness.

To fear is to suffer, is to protest,
To cry and in moments of torment,
To God turn
For peace, for light, forgiveness and love.

To implore on your knees,
To listen to words of good fortune,
Of tenderness, of affection...
And from darkness
And from incomprehension nothing hear.

Once again, writing from her heart left Arizle in a calm, restful state, forgetting her responsibilities and the chores that waited for her. Her eyes drank in the beauty of her surroundings, and her ears reveled in the sounds of nature, as it felt alive around her. Arizle no longer felt alone. She listened to the wonderful melody of the wind in the trees. She wanted to have time stop, the wind cease, and the trees and flowers frozen in their beauty. She wanted her days to be just like that moment–sublime!

Leumas's working days were long and exhausting. He walked miles across the seemingly endless landscape, carrying his surveying instruments. Many times he had students trudging alongside him, learning the art of surveying. The tropical sun was torrid, the days were long, and the only rest he had was when he stopped for a sip of tepid water from his canteen or halted at noon to search for some shade in which to eat his lunch.

Arizle prepared his lunch everyday at daybreak. She got up at four o'clock and cooked fresh rice, warmed up the black beans, and put a pork steak and fried egg on top of the rice. The food was placed in a shallow metal pan with a lid. It could be heated by placing the pan over a cooking fire, but it was usually kept hot enough by the scorching sun of the high plains. Leumas's students were envious of his lunches, because each day Arizle would prepare something different for him.

Leumas was a good husband, patient and tolerant. During the week, he arrived home with little energy to talk or tell his wife about his day in the wilderness. Sometimes he would describe the magnificent colors he had seen in a rare bird or the frightening black scorpions he had seen crawling out of rotten tree stumps. Occasionally, he would come across rattlesnakes that came out in the sun to get warm. Life, however, was monotonous and uninteresting for a fifteen-year-old girl who had read the classics and had high ideals, ambition and zest for life. The backcountry did not fit the dreams of a vivacious, curious and intellectually demanding young woman.

During early spring, the days were glorious, with the sun shining in the cobalt blue skies as if it would never set, never fade away, never depart from her eyes. Arizle loved that fireball. She flung herself on the grass and shaded her eyes from the sun so that she could look directly into it. Its rays showed a thousand colors and she was mesmerized by their beauty. She felt inspired, turned over, picked up her note pad and wrote:

Lisa Whatley

I will go after him!

Satin shoes on my feet,
Light and a vaporous tulle envelop me,
Black hair flies loosely on my shoulders,
Cheek to cheek we dance.
The moonlight is bright
And so is his glance.
I glide on the floor and I see a smiling face.
Masculine, it is not a face of a man,
It is the face of my dream!
Cradled by him, I close my eyes and we dance.
My ideals dance and so does my youth.
Everything is exquisite and I feel at peace.
The moon gleams, the terrace is empty and I am
alone.
I dream!
Why? Why was it not like this?
I go back to reality. I have seen so many,
But not the man of my dreams!

5

Leumas wanted a child with Arizle, and he decided to talk with her about it. At first she did not like the idea, but then as she thought more and more about it, she seemed to feel that a child would fill the emotional void she experienced and would keep her company, and she would feel less lonely. Leumas promised to help her with the baby and take care of the child on weekends, so that she could rest and write. Arizle thought Leumas would make a great father, for he was a patient and a very caring human being. After some deliberation, Arizle decided she also wanted a child.

The nine months spent waiting for the baby to be born were long ones for Arizle. Her pregnancy was not an easy one. She continued to do all the chores, and as the months went by, Arizle became sluggish and tired easily. In the beginning, nausea prevented her from eating much and toward the end, she felt too tired to eat. She was just skin and bones and a big belly, which just kept on getting bigger. She could not find a comfortable position to sleep in and spent many restless nights. She thought of her mother several times a day, and held mental conversations with her mother, asking her to give her the patience and the sweetness to endure and not complain.

The last two months were very arduous, for the chores had to be done and restful moments were scarce. The other women helped her with the washing by the river, but the cooking was still up to her. The ranch workers came to eat at noon, after Arizle went outside to clang the big steel bell to signal that the meal was ready. The workers were dirty, and the smell of their sweat was like the odor of rancid butter left in the butter churn. She could hardly stand to be near them. That smell was unbearable, and the heat of the day made it even worse.

The wives of the workers sewed little shirts for Arizle's baby. Some of them were quite adept at embroidering and they all looked forward to helping with the birth of the child. Arizle had already chosen whom she wanted for her midwife, because she had assisted her with several births and had developed a lot of trust in her abilities. Joana was a heavy-set woman, who, despite her rough looks, had very gentle hands. She was a gift from God, a celestial bearer of comfort and security as she talked to the women in labor. She treated them as if they were her own daughters. No one on the ranch had more godchildren than Joana. Despite that, Arizle was not looking forward to experiencing the pain of childbirth that she had witnessed so often.

When the day arrived for Arizle, she found a piece of thick wood to bite on so that she would not scream. She did not want to scare Leumas, who was frightened and concerned for her safety and that of the child. After hours of labor and horrendous contractions, the baby was finally out of Arizle's womb and lying by Arizle's side. Arizle was exhausted and bathed in perspiration. Joana was going to replace her wet clothes with dry ones, but instead she sat and stroked Arizle's hair softly, saying, "It is over, thank God, and you have a beautiful baby boy." Arizle opened her eyes just enough to look at her son. The love she experienced was indeed sublime. She adored her son already, in just the few short minutes she had known him. She held him close and promised him that she would always love him.

The little boy was named Marcos, and Leumas was enchanted with his son. Marcos was baptized in the ranch's family chapel. The little boy was blond with hazel eyes like his father. He had the same nose, lips and delicately designed mouth as his father, and the shape of his eyes and forehead were like his mother's.

Marcos was not a healthy boy. Arizle spent many wakeful nights caring for him. He had one cold after another, earaches, and sore throats. She woke up whenever Marcos moved in his crib. She also changed him several times during the night so that he would never stay wet too long. Arizle adored her son and could not stand to think of the possibility of losing him. She talked to him all the time as if he understood her every word. Many times she felt that he could understand her, because his eyes would shine and he would smile, or his forehead would wrinkle and frown as she chattered nonstop. Most of the time he seemed to recognize and enjoy her voice.

Marcos's crib had been constructed by one of Leumas's students, modeled on the design of a seven-

37

teenth century child's bed. The crib was placed near Arizle's bed and she spent many hours watching her tow-headed son sleep. Marcos did not mind being in his crib as long as his mother was nearby. When Arizle resumed her regular chores, she took Marcos with her, and while she scrubbed the pants and shirts of the ranch workers, she talked to Marcos, telling him about his grandmother and his great grandmother, the Baroness. Arizle told Marcos the stories she had heard from her nanny Emilinha and her grandmother.

Arizle loved to describe the house in Sabará to Marcos. When she talked to him, her eyes were alive, her face was radiant, and her voice was animated.

"The jasmine bush outside the house filled the area with its aroma, Marcos," she told him. "Sometimes I sat on the window seat above it, mesmerized by the perfume. Now when I smell the fragrance of jasmine, I remember the times when I visited grandmother Rapôso and how happy I felt to be part of her household." Arizle remembered how Emilinha loved to sing when she was near the white jasmine tree. Her song told of a coat covered with stars, as her feet tapped on the floor. The song was about a very kind woman who had received a coat full of stars from Jesus as a gift. As Emilinha sang, Arizle recalled looking at the tiny piece of the sky visible through the window glass, framed by the delicate jasmine flowers. Suddenly Emilinha's song sounded real, not solely from the imagination of an old slave daughter. Arizle saw the coat of stars and she was sure in her mind that it had to have been a gift from Jesus. Marcos smiled at Arizle.

"Marcos," said Arizle, "if this song was sung by someone else in a different location, without the perfume of the jasmine shrub to accompany it, it would not be nearly so enchanting!"

Every Sunday in Sabará, Arizle told him, the children would go to mass at the chapel of the hospital for indigents. After the mass, the children had to take money to the sick. The children also carried baskets full of homemade marmalade, cookies, crocheted slippers and hats, and candied figs. They went from bed to bed sharing the goodies. "My eyes," said Arizle, "never left the cookies, and I wondered why it was that sick people liked them so much."

She continued, "How I enjoyed it when I visited my grandmother! Her cook's name was Sá Barbara. She cooked okra with ground meat and cornmeal. Oh, how I miss eating that delicious dish cooked by Sá Barbara." Arizle remembered how Sá Barbara stuttered when she got mad and how she would start an argument for no special reason. The only thing that she really liked was to pray at the church. The Baroness made excuses for Sá Barbara's temper, saying that she was a spinster, and everyone needed to be patient with her. When Arizle heard her grandmother say that, she wished she could grow up to be a spinster also, for then she could be rude like Sá Barbara and still be forgiven by all.

Marcos fell asleep listening to his mother's memories and stories. As Marcos grew up, he was delighted by his mother's stories and memories of her childhood. Marcos learned how to read when he was four. Arizle asked everyone who came from a big city to bring children's books for Marcos. Mother and son read together many afternoons in the shade of the trees that protected them from the hot sun.

One evening, Arizle fainted. She had not been feeling very well for several days. That night it was

Marcos who stayed by his mother's bedside the whole night. A doctor was called to examine Arizle and he diagnosed malaria. Leumas was devastated by the news. Joana told him that since they did not have antibiotics, he had to keep giving her tepid baths to lower her fever while giving her plenty of liquids. He spent every minute he could, giving Arizle baths and changing the cold compresses on her forehead. Leumas placed her in a large aluminum washbasin filled with cool water several times in an attempt to bring her fever down. Marcos was scared and he did not leave her side day or night. He slept on the floor near her bed. He did not want his mother to die.

After Arizle recovered from the bout of malaria, she thought she was well; however, a few months later, she developed yellow fever. She had jaundice and experienced excruciating headaches. Her legs, back, and neck ached as well. Leumas was afraid she would have kidney and liver failure, so he quickly made arrangements for Arizle to be taken to the nearest city for treatment. The hospital was poor, but the beds were clean and the nurses were kind and conscientious. Arizle arrived with Marcos holding her sleeve. The nurses immediately sent Marcos back home with Joana, who had accompanied Arizle into town. Marcos cried all the way back home. He ate poorly and missed his mother immensely. Arizle stayed in the little hospital for ten days. While in the hospital, she had two blood transfusions.

She made many friends among the other sick people whom she helped with words of support and reassurance. Nevertheless, she missed her son tremendously. She could not wait to see Marcos and hug him tightly. Leumas came to see her three times during her stay and brought news of Marcos. Arizle wanted to know if he was well, if he was eating properly and if he was crying for her. Leumas always answered yes to all her questions. Marcos cried everyday, wanting his mommy.

The day finally came for Arizle to go home. Marcos came with his father to pick her up. Arizle and Marcos were glued together during the trip back home. In the days afterward, Marcos did not want to leave his mother for one second, not even when she needed to use the outhouse. Marcos sat on the dirt outside the door and waited for her. He smiled at her when she got out and grabbed her sleeve again, holding on to it. He was then six years old and had grown to be a loving, caring, chubby little boy.

Arizle taught Marcos never to kill any animal. She always helped him take any crickets and butterflies that entered the house back outside, delicately placing them on a leaf or twig. Marcos and Arizle watched the ants build their hills, watched them carry their food into their holes, and enjoyed observing globefish develop into toads. They were inseparable friends. Marcos and Arizle especially enjoyed it when Marcos read aloud to his mother.

6

The work ended at the ranch, and Leumas moved back to Rio de Janeiro with his family. He obtained a job working for the Estrada de Ferro Central do Brasil, the main railway of the country. Leumas's responsibilities now were to check bridges and tracks, and to ensure safety for the trains that brought the daily commuters from the suburbs to the center of the city. In Brazil, the poor people lived in the suburbs and the wealthy people lived in the city.

Leumas and Arizle moved into a house by the railroad tracks in Madureira, a suburb that had its own shopping areas, hospital, and schools. Leumas and Arizle had no furniture, so Arizle bought several crates from a nearby store and built furniture with the wood from them. She painted them and arranged them so nicely that the bed tables, dresser, and coffee table all looked like they had been purchased at a furniture store. Everyone who came to visit was astounded by her ability to beautify even the most modest home. The front of the house had a large window that did not open. Arizle painted a cherry tree in bloom on it that was admired by passers-by. She also kept her home quite clean. Her pots and pans were polished with fine sand, and she set them on the back windowsill to dry. She had to move them after she received complaints from train engineers, who were blinded by the glare from them as they reflected the afternoon sun.

Marcos was placed in second grade. He read better than any other child his age, and sometimes even better than the teacher, who was always proud of and delighted by Marcos's intelligence. Marcos was extremely bright and advanced for his age. He already knew about botany, lepidopterology, solids and liquids, and volume, yet he still read constantly. At school he wrote plays, ballets and short stories, and composed music, as well. The teachers did not keep him for too long in second grade, for they decided with the director of the school that Marcos needed to be in fourth grade. Nevertheless, he was still bored with what the other students were learning, since he already knew much of it. He was only six and a half years old.

Marcos and Arizle continued to be inseparable. They read together, painted together, played together, and exchanged ideas and theories about what each other had read. Marcos was particularly interested in learning more about his mother's childhood and frequently he asked that she tell him more about the people of Sabará, their lifestyle and their folklore. Arizle had started collecting some of her writings for Marcos, and among them were stories about how her grandmother entertained guests. No one ever left the house without having had good conversation, a demitasse of freshly ground coffee with shavings of raw brown sugar, as customarily prepared in the state of Minas Gerais, and fluffy cookies made of manioc flour. That was not all. Everyone carried home a bouquet of flowers from the garden.

The main gate to the house was never locked so that the poor and hungry would always have access to the little room with the small bed and hot food. While everyone in the household slept upstairs, a poor person slept downstairs in the small room, well-fed and protected from the cold winter nights. In the morning, Sá Barbara went downstairs with a large black iron kettle with boiling water. She splashed the boiling water on the steps, scrubbed and washed the floor and the gate, upset because it was dirty. Behind her was Arizle asking all sorts of questions, "Why do you throw hot water on the steps, Sá Barbara? Why are you scrubbing the gate, Sá Barbara?" Arizle's nickname was "Why."

"Why do you let them sleep there, Sá Barbara?" That was a child's logic—why be upset if they will be sleeping there every night?

Sá Barbara answered, "It is your grandmother's idea, not mine." Not happy with this answer, Arizle continued, "Why do you think she wants them to sleep there, Sá Barbara?"

Arizle remembered her grandmother's rosary. It was made of crystal beads showing scenes of the life and death of Christ. Arizle loved to touch the beads while her grandmother prayed, and sometimes by pulling them too far, she made the Baroness lose count of her Ave Marias. Arizle also told Marcos of the big clock in the foyer of the house. When the hours struck, a friar would come out, and if it was raining, the friar had on his hood; if it was sunny, he would come out without his hood and strike the hour with a small hammer and then disappear inside the clock. The clock itself looked like a monastery. Arizle told Marcos that she would never forget Sabará and the generosity and love of her grandmother.

Leumas climbed the company ladder fast. He was a hard-working, competent man, and a considerate co-worker, who helped everyone everywhere. Soon after his second promotion, they moved to a better house in Engênho de Dentro, another suburb closer to the center of the city. His office was now in the building of the main railroad station. They had only lived a few months in the new house when he was offered a better house, this time underneath the Viaduct of Mangueira, in a private area where only employees of the railroad lived. The house was old, but solid, and Arizle spent countless hours arranging it, so that it would look like a real home for Leumas and Marcos.

When they moved back to the suburbs of Rio de Janeiro, Arizle had to get used to the loud whistles of locomotives approaching the city crossings. At first, she woke up every time the whistles sounded, but with the passing of the years, she had resigned herself to the fact that the wife of a graduate civil engineer had to live near railroad tracks and trains. Finally, she no longer noticed their shrill cries.

Leumas prospered rapidly, receiving many raises in pay, and in the following year, Leumas could afford to make some changes in the house. Arizle knew right away what she wanted done with the house, and she sketched the plans herself. A group of workers from the railroad came to do the remodeling. The first floor had three small rooms that Arizle changed into two larger rooms; new fixtures replaced old ones in the bathroom; and a small room and bathroom were built on the back of the house for a future full-time maid. Clothes closets were built in all of the bedrooms. On the first floor, a dining room was separated from the living room, the kitchen was enlarged and the pantry was provided with an abundance of cupboards. Marcos was eight years old and had his own bedroom. Arizle sewed two beautiful cushions for the living room and they also purchased two sofas and two coffee tables. This became the first comfortable home they had ever shared together. Leumas bought a phonograph and Marcos enjoyed playing his classical music, while Arizle loved the music of the twenties and the thirties. Arizle frequently danced alone while she cleaned and dusted the house.

Even though Arizle was living in the city, she saw very little of her father. Arizle's father had married a widow with four children, and they were living in Engênho de Dentro, not too far from Arizle. Arizle did not visit her father very often, for the stepmother did not want close ties with Cantarini Somar's children. She was very demanding, but Cantarini had mellowed and had become less overbearing in his older years.

Arizle heard from her sister, Laura, that her father was unhappy in the marriage, because his wife's children did not have much respect or love for him. Arizle discussed the problem with Leumas, who thought she should stay out of the situation, but be prepared to offer help if Cantarini called her for assistance. Arizle continued to hear dreadful stories about her father's treatment, but suffered in silence without taking a stand. Cantarini continued to keep his dogs, and apparently, his new wife did not like having dogs. To punish him, she would not feed the dogs, so they were always starving whenever their master of hunting expeditions approached them. Cantarini had always treated his dogs well, and for him to see that they were being mistreated was a sad experience. He had become a submissive man. Suffering at the hands of his new wife and making an effort to cope with his new life had changed him a lot. It seemed useless to complain, and it only aggravated the situation, since he had to live under the same roof with his stepchildren.

His stepchildren did not have jobs and frequently stole money from his wallet while he slept. They also asked him for money for everything, and the fact that they did not even want to get jobs upset him greatly. He had been a demanding man, often a brutal father, but he had worked hard all his life and had never asked for anybody's help regarding money. He had learned from an early age to make his own living and to be independent. He never asked the Rapôsos for financial help. If he had the money, he bought; if he did not, he did not buy. This state of affairs was making Cantarini sick. He could not say anything, because his wife would jump to the defense of her "babies." They were in their mid-twenties, no longer teenagers much less babies. Cantarini wanted them to develop a trade and get out of the house, but what Cantarini wanted no longer seemed to matter.

7

Carnaval season was approaching, and Arizle had never been to a Carnaval ball. She loved to dance but rarely did except when alone in the house. Then she would take hold of the broom and pretend that she had a man with whom to dance. Laura was going to a big ball in the city and invited Arizle to go with her. Arizle did not want to ask Leumas on her own if she could go, but she got together with Laura and a few other friends, who all together went to Leumas to ask him if he minded if Arizle went to the Municipal ball with them. Laura was paying for Arizle's ticket. Leumas agreed to let Arizle join the group of friends and attend the ball. Arizle made a beautiful gypsy costume for herself. The lower part of her face was covered, but her green eyes sparkled with the anticipation of attending the most famous ball in the country.

Arizle dreamed about the ball every night. She was beside herself with enthusiasm and excitement.

She tried on her costume several times and was delighted with the thought of dancing the whole night long with Laura and her friends.

On the evening of the ball, Arizle was euphoric. She set her hair, worked on her nails in the afternoon, and finally at ten o'clock, she was ready to be picked up. Marcos was reading in his room and Leumas was sitting in the living room trying to calm down Arizle. She had never been to any ball, much less one of this dimension. The Municipal ball was the society night in Rio de Janeiro. Leumas told her that she would enjoy it tremendously and that she looked beautiful.

Five minutes after ten, a car blew its horn softly at the front of the house. Her sister came into the house with her friend Miguel to fetch Arizle. They greeted Leumas and then left with Arizle. Leumas went upstairs to check on Marcos who seemed to have fallen asleep. Leumas picked up an engineering book and began to read it.

In the car, laughter was contagious. Arizle laughed for the pleasure of laughing, without totally understanding why they were laughing. The ride took twenty-five minutes, and they arrived precisely at a quarter to eleven. The streets were full of people dancing, singing and enjoying themselves. Sambas were being played everywhere and small groups of dancers moved their hips and feet in an extraordinary frenzy. Large groups of fifty to a hundred dancers where seen scattered all over the streets. The sidewalks were covered with confetti and serpentina, a multicolored Carnaval paper ribbon. Jesters and buffoons sang and greeted one another convivially.

The car stopped, and there were five friends waiting for Laura, Miguel and Arizle to arrive. When they saw Laura, they came to greet everyone. Miguel had to go park the car, and everyone else stood on the sidewalk waiting for his return.

Arizle immediately noticed a reserved individual standing at the base of the entrance ramp to the Teatro Municipal. She did not know who he was or what to say to him, but his eyes were on her as if he were seeing a vision. He was an incredibly handsome man with deep-set eyes, a finely sculptured nose, lustrous dark brown hair, beautiful teeth, and well-shaped lips with a meticulously trimmed mustache. Everything about him was sensational. Arizle thought he was as handsome as Clark Gable. As their eyes met, her heart began pounding uncontrollably, and her hands were shaking and perspiring profusely.

Miguel finally parked the car and returned to the group, and they all walked toward the large platform built exclusively for the street crowds to watch the famous and spectacular costume parade of revelers entering the theater. Arizle felt like an important person, walking on the platform toward the main door of the theater, and she even strutted a little. She wanted to be perceived as independent and self-assured, but it was really impossible for her to pretend to be someone that she was not.

Arizle had finally met the man of her dreams, and she did not know what to say or how to behave. She felt very insignificant near this man who looked young, handsome, and prosperous, yet vulnerable, too. She prayed silently to think of something intelligent to say, but her mind was drawing a total blank. She could not, for the first time in her life, think of anything appropriate to say as they all walked toward their table in the middle of the stage.

Every year the opera house known as the Teatro Municipal became the location for the Carnaval ball. A large wooden dance floor was built over the orchestra pit, and the stage became the area where the tables were set. The theater was richly decorated for the festivities. Three thousand American tourists were in Rio and at least three hundred were participating in this big event. The costumes were dazzling; plumes, feathers, pearls and semi-precious stones adorned the skirts and the tight-fitting pants. The women were beautiful, with supple skin, perfect makeup, glittering nails, and elegant hairdos styled by famous salons. Everywhere men looked, there were the women: gorgeous, sensual and ready to flirt.

There was a lot to see, and Arizle did not want to miss anything, but her eyes from time to time would meet the eyes of the young man. She whispered to Laura, "What is his name?"

Laura whispered back, "Miguel told me that his name is Rameda."

It was the most beautiful name she had ever heard. Rameda!

Arizle and Rameda could not stop gazing at each other. Arizle noticed his hands, with his long and sensual fingers. Rameda gazed incessantly into her emerald eyes. Laura noticed the silent connection that was kindling between the two, and decided to remind Arizle that the evening was an occasion for dancing with friends and not for romance. Laura leaned toward Arizle and whispered in her ear that she should not forget that she was married and had an eight-year-old son. Arizle's mind was far away. Her sister's words echoed only distantly. The music was loud and she was completely enthralled.

Rameda arose from his seat, came toward Arizle, and invited her to dance. She moved so quickly toward the dance floor that she forgot she had left her evening bag on top of the table. She had meant to place it on the floor underneath her chair, but it was too late to go back for it now. She did not want to delay dancing with Rameda for a single second. Rameda touched her hands and a searing tingle shot up her spine. The music was too loud to talk, and it was a relief for Arizle, who could not speak—her mouth was dry and her throat scratchy. Rameda did not remove his eyes from hers, and they danced the whole night, retreating to the table briefly for refreshments, but returning to the dance floor as soon as they could.

Rameda asked Arizle to remove the veil covering half of her face. She declined, saying that she was very ugly and deformed on the lower part of her face, and so she could not remove it. His curiosity increased with each hour that passed, but Arizle kept her veil in place, removing it only once in the ladies room where she went to powder her nose. When she left the powder room, Rameda was outside, smoking while he waited for her. He took her hand, and they returned to the dance floor.

It was three in the morning, and Arizle and Rameda were dancing cheek-to-cheek. They did not say much to each other, but as time passed, and the moment neared that would end the enchanting night, Rameda insisted that he had to see Arizle again. She did not tell him that she was married or that she had a son.

It was now five-thirty in the morning and everyone in the group was exhausted. The only time that they had only stopped dancing was to watch the dazzling costume parade that was the highlight of the ball. Laura knew that it was time for her and Miguel to take Arizle home. They rose from the table, saying goodbye to one another. Arizle wrote her phone number on a napkin and discreetly gave it to Rameda. Rameda walked to the door with them.

At the door, Rameda kissed Arizle's hands, then gave her a soft kiss on the cheek. Arizle had thanked everyone for the wonderful time and begun to follow her sister, when Rameda said he wanted to walk her to her car. Arizle said nothing, so he took her hand as they left the theater and did not relinquish it until they reached the car. Laura was very apprehensive. She was thinking how much her cousin Leumas had trusted her and that now she could lose his respect, friendship and affection because of Rameda's and Arizle's actions. How was she going to explain that Arizle had danced and held hands the whole night with Rameda? Who was Rameda, anyway? She knew nothing of him or his family, since she herself had only met him that night.

As they arrived at the parked car, Rameda once again kissed Arizle's cheek. When Arizle got into the car and they had started moving, Laura told Arizle that she was very upset by her behavior and that she wanted to talk with her later that day. It was close to six o'clock.

When Arizle arrived home, Leumas was having coffee in the pantry. Arizle said good morning to him, explaining that she was tired and needed to sleep for a few hours. It was Tuesday morning, and Leumas responded that he was going to read the newspaper, water the plants, and go to the vegetable market for her. Meanwhile, he said in a fatherly manner, he thought she should rest, for she looked weary.

Carnaval festivities took place just before Lent began and lasted for three days and four nights. In those times, the event was a family occasion, and there was little crime. Children, parents, and friends danced freely in the streets, on buses, streetcars, and in open cars. There was no other party in the whole world like Brazilian Carnaval. People from all walks of life talked to each other and danced together as if they had known each other for many years. It was the feast of the masses, but the masses then had self-control and social graces. All the stores and businesses closed for those three days. Only a few food shops and restaurants kept their doors open. Arizle had enjoyed taking part in Carnaval for the first time in her life. She saw that she was not the only one fond of dancing and music. She had seen thousands like her that evening.

Arizle brushed her teeth, took a shower and went to bed. Though exhausted, she could not sleep, and she could think of nothing but Rameda. She could feel his hands touching hers, feel his last kiss on her cheek, feel his eyes watching her, and sense the proximity of his body near hers as they danced at the end of the evening as dawn was about to break. The image was so vivid that she felt the heat of his presence in the bed with her. She imagined kissing his lips and tasting the flavor of his saliva in her mouth. Never had she felt for Leumas what she was experiencing just thinking of Rameda. She sensed that her life was about to change forever.

Arizle was too immersed in her thoughts of Rameda to feel any guilt about her new feelings. She did not want to think of the present—only the future mattered. In a few hours, she knew Rameda would call, and she needed to rest and to decide whether she should tell him the truth. Fear shadowed her thoughts, for Rameda was so handsome, so debonair, that if he knew she was married, he would not want to see her again. He should fall in love with a single girl, one of those gorgeous young women whom she had seen dancing at the ball. This thought saddened her and tears ran down her cheeks. As she dropped off to a deep sleep, the last words she mumbled were addressed to her mother's spirit. "Please, Mother dearest, help your daughter!"

Leumas went into the bedroom to check whether she was asleep. Marcos also had gone to spy on his mother. He could not remember ever seeing her sleep so late. He asked his father what time she had come home, and he laughed when his father told him that she had probably had fallen asleep around seven o'clock.

Arizle woke up at one-thirty in the afternoon. From bed, she went straight to the shower, spending ten minutes under the hot, pounding water. She dressed and went downstairs for a weak cup of coffee. Marcos and Leumas wanted to know all the details of the ball. Arizle had to make an effort to describe what she had seen without mentioning Rameda. She told them of the wealth of costumes parading before her eyes, of the beautiful women in opulent attire who danced with men in elegant tuxedos. She told them of the dazzling decorations adorning the theater. Leumas asked her who else she had met at the ball and whether she had danced. Arizle carefully answered that she had danced with Laura's group of friends. "They are the same people with whom Laura goes out all the time," Arizle said casually. She ended the conversation suddenly by saying that she had to check the refrigerator to see what she needed to purchase, if anything, to cook for dinner.

Marcos went to watch his mother check for salad greens and wash the few dishes left from their breakfast. Arizle seemed distracted, and Marcos had to ask questions twice before she answered him.

"Mommy," he asked kindly, "why are you not paying attention to what I am saying?" Arizle dismissed his question by asking him if he had finished the oil painting that he had been working on the day before. Marcos responded that he had a little more painting to do in order to finish it. Arizle then suggested to him that he should finish it, for they needed a painting to hang on the west wall of the living room, and his landscape would be ideal for the location. Marcos agreed, kissed her and went upstairs to his room.

Arizle was alone with her thoughts once again, and her mind was on Rameda. She began to daydream over the dishes. "What an enchanting man!" she thought, as she imagined herself in his arms. She felt slightly embarrassed by her thoughts, but then her mind quickly raced ahead to thinking about how life would be with Rameda, how it would be to be kissed by him, make love to him, spend all night sleeping by his side in his arms, to have his child. It would be marvelous, she thought. Nothing could be more divine, more romantic, more inspiring. As she washed the dishes, she looked at her hands and thought that she should be more careful with them. The skin was very dry and rough. Perhaps she should buy some rubber gloves and use hand lotion every time she had them in water. She should take care of her hands for Rameda. He had kissed her hands twice, and he would kiss them again if they were soft and showed no calluses.

She was very quiet the rest of the afternoon and into the early evening. She could not think of anyone but Rameda. She was afraid that Leumas or Marcos would answer the phone when he called. She did not know how to cope with the devious thoughts she was having. She had decided not to tell Rameda that she was married, not immediately. She also was not going to tell Leumas that she had met another man just a few hours ago and had fallen hopelessly in love with him. Leumas would laugh at her and say that it was just a girlish infatuation on her part.

Above all, she did not want to hurt Leumas or Marcos. What was she going to do? At that very instant, the phone rang. She jumped and went running toward the phone. Fortunately, Leumas was at the dining room table, working on a bridge design and did not notice her hasty move toward the phone. She picked up the receiver and said, "Hello" in a faint voice. She wanted to sound more confident, but her voice would not come out. She heard Rameda's voice on the other end. An electric charge raced through her spine.

Rameda said, "Hello, Arizle. Were you able to sleep?"

"Not too well. I had problems falling asleep." Rameda said that he had not been able to sleep at all, and that he wanted to see her again. Arizle was concerned that Leumas, who was in the same room, would overhear, but Leumas was immersed in his project and did not hear a word she said. Arizle asked Rameda when he wanted to see her.

He promptly answered, "Within the hour. I will come and pick you up at your home." Her heart started to beat so fast that she felt faint and thought it should surely burst through her chest. She did not want to say no to Rameda, for she did not want him to think that she was not as interested as he was. But he couldn't come to the house, and how was she going to leave on the evening of the last day of Carnaval without it seeming suspicious and unnatural? She hesitated for a second, then said that she could not leave her father, for he was elderly, sick man, but tomorrow if it was convenient for Rameda, she would meet him downtown in front of the Municipal Theater. He answered that he would pick her up at her home the next day, but she replied quickly that she was going to be shopping downtown with Laura that day, and so it would be easier to go and meet him there so that he would not have to come all the way to Mangueira to fetch her. He said that he would be waiting for her at 2:00 p.m.

Arizle was frantic when she hung up the phone. She was gasping for breath, her heart was palpitating, and her forehead was covered with perspiration. Leumas seemed too involved in his blueprints and plans to notice anything. She went into the bathroom and sat down on the toilet seat to think. What was she going to do? The thought of deceiving Leumas put her mind in turmoil. She did not have the heart to remind him of his promise of almost nine years before, when he said he would give her freedom if she fell in love with another man. His words echoed in her brain, and she was anxious, unhappy and confused by the conflict between her duty as a wife to Leumas and her strong feelings of love for a man whom she had only seen once.

At this moment, there was a knock on the door. "Mommy," Marcos called out, "I finished the painting." Arizle asked Marcos what time it was. He answered that it was seven o'clock. She realized that she had been sitting there for two hours. She opened the door, and Marcos hugged her joyfully and took her into his bedroom. His painting was lovely, she thought, and she complimented his work and left the room to get a hammer and nail. The painting looked wonderful on the wall, and all it needed was an attractive wooden frame. Marcos was so proud and happy that his mother liked his work. Leumas also commented that the painting was beautiful and that he had a very talented son. From then on, Marcos worked hard at sculpting such things as Indians, falcons and airplanes out of long bars of soap to adorn the living room. After Marcos finished the sculptures, he would coat them with clear varnish. When the Indian, falcon, lion and horse heads were varnished, they looked like they were made of soapstone. Arizle thought her son was an extraordinary child. His talents were diverse, and she thanked God many times for giving her such a talented and intelligent son.

The next day, Arizle arose early to wash her hair and patch up her nails, which had chipped when she was washing dishes. She had read that women with her skin color should use red nail polish. She selected a dress from the limited choices in her meager wardrobe. She wished she had a new dress to wear, but her small allowance went to buy supplies for Marcos's creative endeavors. Her sandals were not new, but she removed the marks on the front and heels and polished them.

She told Leumas that she was meeting Laura downtown to accompany her to the doctor. She called Laura while Leumas was in the shower, and begged her to cover for her if Leumas happened to ask her about the visit to the doctor. Laura was the product of Catholic schools and was against Arizle's meeting with Rameda. Nevertheless, she had known for many years that her sister had been miserably unhappy in her marriage to Leumas, and reluctantly, she agreed to

help her.   However, she warned Arizle that she was
about to commit a sin by meeting a man other than
her husband.   Arizle did not need to be reminded, for
she knew that society would condemn her and that the
Catholic church would excommunicate her if either
one found out about her infidelity.   She had never
been a practicing Catholic, even though she was a de-
vout follower of St. Anthony and other saints whom
she admired and loved. Arizle prayed frequently, without being aware that her words were different and
more personally meaningful than the set prayers in the
Missal.   She talked to God frequently, asking Him to
help the sick and injured whenever an ambulance
passed by. She asked God to bless the flowers and the
birds. She thanked God for the moonlight, the sunset
and all the wonders of nature.   Nevertheless, anytime
she was asked about her religious preference, she
would answer that she did not have one.

Living in a Catholic country had many implica-
tions regarding an individual's freedoms versus a strict
moral religious code.   There was no divorce, only legal
separation, and if a couple had married in one of the
nearby countries, such as Mexico or Uruguay, which
had legalized divorce, the marriage was not legal in
Brazil. In the eyes of the church, marriage was a permanent pact.   There was absolutely no recourse from
the signed document in the religious or the civil
courts. As a result, the country always had a multi-
tude of couples who, according to both sets of rules,
lived in sin.   These unions, sometimes of twenty or
more years, were taken seriously by the families and
their children, despite the rules of the church and the
government.   They were reason for gossip, alienation
by society and scorn by acquaintances. Children from
a union other than the one with the legal spouse were

considered to be the children of the legal husband. The real father could not register them and take paternal rights over them. They were illegitimate and society let them know in many ways that they had no value as human beings. Napoleonic Law covered the rights of the citizens and there were many incongruities and paradoxes beyond the understanding of any sensible and practical mind. Women in those years had little say in the eyes of the law. Frequently generations of families were divided, because children had left an unbearable conjugal situation to build a different life for themselves. Parents did not talk to their children for ten or twelve years at a time, or even a lifetime, because their children had left their legal spouses to live with another individual.

Arizle was cognizant of all that, and she knew what was expected of her, if and when she decided to leave Leumas. Even Leumas's consent would not guard her from prejudice and judgement by others. People thought that living with another person who was not one's legal spouse was living in sin, and that was that. The fact that the "sinful" parties became emotionally scarred was not taken into account.

Arizle left the house around 12:30 p.m. The bus ride could not take much more than an hour, she thought, and she did not want to be late. She walked briskly from her home to the bus stop, waiting for the right bus for about ten minutes. She wanted Rameda to think her elegant and beautiful, but she thought this was impossible, since she always thought of herself as an unattractive woman. The source of this notion was the fact that her lower teeth were slightly crooked. Though nearly unnoticeable to others, it was magnified ten times in her mind. Braces were unheard of in Brazil, and orthodontists did not even exist. Arizle had read that in Switzerland, children were starting to wear corrective appliances on their teeth. Arizle did not expect this technology to come to Brazil any time soon.

Arizle knew that she had to change the alignment of her teeth on her own, even though no one but her noticed this peculiarity. She exercised her jaw daily, pulling her chin backward to get her upper teeth to close over her lower teeth. She tied a strap around her chin and the back of her head at night to force the lower teeth into place. She was a woman with perseverance and tremendous self-discipline. Arizle made up her mind that she would conquer her problem by the time she reached twenty-five. She did her exercises religiously every day, and Leumas and Marcos admired her fortitude. They often told her that she was a beautiful woman, despite the slight malocclusion in her bite. The daily exercises and her determination eventually paid off when her bite finally became normal.

Arizle changed the position of her teeth, but she did not change her mental image of the deformity. Her teeth were not out of alignment, and her bite looked right; nevertheless, the thought that she was not an attractive woman haunted her all her life. Only Leumas knew how she felt. Leumas was the only person she trusted with her insecurities. For the outside world, she managed to put on a brave front. She knew Leumas loved her, no matter how she looked.

8

Rameda was waiting for Arizle in front of the Municipal Theater. He was certainly dressed very fashionably, and he looked very dashing to Arizle. She saw him before he spotted her, and thus had a few seconds to admire him and see the other women looking at him as well. He was dressed in a beige gabardine suit, light blue shirt with his monogram on the sleeve cuffs, a beige, cinnamon, and chocolate silk tie, brown socks, brown shoes and a brown belt with his initials on the gold buckle. On his head, he wore a raffia fedora with a dark brown hatband. She felt insecure and out of place in her old dress and well-used sandals. He saw her and went hurriedly toward her. He took her hands and kissed them both. Her mouth was dry, just like the last time they said goodbye. She had to make an effort to move her tongue and enunciate the words with which she had thought of greeting him. A fuzzy "Hello" came out, as if she were trying to swallow and talk at the same time. She was petrified that he would not want her, for she knew she was ugly.

Rameda did not compliment her dress or how she looked. Instead he asked her if she wanted to have grape juice and fruit sherbet and go to a movie. She opted for the grape juice. At the café he kept reaching for her hand, but she was afraid that a family member or an employee of Leumas would see her holding the hand of a stranger. Arizle tactfully would pretend that she was checking her handbag or fixing her hair with her hand. She looked nervous and vulnerable. Rameda paid for the fruit juice and they left, with Rameda holding her elbow as they walked side by side. He asked her how long she had been living with her father. She answered that she had been living with him for over three years and that she had a godson who lived with them as well. She quickly changed the conversation by asking him if he had any brothers or sisters. He told her that he had nine, and that his father and his uncles, a total of six men, had married six sisters. Arizle asked if they were cousins, and Rameda said that they were distant cousins. "Some day," he added, "I will show you the pictures of them all together on the wedding day they all shared."

Rameda, Arizle thought, had to have money for he was dressed impeccably and his jewelry was of real gold. On his left ring finger, he had an engineer's ring. Every profession had a special type of ring: a lawyer's ring had rubies, a medical doctor's had emeralds, and an engineer's had sapphires. These three professions required a doctorate, and very few could afford to enter one of them. He saw her looking at his ring, and he commented casually that he had received it as a gift from his father when he had finished his doctorate in engineering. His ring was beautiful; it had two large diamonds next to the big sapphire in the center. One side had the insignia of engineers and the other side another design that she did not recognize. His hands were gorgeous and his palms without calluses. Arizle was completely enchanted with the man at her side.

Rameda broke the silence by telling her that she had the most beautiful eyes he had ever seen. He added that her hands were beautiful, her fingernails lovely, her black curly hair dazzling, and that she walked with the grace and delicacy of a small pigeon. She thought of her father, who had described her mother's walk in the same manner. She smiled and did not comment.

He stopped and put his arm around her shoulders before they walked on. She became worried that she would be seen being embraced by a man other than Leumas. Her concerns subsided when they arrived at the cinema and he had to let go of her to buy the tickets. When they entered, they sat down in the seats in the last row. He leaned toward her and kissed her on the cheek. She did not know how to behave or what to say. Her mouth was still dry, despite the grape juice and ice water she had drunk. The lights went out, and the world news came on the screen. He turned her head toward him and kissed her on her lips. She felt numb. She could not hear any sound, and his tongue was moving inside of her mouth like a fire swirl. She thought of pushing him away from her, but she could not do it. They kissed passionately during the whole movie, and he could not let go of her.

Those kisses were like firebombs hitting her heart. She could not breathe, she could not talk; she just felt the heat of his long, wet kisses. The movie ended and they both had no idea what they had seen. They were almost anonymous in the back row, and fortunately at that time of the day, few people had gone to the movies.

As they walked out in silence, she immediately put on her dark glasses. She kept looking in the shop windows as they went by, to see if her lipstick had smeared, but she could not see anything. She told him that it was nearly six o'clock, and that she had to go home and prepare dinner for her father. He asked her to stay, but she sadly replied that she really could not. He asked her when he would see her again. She replied that her godson needed her help with homework, and that her father was very strict and did not like her to date. All her excuses served to add some mystery and intrigue to their relationship. He was in love with her. His eyes told her that every minute. She was desperately in love with him. She wanted what she felt to be desire, to be only desire, but it was more than that: they were totally in love with each other.

He told her that he would call her next day. He placed her in a taxi, paid the driver, and walked away, looking at her until the car disappeared in the long Rio Branco Avenue. She arrived home. Leumas had been worried about her. He had called Laura's home, but there was no answer. Marcos was happy to see his mother, for he was used to being in her company, and without her, the house felt deserted. They had hired a full-time maid a week prior to the start of Carnaval. Even though she had started working for them immediately, she informed them that she would not work during those three days and would only be back on Ash Wednesday. Francisca was her name and she liked children, but Marcos thought she was very boring, always repeating herself when she talked.

Arizle sat at the dinner table with them, but ate very little. She claimed Laura had taken her for a refresco, and that she had eaten too much cake and ice cream. Marcos wanted to tell her what he had read and what had occurred at school, but she seemed distracted and her mind appeared to be far way. He called upon her to pay attention sweetly.

"Mommy," he said, "why are you not paying attention to me?" Arizle denied not being attentive and asked him to repeat what he had asked her before. He did, but he did not hide his annoyance with her. She placed her arms around him and kissed him on both of his cheeks, his hair, and his eyes, and told him that she adored him. He smiled and kissed her back, telling her he loved her deeply.

Leumas finished his dinner and went to do some reading for his job, sitting on the sofa in the living room. Arizle and Marcos went upstairs to read stories together. The maid Francisca cleared the table, washed the dishes, and went to her room. Marcos and Arizle heard Francisca turn on the radio in her room. Arizle asked Marcos if he would read aloud to her. He agreed and began to read a new book about butterflies that his father had given him, but Arizle's could only focus on Rameda and her actions. She felt terrible that she had told so many lies. She hated herself for not having the courage to tell Leumas, but she had no idea what she was going to do or what the future held for her. She felt like a criminal, a horrible, despicable human being who should have no right to happiness.

Marcos got up to brush his teeth after an hour of reading. His mother followed him into the bathroom and sat on one side of the bidet, while he stood in front of the sink, using dental floss and massaging his gums. Arizle had taught him all about what she had read in a periodontic journal on her last visit to a dentist. Marcos excused himself and asked her to wait outside while he went to the bathroom. She had also taught him about refinement and manners. She went out to sit on his bed and wait for him.

Marcos opened the door and jumped in bed with her. Now it was her turn to read aloud, and she continued for another half-hour until he fell asleep. She got up from his bed and went to take a bath. She was physically and mentally tired, and the hot water soothed her back and her spirits. While in the tub full of hot water and aromatic salts, she looked at her breasts, her body, her legs, and her feet and thought they were quite lovely. She indeed had a beautiful body and nice, shapely legs. Her ankles were thin, as were her wrists, and these she had read in a book were the signs of an elegant and refined woman. She wanted to be refined, and she did not realize that she had always seemed to be refined, having been brought up by a refined woman, her mother.

Leumas knocked on the bathroom door. She told him that she had a headache and was trying to get rid of it by relaxing in hot water. She told him to go ahead and come in, brush his teeth and get ready for bed, for she was going to stay in the tub for another ten minutes or so. When she finally went to bed, he was already asleep. She was glad that she did not have to share the details of her afternoon with him.

The next day, Leumas left early for the office; Marcos left with his father, who was going to drop him off at school. Marcos attended an American school called Colégio Anglo Americano. This was a school for children of American diplomats and businessmen who lived in Rio de Janeiro and worked for branches of American businesses. The school was very advanced, and Marcos enjoyed being with other children of his intellectual level. Marcos had jumped two grades once again, and he was happy in high school despite being only eight years old. Luckily, the school offered extra curriculum courses during the months of January and February. Marcos did not have to be on vacation for the entire summer. He enjoyed going to school and this activity kept him from being surrounded by adults all the time. Arizle wanted him to develop friends other than his parents.

When Leumas and Marcos left, Arizle was alone with the maid. She told Francisca that she was going to clean upstairs on her own and Francisca did not need to worry about the second floor that day. Arizle took the opportunity to call Laura. Laura was not supportive of her actions, but did promise to help her whenever she needed it. Arizle shared with Laura that she was in love with Rameda and in total turmoil for having to lie to Marcos and Leumas. She related to Laura that she felt guilty and ashamed of her behavior and deception. Laura warned her that she was going to create serious problems with her behavior and that she hoped that Arizle would find happiness in the midst of all the complexities that awaited her. She told Arizle that she was quite sure that Rameda came from a very wealthy family who was very Catholic. Laura added that Rameda and she would never be able to marry and that the situation would eventually become too much for Arizle to handle.

"What are you going to do, Arizle," Laura asked, "when Rameda's family repudiates you? How are you going to feel if Rameda's brothers and sisters refuse to accept you? Arizle," Laura declared, "you are playing with fire!" Arizle had thought about all that. Their love, she thought, would break through all barriers. She just wanted to be with him.

As time went on, it became easier for Arizle to lie, even though deep down she knew it was destroying her. Within the six months that Arizle and Rameda had been seeing each other, Rameda had rented an apartment in Tijuca, a lovely barrio where many traditional families had their homes. That apartment became their meeting place, and in it Arizle lived the best moments of her youth, making love to a man that she adored. Their sexual relationship was sublime in terms of the tremendous respect they had for each other's feelings. He took his time kissing her and caressing her beautiful body. He loved the softness of her skin. She adored feeling him inside her. An orgasm with him was a fleeting manifestation of an overwhelming feeling of belonging, of loving with all the passion of her young heart. She understood what the heroines in the books felt when they were possessed by men they adored.

One rainy afternoon, Arizle had to disclose to Rameda that she was pregnant. No one knew except the doctor that she had gone to see. It was time for Arizle to tell the truth, not only to Rameda, but also to Marcos and Leumas.

9

Arizle never forgot that afternoon for the rest of her life. She told Rameda that she was married, had an eight-year-old son, and that Leumas had promised her freedom if she fell in love with another man. Rameda was angry; he shouted at her that she had kept the truth from him for all those months, that she had lied to him, to Leumas, to Marcos, and above all to herself! He stormed out of the room without saying goodbye.

She threw herself on their bed and cried until her face was swollen and she no longer had any tears to shed. She was desperate. She did not know if she would ever see Rameda again. And what if he abandoned her forever? She thought of killing herself, of ending this tragic problem she had created, of telling Leumas and Marcos the truth and then ending her life. Leumas and Marcos were better off without her, her lies and her unforgivable deceit. She did not deserve Marcos; she was an evil woman. She was not a kind mother, not a truthful friend or wife. She felt sorry for Leumas, for Rameda, for Marcos and for Laura. What had she done, involving all these innocent people in a spider web from which they could not get away? This deep labyrinth of lies had extinguished her soul, and killing her body would not be of any importance, for her soul was already dead. She lost track of the hours, and when she looked at the clock on the bed table, it was close to 10:30 p.m. She picked up the phone and called her home. Marcos answered the phone frantically.

"Mommy," he cried desperately. "Where are you? Dad already called the hospitals, and the police have been looking for you. Are you all right, Mommy? Please come home or tell us where you are so that we can come and get you."

Arizle replied in a soft, sad voice, "I will be home in twenty minutes," and then hung up the phone, not giving Marcos the chance to say anything or ask more questions. She quickly picked up her make-up, threw everything into her bag, and without washing her face or combing her hair, she took the elevator down to look for a taxi. She did not care what happened to her, and the only reason she was going home at all was to tell Marcos goodbye before she ended her life.

The taxi driver asked her if she was all right. She answered, "Yes," and asked him if he would drive a little faster. The old driver was sincerely concerned about this young woman with a swollen, red face, who looked so desperate and sad. Arizle did not want to talk; she wanted to be left alone.

"I just need to think," she sighed.

"Sure," he answered. "I will say no more." When the taxi stopped at the curb, Marcos and Leumas were waiting outside the gate. She paid the driver and thanked him for not talking and respecting her private thoughts. She opened the door of the car, and assisted out by Leumas, she fell to her knees and into Marcos's arms. She rocked back and forth, weeping, and Marcos, astounded, did not know what to do for his mother. Marcos started to cry with her. They hugged each other, sobbing, for several minutes. Leumas stood by in silence. Her red and swollen face only emphasized her suffering, and all that mattered to Leumas and Marcos was that she was alive and there.

After a few minutes, Marcos and his mother slowly walked past the gate, through the garden, and then into the house. Marcos would not let go of his mother, and Arizle sprawled on the first chair she found, speechless. Leumas touched her hair in an affectionate and paternal manner. He said that she needed to say nothing more that night, that she needed to rest and that the next day they could talk if she felt like it. Leumas helped Arizle to the bathroom, and stayed by the door while she brushed her teeth and washed her face. Leumas knew something was tormenting her. When she finished, he accompanied her to the bedroom, helping her get under the covers. Marcos was lying in her bed, waiting for her. Marcos slept all night with his mother, and Leumas left mother and son together and went to sleep on Marcos's bed.

Fortunately, the following day was a Sunday and Leumas decided not to go to work for the half day but instead to stay home to talk to his wife. Arizle came downstairs, and her face was more swollen than it was the night before. She poured a cup of coffee that she diluted by adding hot water to her cup. She sat at the table looking at Leumas, but he sensed that she was not seeing him. Despite his external serenity, he was quite angry with her. Marcos came to sit near his mother. Leumas told Marcos that he was going to take him to spend the day with one of his uncles because he and his mother needed to talk privately. Marcos insisted that he preferred to stay in his room, and that he would not interfere with their conversation, but Leumas wanted Marcos out of the house and away from whatever had to be said. He felt that Marcos could get an explanation at a later date after emotions had cooled. Marcos went to get dressed and Leumas drove him to his parents' home to stay with one of his uncles. Leumas promised Marcos that he would pick him up in the afternoon around six o'clock. Marcos was not happy, but he went to see his uncle's airplane models after he said goodbye to his father, and the distraction took his mind off his mother for awhile.

Leumas was concerned with Marcos's feelings, but he needed to talk to Arizle without worrying about Marcos's overhearing them. He drove back to his house, lost in thought. He knew something was wrong in their lives. He knew that Arizle went out almost every day with excuses that many times were ridiculous. Was it possible that Arizle thought that he, Leumas, was that naïve and stupid?

He was not a weak man; he was a calm man who did not want to lose the wife whom he had married and had loved all his life. But now he felt he was losing her. He recalled giving her his word of honor that he would give her the freedom to choose another life. He had been crazy, he thought, making her that promise. How could he have promised her such a thing! Of course, back then he was sure that that something of this nature could never come to pass.

Furious and scared, with tears welling up in his eyes, he could hardly see the road in front of him. He experienced a stabbing pain in his chest. He felt physically weak and mentally exhausted. He did not want to hear from her that she was going to leave him. That could not be. He could not bear the thought of not seeing her anymore. This would be his death, he thought.

When he stopped in front of his house, he did not know how he had driven there. His mind was a total blank, and the pain in his chest had not gone away. He locked his car and went slowly through the gate, along the flowerbeds that she had planted, with one thought in his mind—to say "No" to her request for freedom or whatever it was she wanted, and let her suffer for the rest of her life!

He opened the door and found her still sitting in the same place and position in which he had left her. In her hands there were four hand-written pages. She had been writing him a letter, a letter that she quickly hid from him when she saw him enter the room, a letter that she never gave him to read. She had written it in anger, and her words were caustic.

Leumas,

I do not know which one of us was more deceived by the other. Was I the one to deceive you, when I always told you that I was not in love with you, or was it you who deceived me with promises that love would come to me later? I would not complain if you loved and married another woman. No, I complain of how your affection and your friendship for me are gone so suddenly. I saw it on your face this morning. I have always done everything I could to assist you; God only knows that it is true. You will suffer more, because ugly human beings like you and me should never fall in love. Humanity adores beauty, and though a bit late, I now understand this truth. I, however, have my mission to fulfill with this baby I am carrying, and so I will fulfill it. Afterward, the end will be brief for one who does not believe anymore in anybody or anything. Marcos will certainly hate me, and you will not remember that I have existed. Neither run away from yourself nor from your conscience. I feel exhausted after all that has happened in my life lately. I have always helped you in your difficult moments, and I will help you again with a marriage annulment.

I was not a saint, but I have been your friend, and in my heart you have always had a large place—so large, Leumas, that everything, even the prospect of happiness, seems strange and far away without your presence and your affection. I believe you will be happier without me and wish you happiness, even if sometimes I will seem to you unjust and evil. It will be because of my hurt and grief for the absence of your affection. I know that you do not need me, but I need you, though you may believe that I do not. Farewell, Leumas! You will be happy if you accept my advice: Do not love too much. Try to always love less, so that you will not suffer again as I suffer now. May God bless you always.

Accept the desperation of your wife,
Arizle
P.S. I have been asking God to forgive me,
and I ask you, too, to forgive me for the
evil I have done against you.

When Leumas entered the house, the look of
rage in his eyes met the acute pain in hers. Silence.
His face was no longer that of an angry man; his heart
began to crumble inside of him. More silence. He
asked her if she wanted a glass of water. She responded that she did not, but she got up to get a glass
of water for him instead. He sat down and waited for
her return. He took the glass from her hands and
drank it all. His forehead was covered with beads of
perspiration, his hands were shaking, and his voice
was low and despondent. He waited for her to start.
She waited for him to ask. Neither one said a word for
several minutes.

Suddenly, weakly, she said, "I betrayed you,
Leumas. I deserve to be thrown out of this house and
never again be allowed inside. The only thing that I
ask," she whispered, "is that you allow me to see Marcos from time to time."

He immediately said, "I would never take Marcos
away from you; you must know better."

When she heard him say that, she started to sob
uncontrollably. While he waited for her to calm herself
once again, he stroked her head softly, as a caring father does to a child in despair.

She raised her head and said, crying, "I am
pregnant, and the father of this child abandoned me."
When Leumas heard these last words, he lowered his
head in his hands and cried. Arizle wanted to hug him
and ask him to forgive her, but she felt dirty, unworthy

of him, and she could not move to him. As she knew he wished her to say something, so she, too, waited for him to say something. After a while, he searched for his handkerchief, blew his nose, and dried his eyes.

He looked at her and said, "This man does not deserve your love," he stated in a matter-of-fact manner, "if he leaves you with his child." She did not answer him.

"Do you really love him?" he asked her.

She answered, "Yes, I do. Desperately."

"When and where did you meet him?"

"It was on the evening of the Baile de Carnaval at the Teatro Municipal."

Leumas said in a sad voice, "I sensed something had happened that night. I feel sorry for you, Arizle. How much torment you must have experienced within yourself all these months! You, above everyone else, know how much I detest lies!"

Arizle sat in silence. She could not even look into his eyes. She felt so inferior to him. Why was he not telling her to leave the house? Why was he not screaming at her, telling her that he no longer wanted her in his house? She loved him as a friend, and hated him as a man for being so magnanimous.

He asked her, "How long have you been pregnant?"

She answered, "I found out only two days ago. The doctor said I am three months pregnant."

Leumas sighed deeply. Arizle paid attention to all his body language and knew what his face looked like, even though she had not even looked at him once. Leumas seemed to be immersed in deep thought. His hands were shaking, and Arizle interpreted this as his being so angry that he could hardly control himself.

She knew she had broken his heart, and she knew their relationship had changed in that moment.

"What are you going to tell Marcos?" he asked.

She replied, "The truth, I imagine. Don't you think I have lied enough?"

He did not say a word, even though he felt empathy for her problems. He was furious and hurt, tremendously hurt. He closed his eyes briefly and again lowered his head in his hands, his elbows resting on the table. They both remained in silence for a long time. What more was there to say? Arizle thought she had destroyed her chances of regaining his trust. She was not sure he believed her story.

Leumas went to pick up Marcos at six o'clock, as he had promised. Marcos was waiting for his father on the sidewalk in front of the house. Marcos saw his father's car coming and said goodbye to his uncle, grandfather, and grandmother with a hug. When the car stopped, Marcos got into the front seat. The first question he had was about his mother.

"Where is Mommy?"

"At home waiting for you," his father replied.

"Is she still crying?"

"I do not know, son."

Marcos became silent. He was afraid to ask his father any more questions, for he sensed that the answers would make him anxious and unhappy. Leumas quietly and carefully drove the rest of the way home.

When they arrived, Marcos did not wait for his father to park the car in the garage; he ran to his mother. No matter what had happened, he wanted to see her and make sure that she was still there. Marcos feared that something horrible was about to be told to him and he did not know whether he could wait any longer. He had to know.

Arizle went running toward him, hugging him and kissing him as she started crying, afraid that he would not love her anymore. Marcos, though intelligent, was too young to understand her pain, but he did not want her to hurt.

He looked at her and said, "Mommy, what can I say to you that will make you stop crying?"

At that, she cried even more. She could not stand herself. She did not deserve to hug him; she did not deserve to be his mother. She wanted to tell him that, but would he understand her? She stopped crying, blew her nose in a small towel she had in her skirt pocket and turned to him with immense humility and tenderness.

"Darling Marcos," she said, "I am going to have another baby and it is not your father's baby." Marcos knew what that meant. They had discussed procreation between animals and between humans. He had come back from school on his second day of classes with a vulgar vocabulary relating to sex. She did not tell him any lies, but picked up the encyclopedia and a medical book to show him how everything happened in a scientific manner. He was both surprised and intrigued. She showed him pictures and told him the correct terminology. He took it all in as just another one of life's realities. He did not seem to be disgusted, for he had seen dogs and other animals copulating when he was outside in his grandfather's yard. He was just surprised that humans copulated just as other animals did.

Marcos asked her, "Why did you make a baby with a man other than Dad?"

She answered, "Because I was weak, and because I am in love with him."

"You must not love Dad any more," Marcos insisted.

Arizle answered quickly, "No, I do still love your father, but as a cousin, a best friend, a father."

Marcos did not give up so easily. "Does that mean that you will leave us forever?"

"No," Arizle said with assurance, "I would never abandon either of you! I could not live with myself if I did that to you, Marcos. Don't you know how much I adore you, my Marcos? I did not fall in love with another man because I no longer love you! You are my son, my blood, my flesh, I can never stop loving you."

"How about Dad," Marcos inquired. "Can you leave him for this man?" Arizle felt compelled to tell Marcos that "this man" had left her when he found out that she also had lied to him about being a married woman with an eight-year-old son. Marcos asked her another question before she could say anything else.

"Are you going to love this baby more than you love me?" Marcos asked with tears in his eyes. Arizle felt a sharp pain in her heart, and she choked. She quickly coughed and tried to regain her voice.

"Marcos, darling," she said tenderly, "you were my first child. A mother feels closer to her first child. Besides," she continued, "how can I love anyone more than I love you? The love for a son is very different than the love a woman feels for a man. Mothers love their children equally, for they all come from them; they all have their blood. Mothers carry children in their wombs for nine months. During this time we get attached to our babies as if they were pieces of our souls. In no way, darling Marcos, will I love another child more than I love you. I have lied to you and to your father, but I swear on my mother's spirit that I will never abandon you or love you less than I love you today."

She paused to see his reaction. "Do you believe me, Marcos? You must believe me," she implored. He nodded his head and put his arms around her. She thought that he was an outstanding child to react to her intimate revelation in such a manner. Her eyes were filled with tears, and once again, she felt undeserving of her son. Marcos let go of her neck and whispered to her that he had to go to the bathroom.

Leumas had been watching them from a short distance. Marcos's maturity, understanding and tolerance bewildered him. Had Marcos really understood, he asked himself? He was amazed at what he had just witnessed.

"Our son, Arizle, is an old spirit," Leumas remarked. Arizle did not answer; she just nodded her head in agreement. Leumas told Arizle that Francisca had had dinner ready for them for two hours. He added that he told her to go ahead and eat and retire to her room and leave everything on the stove for them. She had done so, and now everything needed to be reheated at least, he added, for Marcos's benefit, for he ought to be hungry.

Arizle got up from her chair and went to reheat their dinner. She worked for fifteen minutes and then began to take the food to the table. Marcos was behind her, waiting to take a few dishes to the table for her. She gave him the rice dish and followed him with the roasted chicken and vegetables. The salad had withered, and she had to dispose of the lettuce. Francisca had forgotten to place the greens in the refrigerator, perhaps because she had no idea that they would take so long to eat. She had retired at eight o'clock and it was now close to ten. She apologized to Marcos for serving the dinner so late. He had school the next day and she said she was terribly sorry. To Leumas she did not apologize. He deserved a much bigger apology, and she was not sure there would be one suitable for what she had done to him.

They sat at the table in silence. She waited for Marcos and Leumas to help themselves before she took a portion only fit for a tiny bird. Then she did not even eat that. When they finished, she took all the plates back to the sink and cleaned them, throwing the few remains of the food into the trash and piling the dishes up for Francisca to wash the next day.

When she felt everything was organized and in order, she took Marcos by his hand and said to him in a very soft voice, "Marcos, let me tuck you into bed and read you a story. Would you like me to do that?" Marcos hugged her and kissed her tenderly. He nodded his head in agreement and both went upstairs. Leumas stayed at the table, and shortly after he heard them go into Marcos's bedroom, he moved to the living room. He sat on the sofa, moving one of the cushions she had sewn to the side. He did not turn on the lights; he wanted to think in the dark, and he wanted to be alone.

Arizle came downstairs as soon as Marcos fell asleep. Leumas was sitting in the dark with his head in his hands.

He said, "Who is this man? What is his name?...Do you know where to phone him? I want to speak with him myself."

So, Arizle told him about Rameda. She said that like Leumas, Rameda had a doctorate in civil engineering. She told him everything about his family and that he worked for his father at the Matadouro de

Pachêco (Pachêco Slaughterhouse), the family business. Arizle did not hesitate to give Leumas Rameda's office phone number.

Leumas assured Arizle that he had not forgotten his promise to her. However, he was not going to give her freedom to go with just any man. He wanted to talk to Rameda and find out his intentions toward Arizle. If, after talking to Rameda, he felt that he was a man of honor, he would give Arizle the freedom she so desired.

Arizle could not contain her tears. She knelt on the floor in front of Leumas and placed her head on his knees, asking him to forgive her. Leumas motioned to her to get up and sit on the sofa.

"Arizle, you broke my heart and my soul; my manhood is in pieces, and my ego is dead," he declared. He looked at her with incredible sorrow in his eyes. "But," he added, "I promised you that I would give you your freedom."

"It is my mistake! I should never have put you in such a position," she cried out.

"But I did promise you this, and I will see to it that you get your freedom. Tomorrow, I will call this Rameda to talk to him. I hope to God this man has honor," he added. "I hope that he knows what he did and that he is willing to take responsibility for his actions... I should never have let you go to that ball!" He was almost shouting with anger as he finished speaking. "Laura hid this from me to help you; even Laura lied to me. Where does it end? God help me!"

His anger spent, he rose, touched her head, and walked toward the stairway. There was nothing more he could say to her; he was exhausted. Arizle stayed downstairs. After a while, she removed her shoes, lay down on the sofa, and curled herself into the fetal position until she fell asleep around three o'clock in the morning.

At seven, she awakened to Francisca setting the table for breakfast. She waited for her to go back into the kitchen and then tiptoed upstairs. Leumas was already dressed, and he was helping Marcos get ready for school. Arizle hugged Marcos when she saw him. Marcos placed both arms around her neck. He did not want to let go of her. His father reminded him that he had to eat and that they had to leave in ten minutes. Marcos let go of his mother, picked up his school briefcase and went downstairs with his father.

Arizle went into the bathroom, drew a bath and sat in the tub for more than an hour. She touched her belly that she thought was starting to protrude. She caressed this baby who, at the moment, had no father, only a mother who happened to be stupid and in love with its father.

Leumas left without saying goodbye to Arizle, but Marcos went upstairs, knocked on the door and said, "Mommy, I love you! I need you, Mommy."

Arizle wept. "God bless you, Marcos. I love you too, deeply, my darling son!" Marcos went back to the dining room where his father was waiting.

"Do you hate Mommy, Dad?"

"No, I do not, Marcos," replied Leumas.

The ride to the school was a silent one; neither one said anything to the other. Marcos said goodbye to his father, thanking him for taking him to school.

When Leumas arrived at his office, he removed the piece of paper with Rameda's number from his coat pocket. He thought it was better to wait for 9:00 a.m. to call. "Wealthy people!" he thought. "God only knows when they arrive at work." He took his drawings out of a large drawer and focused his mind on examining them. At nine o'clock, Leumas picked up the phone to call Rameda. The office informed him that Dr. Rameda was out of town buying cattle. He asked the man who answered the phone whether he knew when Dr. Rameda would be returning to town. He replied that Dr. Rameda would be back in Rio on the following Wednesday.

"Would you like to leave your name?" the male voice asked.

"No," Leumas answered, "I will call him back next Wednesday."

When Marcos and Leumas got home, Arizle was anxious to know whether Leumas had talked to Rameda. Leumas waited for Marcos to go to his room and then told Arizle that Rameda was out of town until the following week. Arizle did not comment, but her face fell, and anxiety creased her forehead. She told Leumas that she had drawn a bath for him and that his pajamas, robe and slippers were all by the bathtub. Leumas nodded his head in understanding and went upstairs. The wooden floors smelled of carnauba wax, the furniture had been oiled, and there was not a speck of dust to be seen anywhere. The drawers of the dresser had been organized, and she had moved his socks and underwear to the upper drawers, giving herself the two lower ones.

She was a hardworking woman, he thought. Since he had married Arizle, he had never seen a hole in one of his socks. After this thought, he shook his head, thinking to himself what a ridiculous thought that was. One of a wife's tasks was to mend her husband's socks, but he remembered his friends' wives and recalled that they never ironed any clothes nor mended any socks for them. Their houses were not as clean as his was. He thought of the pieces of furniture made of crates that Arizle had built. He thought of all the heavy loads of clothing she had carried to the river and washed on the wooden washboard until the skin of her fingers was blistered raw. He thought of the fresh food that she cooked for him every day, and how he had fresh rice to eat every noon. He remembered how malaria and yellow fever had jeopardized her health. Suddenly, he realized what he was thinking and asked himself why he was having those thoughts.

He removed his suit, hung up his trousers and tie in the closet, left his jacket on the bed and went in the bathroom. He had not slept at all comfortably the night before, and the hot water felt good on his back. Arizle had filled the tub to the brim. He remembered how young she had been when he married her. She was just a child, he thought, recriminating himself. She was just a child! He closed his eyes, leaning with his head against the wall and remained motionless.

He heard a knock on the door. It was Arizle asking him if he was all right. He answered, "Yes. I will be out soon." She went downstairs with Marcos and waited for him to come to dinner. Marcos ate very well, but Leumas and Arizle had only a few spoons of soup. Leumas remarked to her that she needed to eat heartily, for she had to eat for two. Marcos looked at her and smiled sweetly.

After dinner, Leumas asked Marcos to give him and his mother a few minutes alone. Marcos agreed and went to read in his room. As soon as he left, Leumas asked Arizle to be sure to take care of herself and the baby. He asked her whether she had appointments to see the doctor and whether she was taking daily vitamins. She answered "No" to his questions and promised him that she would take care of doing both the very next day.

Lisa Whatley

The week went by slowly. Arizle made two table-
cloths, several kitchen towels to dry the dishes, and
covers for the chairs outside on the terrace. She cut
fresh daisies and placed them in a vase on the coffee
table. Marcos loved seeing his mother decorating the
house with fresh flowers. Leumas told Marcos that the
flowers meant that his mother was in better spirits.

Wednesday came quickly for Leumas, who
wanted to talk to Rameda. He again waited until 9:00
a.m. to call Rameda at his office. At nine, he waited
for his secretary to get coffee for herself, closed the
door of his office, and dialed Rameda's number. Once
again, a man answered, but this time it was Rameda.

"Dr. Rameda," Leumas began, "I am Leumas,
Arizle's husband." There was total silence. Leumas
had to say, "Are you there?"

Rameda answered, "Yes, I am here, Dr. Leumas."

Leumas continued, "You know Arizle is pregnant
with your child, do you not?"

Rameda replied, "Yes, I do, Dr. Leumas."

"Well, do you love my wife, sir?"

Rameda was speechless; he could not believe
that he was having this conversation with Arizle's
husband.

"Well?" insisted Leumas.

Rameda said suddenly, "I am in love with Arizle,
Dr. Leumas." Pause. "How much will it cost to set her
free?"

Leumas was furious. "Rameda," he rejoined, his
face flushed with anger, "my wife is not a commodity,
and she is not for sale! If you love her and will honor
her, then I will set her free."

Rameda could not believe what he was hearing.
He stammered awkwardly, "It is very complicated, Dr.
Leumas. My family is devoutly Catholic and will never

accept Arizle. My father will be so upset with me that he might fire me from the job I now have with his company. Even a marriage outside of this country will never be recognized by Brazilian law."

"Well," Leumas roared angrily, "you both should have thought of all this before you decided to make a child." Leumas paused before continuing. "In a war one must behave like a general, not a coward!" There was dead silence.

Rameda asked when he could see Arizle. Leumas replied that he should call her soon, for she had been living in real hell, and that his son, Marcos, and he had also been cast into that hell.

"It is time for you take responsibility for your actions!" Leumas declared before hanging up the phone.

Arizle received a phone call from Rameda that same day. Rameda told her that Leumas had called him. Sobbing, he apologized to her, begging her forgiveness for the madness of his running away from her. He told her that he wanted her and their baby. He pleaded with her to forgive him. She was quiet, but her heart was pounding in her chest. He asked her to please meet him that afternoon. She replied that she could not because she had a doctor's appointment. He insisted that he wanted to go with her to the doctor. Rameda told her that he was taking the day off, and that he would come to the house to pick her up and take her to the doctor in a taxi. Her mouth was dry; she was having difficulty in answering him. She finally pulled herself together and agreed to wait for him; however, she was adamant about not wanting Marcos to see them together, so she made Rameda promise that she could return home alone after she had seen the doctor and talked to him. Rameda agreed. He had never heard her so obstinate. He could not wait to see her again.

At one o'clock, he was at her door. He got out of the taxi, held the door for her and sat beside her without touching her. She looked wonderful, he thought. She was glowing like a rose in bloom. Leumas had made him see that Arizle had value. She was a lady, and Rameda wanted to treat her as such. In the taxi he behaved like a gentleman, and he waited until after the visit to the doctor, when they were alone in their apartment, to kiss her passionately. He told her that he was renting a two-bedroom apartment in Tijuca for them and that he wanted her to help him buy the furnishings, so that they could make a home together. She was so happy hearing his words, yet so distressed, thinking that she could not be with Marcos and Leumas. Who would take care of them? What would Marcos do without her? She thought of taking Marcos with her, but she could not make herself do it. She was leaving Leumas, and she could not also take his son away from him. She was tormented! Her life was disintegrating around her. She wanted Rameda desperately, but she hated to leave her son and her best friend alone.

She told Rameda about her turmoil. Rameda said, "Bring Marcos to live with us."

"I cannot do that to Leumas. Marcos is all he has left!" she wailed miserably and then sobbed. "What shall I do?" she shouted. "I am in love with you, but I love my son, and Leumas has been the father I never had. I do not want to hurt him more than I already have. My God, help me!" she pleaded.

Rameda was kneeling, holding her feet tenderly. She asked him to let go of her feet, because she had to get up and blow her nose. He brought her some

Kleenex. Her face was swollen and red, and her eyes, which were usually large and clear, were small, pink and puffy. Arizle laid her head on his knees. Rameda's fingers stroked her hair softly. He had no words of wisdom for her.

Since he had talked to Leumas, he now understood Arizle's concern for him. He was indeed an unusual man. Leumas loved Arizle more than he loved himself. Leumas had placed Arizle's happiness ahead of his own. Rameda was sure that Leumas adored his wife. He also loved Arizle and could not live without her. What a drama, he thought to himself. How could life be so cruel! Someone's happiness is often at somebody else's expense. He did not know what to say to her. She remained with her head on his knees for a long time. Finally, he had to tell her that he needed to get up and change position because his legs were numb.

She let go of him and went into the bathroom. She came out a few minutes later and told him she needed to go home and pray to her mother's spirit to help her. Marcos, she added, would be frantic if she came home late. Rameda understood and told her he would put her in a taxi so that she could go home to Marcos. He kissed her eyes, her hands, her sleeves, and called for the elevator. When the elevator stopped, he kissed her hands just as he had done the first time they met. He called a taxi, opened the door for her, and whispered in her ear that he adored her, too. She had tears in her eyes when she told him that she needed his love. The car disappeared quickly in the rush hour traffic. He watched the back of her head until it became a minute spot. He had forgotten to tell her that he would call her in the morning.

When she arrived home, the driver wanted to give her the change from the fare Rameda had paid, but she told him that he should keep it. She opened the gate and went into the garden. She walked slowly to the front door, which was open. Leumas and Marcos were waiting for her. She told them that the traffic had been the worst she had encountered coming home by taxi. She hugged Marcos and Leumas in a single embrace. It was the most emotional embrace she had ever given anyone. Leumas did not say anything to her; he knew what awaited him. Marcos was the only one who did not know what was coming.

They sat at the table to eat dinner. Francisca had prepared okra with ground meat and corn meal. When Francisca had started working for the household, Arizle had given her lessons on how to cook certain foods that they all liked. As a mentor, Arizle was very patient and she liked to demonstrate and then have Francisca show her how to make the recipe she had just learned. Arizle also wrote the recipe down, step by step, so that Francisca would not forget it. She thought about Sá Barbara, who was a master when it came to this recipe. She smelled the aroma of the garlic when Sá Barbara sautéed the meat prior to adding the okra. Her thoughts were swirling. She wished she did not have to make these difficult decisions, and that she could go back and hide under Emilinha's skirts once again. God, Arizle thought, it seems so long ago that it might never have happened. Sá Barbara and Emilinha had become mirages in the desert of her life.

After dinner, Leumas suggested to Arizle that they should talk. Arizle kissed and hugged Marcos, asking him if his father and she could be alone. Marcos, sad and disappointed, went to his room. Marcos did not have friends with whom to play. There were other children living on the same street, but he preferred to read or to be in the company of his mother. He looked at his mother from the landing as if he wanted to say something important to her, but he disappeared up the stairs, and softly shut his bedroom door.

Leumas and Arizle left the dining room table and walked into the living room to sit on the sofa. She was apprehensive and lost in thought. She did not recall ever having so many enormous obstacles facing her as she did now. She felt vulnerable and confounded, and there seemed to be no way to make everyone happy. Was there a solution? She knew there was not. She knew that whatever she decided was going to hurt others–Marcos mainly, for he was so young and so attached to her.

She had no idea where to start, but then the words came out spontaneously. "Rameda thinks you adore me and that you are an unusual man, Leumas. What you told him over the phone impressed him as words coming from an extraordinary man. He said that you spoke to him in a very forthright manner, and he said that you were not very tolerant of his actions."

Leumas did not respond to Arizle's statements; instead he told her, "Remember, Arizle, in war, be a general."

Leumas was exhausted. He had been sleeping poorly, and his body seemed to have lived an extra thirty years in the past week. He had a terrible headache, but he never mentioned it to her. Arizle had suffered pains in her stomach, but had said nothing to anyone. Arizle did not want to be seen as a victim, as a martyr, nor as a woman without strength of character. She could not prevent God from seeing her as a sinner, but God knew she was no coward. She had moments of self-doubt, but she was a strong woman with extraordinary will power, and she had endless perseverance, despite her moments of despair. She knew that she alone had to make her decisions, for no one else could make them for her–neither Leumas nor Rameda.

When Rameda called the next day, she asked him to be patient, for she did not have any answers and had not made any decisions. Rameda called every day. Aside from the hours she spent with Marcos after school, she spent her time in solitude and in continuous serious meditation. Two weeks went by, and still she agonized. One night she had a dream about her grandmother.

The Baroness smiled at her. "Beloved granddaughter, always follow your heart. Decisions made from the heart are the learning ones. Listen closely, child. I did not say they are the right ones; I said the learning ones. You, sweet breath of spring, need to learn, and the journey is challenging, for God gives the good students the most difficult problems to solve." Arizle woke up smelling the inebriate aroma of the old jasmine bush at her grandmother's house in Sabará.

She then woke up Leumas, earlier than their regular schedule, and told him that she had made her decision. Arizle told Leumas that she was leaving him to be with Rameda. She assured Leumas that, despite her departure, she would never abandon him or Marcos, and that she wanted Marcos to stay with him, for she could not take from him another being he loved so deeply and totally. Leumas was startled, but resigned himself to Arizle's decision and the difficult journey which they all were now forced to undertake.

Arizle left the room and ran upstairs, locking herself in the bathroom. She cried and agonized over how tremendously difficult it was going to be to tell Marcos of her decision. She prayed for guidance from Emilinha, God, and St. Anthony. None of them answered, but she felt a warm feeling penetrate her body and peace settle within her soul.

Marcos knocked on the door, saying he needed to use the bathroom. Arizle opened the door, touched his face and went to get dressed. At the breakfast table, they chatted normally, as if all was fine in their lives. Marcos finished his chocolate milk, hugged his mother and ran to the gate. Leumas followed him and a few minutes later, they both were gone for the day.

Arizle waited for Rameda to call her so she could tell him what she had decided. When Rameda called around nine o'clock and she told him, he was beside himself with happiness. He asked her if she had talked to Marcos. She answered that she had not done so yet, because Marcos had an exam to take that day. She wanted to wait until he returned home that afternoon. She thought that it was best for Marcos if she talked to him during the week when he was busy with school and would not have much time to dwell upon her leaving. Rameda thought her reasoning made sense and told her that he wanted to meet Marcos, for he wanted to be the one to tell him that he could come to spend time with them for as long as he wanted.

Rameda told Arizle that he had found a three-bedroom apartment in the same building. He wanted Arizle to see it before he signed the contract. Arizle replied that he should take the apartment without her seeing it, for she trusted his judgement. She changed the subject then and asked him whether he had told his family. He answered that he had not done so yet, and that he would do it later, closer to the birth of the baby.

Marcos and Leumas came home at six o'clock. She had been worried about their being late and had called the school and Leumas's office, but she was happy to find that they were well and safe. As soon as Marcos had gone upstairs to change and had something to drink, she took him by the hand and walked in the direction of the garden. She was quiet and pensive. They sat on the double swing by the little pond she had built and designed. The sound of the water falling from a little fountain in the shape of a toad soothed her troubled heart. She did not move the swing; they both just sat still.

Her lips trembled and her forehead perspired. With a dry mouth and her heart pounding in her chest, she took his hand and said, "Marcos, I will be moving out of the house. I have decided to move into an apartment Rameda is renting in Tijuca."

Marcos said nothing, his eyes glaring sternly at hers. His face was expressionless as he moved his hands away from hers. He was mute. She did not get one other word out of her Marcos. She reached for his hands, but he pulled away, out of her reach. There they sat for fifteen minutes without his saying a word to her. She wondered whether he would ever forgive her.

Marcos never did. In his eyes, she had abandoned him, rejected him, and left him to himself. His father was an honest man, a kind man, but Marcos's affinities with his mother could never be replaced. Intellectually and emotionally, he and his father had little in common. The most important friend, whom he trusted and adored, had just walked out on him. No!

Marcos could never forgive his mother for choosing romantic love over parental love.

Marcos's writings from that moment on changed drastically. They became sarcastic, ironic, and antagonistic toward the ideas of others. They were defiant of nature and God and consumed with endless, deep anger. He grew up faster than ever, mentally, but he became a harsh, hard, unsympathetic and emotionless young man. The metamorphosis was so astounding that his father and he began to clash, spiritually and intellectually. That young man was not the Marcos that Arizle and Leumas knew, but a new Marcos, who had changed, locking out the tender love of the mother that he had adored from the moment of birth.

10

Arizle went through the whole house, took inventory of all they had and gave the list to Leumas. She counted the bed and table linens, the bath and face towels, making sure that they had an ample supply to fulfill their needs. She took her whole monthly allowance and bought clothes for Marcos. She made sure his closet was in order and that he had more than enough trousers, shirts and jackets. She did the same for Leumas. Leumas needed dress shirts.

She left the house and bought him three shirts. She called him at the office and told him that she had purchased extra dress shirts for him to wear to work, but not having enough cash, she had asked the store to deliver them to his office where the bill would be paid. He complained and said he did not really need them, but he knew she had always bought all his clothes, and if she thought he needed more shirts, she was probably right.

She called Francisca to talk to her about her leaving. She told Francisca in a dignified way that she was going to live with another man and that she needed to know if Francisca was willing to continue to work for Dr. Leumas and Marcos without her being in the house. Arizle wanted the maid's assurance that Leumas and Marcos could count on her. Francisca mentioned that she was sad to see her leave, but Arizle could count on her to take care of Dr. Leumas and Marcos. Arizle asked Francisca if she would please pay special attention to Marcos. Marcos, Arizle explained, was very attached to his mother and he would be the one to suffer the most. She explained to Francisca that she needed to be informed when Marcos or Dr. Leumas was sick. She wanted Francisca to call her whenever an emergency occurred. She also instructed Francisca about what to cook for every day of the week, what to write on the list for Leumas to buy at the market, and what rooms to clean and wax according to each weekday. She wrote down all of these instructions, saying that as soon as she had her new telephone number, she would call her with it. She told Francisca that she would come back once a month to make sure that Dr. Leumas and Marcos had everything they needed.

Arizle thought of writing them each a letter, but opted not to do it. It was not like she was never going to see them again; she was going to visit them and they would visit her every week. Instead, she wrote a poem describing her anxiety and turmoil.

Miracle

Is it love? I do not know this anxiety,
This insane desire to be close

In the absence to feel all the nostalgia,
The sensation that all is a desert.

Is it love? This anguish I feel throughout
the night,
Dreaming dreams that my heart builds
and unbinds
Between the darkness and the dawn of the
night,

Ah! I wish to be loved, I wish!
To see myself finally captive in chains,
A soul that does not believe, that waits for
nothing...

I wish I could feel secure and conquered,
And give myself happily to the conqueror!
And in an utter miracle in my life,

I wish I could feel secure and conquered,
Feel poor and wanted
Before I die of love!

She left before they came back for dinner.

She remembered that day all of her life. It was
raining, gray and gloomy. The wind was blowing just
like the night her mother died. It was as if a new beginning was ahead of her, but she knew not the extent
of her decision, nor the consequences that would come
later, meeting her head on with no mercy and no forgiveness. She heard thunder far way. She felt her legs
wobbling. She was petrified; she left with one suitcase
in her hand and that only half full.

Her clothes were few, for her allowance had been
spent on Marcos. She did her own hair, her nails, and

her pedicure. She always looked well-dressed even though she only had three good dresses. She had no jewelry, only a gold wedding band she had received from Leumas on the day of their wedding. She only had two pairs of shoes and one pair of sandals. She had a knack for style and had asked Laura to give her the fashion magazines she no longer wanted. She spent time looking at fashion, the position of the models' feet when they stood up, their hair, their nails, and their shoes. She emulated everything she saw that could make her a more refined and good person. She also grew spiritually with every passing day; she learned about new things constantly, and her willingness to grow and improve herself was irrepressible.

Rameda had sent a car to pick her up, and he was waiting for her at their new two-bedroom apartment. The three-bedroom had not become available yet. When he saw her, his face glowed with happiness, and though Arizle seemed sad, she was also very glad to see him. He took her in his arms, and they spent the afternoon on the only soft surface they had, a couch he had purchased for his office. It was short and narrow, but they felt nothing except the heat that emanated from their bodies. He had missed her soft skin. She felt his unshaved beard on her neck, and that sent that familiar electric wave through her spine. Their lovemaking was a mixture of lust and sublimated love. They touched each other's bodies with the gentleness of caring nurses handling babies only a few hours old. He kissed her neck, her breasts and her belly. She had exquisite breasts—big, rosy and firm. He loved touching them, kissing them, and sucking on them, rolling his tongue around the tips of her nipples. They performed their love game with the delicacy of mating butterflies. He loved hearing her moan with pleasure and happiness. Her waist was small and her hips curved elegantly and sensually down to her firm, contoured thighs. Her ankles were thin, feminine and aristocratic. She told him what her mother had said about thin ankles and wrists. He smiled. She had a magnificent body, he thought to himself. He noticed the scar on her thigh and asked her what had happened. She answered that it was a long and sad story, which she did not want to tell at that moment. He did not mind. His attention was on her body, her eyes, and her face, which conveyed pure pleasure.

It was night and they decided to get dressed and try to find a real bed. They walked to the furniture store and saw a large, comfortable bed with a wrought iron headboard. Arizle tried the mattress, liked it, and he bought it. Rameda asked if he paid extra, would they still deliver it today, just two blocks from the store? The owner of the store he said he would do it, mainly after Arizle mentioned that they needed lots of furniture in their new and empty apartment. They rushed next door to a linen shop and purchased sheets, pillows and a blanket. Her favorite color for bedding was mauve, a sort of champagne rose that she had read made one's skin color look lustrous and ethereal. They left the store in a hurry, because they did not want to miss the bed delivery. They acted like two small children around their first Christmas tree.

They did not have a single hanger on which to hang their few pieces of clothing in the large built-in closet. He laughed when he saw her trousseau and told her to go shopping for day dresses, evening dresses, beautiful shoes and handbags while he was at work the next day. He wanted to take her out and show off her figure.

"I have no money, Rameda. I need to get a job, and after I make some money, I will," she replied.

He kissed her on her lips and laughed, "Go to the Imperial Boutique on Ouvidor Street, downtown, choose what you want, buy it, and ask them to send the bill to my office." Smiling, he let her know that she would be sorry if he made a list of what she should buy. Instead, he added, they should make a list of what they needed to buy for their apartment. They sat down on the parquet floor and together made a list of the pieces of furniture they wanted. The list was short, because the apartment, though a two-bedroom, was very small but cozy. After they finished the list, she asked him if they could buy feminine lamps for the bed tables.

"Not more feminine than you are," responded Rameda. She embraced him and gave him a long kiss. He had started to undress her when the bell rang. She quickly buttoned up her blouse and smoothed her hair while he went to open the door. It was their first bed. She was very happy with this purchase, and she asked the two men carrying it to place it against the wall, facing the door. She had read that a bed is the most important piece in a room and that it should always face the bedroom door. When the deliverymen left, she opened the packages of linens and made the bed. The sheets were of a deeper tone of the same color as the blanket. It looked marvelous.

That night they did not feel like eating, and they did not have a single edible item in the refrigerator, anyway. Instead, they made love most of the night and slept curled together until morning.

When he awoke, she had already gone out and purchased bread, butter, coffee, milk and sugar for them to have the typical Brazilian breakfast, café au lait with a piece of fresh, buttered French bread. A variation of this routine was a piece of soft cheese and some fruit. He got up, sat on their bed, and pulled her toward him. She kissed him back, but reminded him between kisses that the coffee was hot and so was the milk. If they did not drink it then, it would get cold. He reluctantly let go of her and went into the bathroom. When he returned, she had set a table on the floor as if they were at a picnic. He had combed his hair, washed his face and brushed his teeth. His mouth smelled fresh when he kissed her on the cheek and lips.

They had their first morning coffee together sitting on the bare floor. She described an imaginary landscape around them, trying to make that moment enchanting and different. She described the countryside around the Rio das Velhas in Sabará. He loved her spontaneous account of the splendid scenery surrounding them. He loved her imagination. He was convinced that she was the most interesting, creative and intelligent woman he had ever known. She had a talent with words and her eloquence was admirable. For a moment, he thought of his father, and if he would only meet her and give her a chance, he was sure Seu Pachêco, his father, would respect her. Like his father, she was self-educated and had worked hard to achieve a place in the sun in a world that was always ready to judge without mercy.

He put on a fresh shirt, the only piece of clothing he had brought with him, and finished getting dressed to go to work. He reminded her to go shopping for her clothes. Also he told her to choose the other furnishings they had written on the list. She commented that she did not want him to spend too much. He replied that she should not worry about money, for that was his job; she should just enjoy her new life. As he mentioned enjoyment, he took her in his arms and started undressing her. She reminded him that he needed to leave, for his father would be upset if he was not in the office by eight-thirty. He left after he tenderly kissed her hands, her feet and her lips.

When she was alone in the apartment, Arizle picked up the phone and called Francisca to tell her the new phone number, and to ask after Marcos. What had he eaten? Had he taken his lunch with him to school? Had he drunk his milk? How did he look? Francisca had received strict orders from Leumas not to worry Arizle with news that was not positive; so, she answered that all was as it should be and that Marcos was fine. Arizle felt there was something wrong with Francisca's response. She knew Marcos was angry and extremely upset and unhappy. She hung up and went to take a shower and get dressed.

Arizle and Rameda had the habit of writing to each other all the time, leaving little love notes on the top of the kitchen counter, the bed, the bathroom sink and any other location they could find. Her notes were beautifully written and his were an attempt to convey his feelings of passion and deep love for her. As she readied herself to leave, she went into the kitchen to pick up the list and found near it several bills and a note saying,

My love,
   Take taxis and be careful. I cannot bear the thought of losing you!
      Yours forever,
      Rameda

Arizle left, still concerned about Marcos and Leumas. As she walked along the sidewalk, she thought of them all the time. "They both hate me," she spoke aloud. She looked around furtively, worried that someone had heard her talking to herself. Arizle flagged a cab and asked the driver to take her to Ouvidor Street. Once in the taxi, her thoughts were again about Marcos. Marcos was only eight years old. Though extremely intelligent, he was still a child. Should she tell Leumas that their son needed to be with her? Should she take Marcos away from Leumas? Arizle was so immersed in thought that the driver had to call her attention twice to the fact that they were at the corner of Ouvidor and the Largo de São Francisco. She apologized and handed him the fare, tipping him well. She began walking toward the middle of the block, looking for the sign that read "Imperial."

The street was narrow, built only for pedestrians, and there were stores of all kinds on both sides. There were many people walking there, some strolling and window shopping, others in a hurry to get somewhere else. Arizle was looking at all stores attentively when she spotted the large sign with neon lights that read Imperial Modas. As she entered, immediately a pleasant, well-dressed young woman approached her, saying that her name was Elza and asking her how she could be of service. Arizle replied that she needed a wardrobe. Elza smiled and replied that she thought she could help her with that. Elza took Arizle to a small elevator, similar to the ones described in the French novels she had read. The elevator was slow, and its cast bronze doors and ceiling were magnificently made. The store was beautiful and elegant, and the furnishings were as lovely as the ones she had seen in the fashion magazines that Laura sent her.

Arizle was invited to sit in a pretty chair and then asked if she wanted coffee, tea or fruit juice. She thanked the young woman and replied that she did not need anything to drink. Elza started bringing the newest fashions for Arizle's review. Arizle had never seen so many suits, dresses, evening dresses, and gorgeous hats. Elza brought her gloves that coordinated with the handbags and shoes. Arizle was mesmerized with so many beautiful accessories. She touched the gloves, and they felt so soft. Elza saw her delight in handling the gloves and told her they were made of leather from an unborn calf. The thought of wearing such gloves distressed her so much that she opted to buy suede gloves instead. Elza laughed respectfully and politely with Arizle, who commented that she was being silly, for no matter how she felt about the material from which the gloves were made, she would still be wearing the skin of an animal.

Arizle bought a lovely trousseau consisting of one evening dress, two street dresses, two dinner dresses, one suit, three hats, handbags, shoes, gloves, stockings, two nightgowns, and a few lingerie pieces. Elza asked her if she liked perfume and brought her a bottle of Fleurs de Rocaille by Caron. Arizle did not know the perfume, but the fragrance reminded her of the aroma of Sabará meadows in bloom, and she purchased it.

When Arizle stated that she had bought enough for the day, the two then went downstairs to sign the bill. While in the elevator, Arizle asked Elza if she could recommend a store for dishes and silverware. Elza replied that Casa Daniel was one of the best and it was not too far from Imperial, on the same street.

"I will look there," Arizle said. When they arrived at the ground floor, Arizle was asked to sit in another nice chair while Elza prepared the invoice and took her purchases to be wrapped. Shortly, Elza came back with the bill for her signature. The package was going to be delivered to Dr. Rameda Pachêco's office that afternoon. She signed Arizle Somar and Elza told her that it had been a pleasure helping her with her purchases.

Elza added, "Please come back again, Madame Somar." Arizle thanked Elza and left the store, thinking that she had to have been dreaming, for she felt like a princess in a fairy tale. In time, Arizle and Elza developed a long business relationship and Arizle became her confidante and mentor.

Arizle strolled toward Casa Daniel. Her thoughts were on how much joy she was experiencing, buying all that she wanted without any concern for the money being spent. She thought about how poor Leumas and she had been and how poor her childhood had been. She asked herself whether money brought any happiness. She answered her own question with "No," for her happiness was not complete without Leumas and Marcos. They were unhappy, she knew. "My God," she thought. How could life become so complex, so very troublesome like this? Was there total happiness? Was there total serenity? Was there total spiritual peace? She was not a kind human being. She was not selfless; she had not had the courage to sacrifice her own happiness on behalf of Marcos's and Leumas's happiness. She was a selfish bitch, she concluded. There was no difference between her actions and the actions of her father nine years before.

"What a horrible woman I am! How can Rameda be in love with me?" She was uncompromising in self-recrimination and self-judgement. Had she fallen in love with Rameda because he was wealthy? No, she was sure that it was not his money that had attracted her to him.

At this moment, she saw the store sign she sought. She stopped to look at their window displays. The sets of dishes were beautiful and refined, the glassware was magnificent and the art objects, though new, were made by Ginori, Baccarat, Sèvres and other designers whose names she had seen in various issues of *Architectural Digest*. She went into the store and was greeted by Senhor Daniel, the owner of Casa Daniel.

She introduced herself as Arizle Somar and immediately he asked, "How may I help you, Madame Somar?" Arizle replied that she needed to buy dishes, glassware and silverware. He asked her to follow him to a section of the store that specialized in dinnerware. Senhor Daniel asked a store salesperson to assist Madame Somar with finding what she liked. Arizle thanked him and began examining the different china displays. She saw a Bavarian set that she adored for its simplicity, loveliness and refined design. After deciding on the dishes, she chose a beautiful set of Baccarat crystal. The silverware was simple and practical. She also purchased some glasses for everyday use, place mats with matching napkins, and a table centerpiece and two candlesticks of Bohemian crystal. As she was finishing her purchases, she spotted a lovely maroon Sèvres pedestal cake plate. She added the piece to her other purchases and finally, she said that she did not want to look any more, for she had all that she needed. She arranged for the package to be delivered to her residence after the bill was submitted for payment at Dr. Rameda Pachêco's office. Senhor

Daniel shook her hand, thanking her for choosing his store. Arizle remarked that he had magnificent merchandise, and she was happy that her saleslady at Imperial had suggested his store.

She left and began walking toward the Largo de San Francisco, but returned to Casa Daniel to ask where she might find a store for kitchen utensils. The saleslady who had helped her recommended Loja Dragão (Dragon Store) on Alfandega Street, telling her how to get there. She thanked the woman and left.

She walked for at least fifteen minutes before she saw the street and the store signs. She saw one store after another, all displaying pots, pans, and all kinds of cooking utensils behind their plate glass windows.

She entered the second store from the corner and found the quality of the merchandise was much more modest than that on Ouvidor Street. She began browsing, picking up some heavy pots and pans she had found, when a man approached her, asking whether she wanted him to hold those items for her. She nodded her head and added that she probably would have a lot of utensils to purchase, but she needed his help to find all of them. She spent more time in that store than at Imperial or Casa Daniel. The store was crowded, and just making her way through the people to make her choices took time. After one and a half hours, Arizle finally had all that she needed to prepare Rameda's meals. She left after signing the bill and asking them to have everything delivered to Dr. Pachêco's office.

She was tired and her feet ached from standing and walking for the last six hours. She was getting hungry and thirsty, so she decided to go back to their apartment. She left the noisy, crowded store and walked toward a row of taxis parked on the next block. She opened the door of the first taxi parked by the curb and asked to be taken to Tijuca, 47 Guapeni Street.

Arizle only returned fifteen minutes ahead of Rameda. When he opened the door, he found her sitting in bed, massaging her feet. He promptly told her that massaging her feet was his job. He kissed her, happy to see that she had not changed her mind and gone back to Leumas. He took over massaging her feet, and she reclined backward on the bed, keeping both feet on his lap. He asked her if she had had fun shopping for herself and their apartment. Instead of answering him, she thanked him for rubbing her feet and sat up in bed close to him. Her eyes were shining as she described all the outfits that she had bought.

He kissed her lips and she returned his kiss, thanking him for the lovely and elegant clothes she had been able to buy due to his generosity. He interrupted her and interjected that he saw her as his wife, his responsibility, and that he was not being generous; instead, he felt he was being selfish, for he wanted her to dress beautifully so that he could show her off to his friends. She commented that she needed to wear everything that she had bought quickly, for within a few weeks, they would certainly not fit her for a few months.

He got up, walked toward the small entrance hall and brought her four large boxes from Imperial and three boxes from the Leão da Lapa, the store in which she had purchased the kitchen utensils. He told her that Casa Daniel had called and apologized for not being able to deliver her purchases today. Their delivery truck had broken down, and they would be delivering the boxes to the apartment tomorrow.

"Did you have anything to eat?" he asked her affectionately.

"No," she replied, "I did not take time to stop for lunch. Also, I would not go alone to a restaurant." He stood in front of her and asked,

"Do you prefer to make love or go out to eat?"

She laughed, pulling him to her. "I want both."

"In which order?" he asked with a playful look.

She hugged him, but stated that she was going to faint if she did not eat first. Nevertheless, she added, "You might be able take advantage of me now because I am feeble."

He helped her up and said, "Let us go eat first, for I have a surprise for you."

She went into the bathroom, quickly combed her hair, put her nylons back on, and put on her shoes. He took her hand, and they left as if they had no worries in the world.

They went to a neighborhood restaurant and were greeted effusively by the maître d'. They chose a table in the corner near a large fish tank. He ordered a red wine after asking her if she liked it. She replied that she did, but she thought it was better for her not to drink because of the baby. He agreed with her and instead ordered mineral water for them both. As soon as the waiter left, he placed his hands in his pocket, took out a small box and gave it to her. She opened it with excitement and anticipation and found two gold wedding bands inside.

Looking at her with loving eyes, he said, "I thought we should be married in the eyes of God before we start our life together." He removed Leumas's wedding band from her finger and placed a small wedding band on the ring finger on her left hand. "Is it too tight, or did I get your size right?" he asked solicitously. He handled her old wedding band carefully, placing it in the empty box, and gave it back to her.

"It is beautiful," she replied, holding both his hands and squeezing them with hers. Then she took the larger band and placed it on his left ring finger.

Suddenly, her eyes filled with tears and her brow furrowed pensively. He asked her what was she thinking about.

She hesitated for a second, then said, "I was thinking about Marcos being downhearted in his room while I am so happy. I want to make you happy, Rameda, for I love you deeply, and I am sorry if I think of Marcos and Leumas in my moments of deep happiness," she remarked dismally. "I wish they could be here with me." She knew her statement sounded nonsensical and deranged. Deep in her heart, her happiness was not complete without Leumas and Marcos participating in her glorious moments. She knew it was very selfish of her to want Leumas to support and be interested in her when she was putting someone else's wedding band on her finger. She had thought of removing Leumas's wedding band the day she left their house, but had decided to leave it on her finger. Several times after she arrived at their apartment, she had thought of placing it in her bag and just carrying it with her, but she did not. She felt incompletely dressed without it.

Rameda perceived her torment. He looked into her eyes and voiced his understanding of what she was going through. He added that he thought it was perfectly normal for her to think of her son and the man she had married and had grown to love and respect like a father.

She looked at him and whispered, "Thank you for understanding and loving me!"

The waiter brought the water and gave them the menu. They made their choices, and the waiter left them to their thoughts.

"Rameda," she said, interrupting the silence, "the Chinese philosopher, Lin Yutang, wrote that happiness is never complete. Have you ever read *The Wisdom of China and India?*"

"No, Darling," he answered, "tell me about it."

She described to him what she had read about happiness and love. Lin Yutang's beliefs were that victory caused hatred, and that the victorious ones were unhappy, while those who abandoned victory or were defeated were the serene ones.

"He believes that only truth brings happiness, and we then live free from ambition, among the ambitious. There is no fire similar to the fire of passion," Arizle continued, "but passion does not bring serenity."

"Arizle," he said, "this is too deep for me." Arizle was embarrassed and changed the conversation by telling him that the wedding bands were heavy and beautiful. She particularly loved the inscription inside the bands. Hers had his name and his had her name. She thanked him once again, blowing him a kiss.

When the food came, they ate quickly for they both had missed lunch, and they were starved. After having cafésinho, they walked hand in hand to the furniture store. The coffee demitasse was strong and had renewed their energy. Arizle stopped to look at the window display. She saw two bedside tables that were just what she wanted. He saw her eyes on the tables, and pulled her inside, so that she could see the tables up close. They walked toward the dining room sets and she spotted a Jacarandá, a round dining table for four. The wooden table was gorgeous, with carvings all around the edges and on its feet. It was massive and looked to be quite heavy. The carvings on the chairs matched the designs on the table. He asked her if she liked it, and she responded that she loved it. He called a salesman and purchased the two bedside tables and the dining set. He reminded her that they needed a piece of furniture with drawers in which to place some of their smaller clothes items. She asked him if a dresser would be what he was thinking about. He nodded his head, and they examined a large dresser in Chippendale style. She liked it, and he bought it. The pieces could not be delivered for three days because, even though they lived very close, the delivery trucks were fully scheduled with previous deliveries. Rameda asked to speak to the owner whom he had met when they had purchased their bed. The owner was not in that evening, but the salesman told Rameda that he would speak to him about arranging for an earlier delivery if possible. Rameda wrote a check, and they left the store, happy that their apartment was shaping up and, little by little, was turning into a lovely home.

The next day after Rameda left, Arizle called Francisca to ask her about Marcos. Francisca was not very talkative; she told Arizle in a few words that Marcos had a fever and had not gone to school. He was in bed. Arizle did not ask anything else. She told Francisca that she would be there in twenty minutes.

Arizle took a shower, got dressed and left. She walked to the corner and took a taxi to Leumas's home. Francisca met her at the gate and warned her that she had not said anything to Marcos about her coming to see him. Marcos never mentioned his mother's name and Francisca was concerned that he would be upset with her. Arizle walked quickly into the house, going straight upstairs.

Marcos was surprised to see her. She could see he was still angry with her. He acted very cold toward his mother, despite Arizle's arms being extended to him. Arizle took his temperature, which was slightly elevated. His nose was running and he had a headache. She asked him whether he had taken any aspirin. He nodded his head and said that his uncle was coming to keep him company and that his father was calling every two hours to check on him. She did not need to be concerned, for at least his father had taken good care of him.

She asked him if she could read to him. He replied that he had a headache and did not want her to read to him. She stayed with him for an hour and talked, but he only answered her questions with disdain and disinterest. After she heard from Francisca that Marcos's uncle was on his way there, she kissed Marcos on his forehead and left. She did not know what to do about Marcos's attitude and deep resentment. Her victory in being able to leave Leumas was looking more like her defeat. She had lost the war to her son. Being a strong general did not seem important any longer. She felt she had lost Marcos's love and respect.

That afternoon, Leumas called her and asked her not to see Marcos for a time. He seemed to be angered by her visit. He said Arizle needed to stay away awhile; she needed to give Marcos time to reflect and become more accepting of her presence in his life. Arizle cried alone in her bed. Her situation was a paradox to her. She had gained the life she wanted with Rameda, but the price she had to pay for her freedom seemed exorbitant.

She phoned Laura, with whom she had not spoken since she had left Leumas. Laura sided with

119

Leumas and told her she had committed a sin by abandoning her son and a man who loved her. In addition, Laura shared with her that their father was furious at her actions and had no interest in seeing her any longer. She had gone to see him only once after she moved to Rio de Janeiro.

"You, Arizle, ruined the family's reputation," asserted Laura. "You ought to think it over, and if Leumas accepts you back, that is where you should go, back to your husband and son!"

Arizle cried after she hung up with Laura. She felt lonely and in despair. The phone rang, and she quickly answered, trying to regain her composure. It was Rameda.

He said to her, "Prepare yourself, for we are going to the Casino da Urca tonight. Carlos Gardel, who I know is one of your favorite singers, is singing the Argentinean tangos you love so much." She pretended everything was all right. She said her tears were caused by a sad story she had heard from Laura. He sensed she was telling him a fib, but he did not insist on knowing what had really happened, for he had someone in the office and could not talk freely.

When Rameda came home that night, he had two large suitcases with him. He had brought his clothes to hang up in their closet. She helped him hang his suits, while she had on a beautiful lingerie robe she had bought at Imperial. He commented on how attractive her hair looked. She had gone to the hairdresser and had also had a manicure and pedicure. Her makeup was appropriate for the soft moss color dress she was wearing that evening. She looked alluring and full of self-confidence.

That night they had a splendid time at the casino. They danced cheek-to-cheek, as if their world were at peace and their lives were enveloped by constant joy. It was glorious to experience such happiness, Arizle thought. She remembered Lin Yutang's words that real happiness was a state of the soul and not a feeling that would last indefinitely.

For the next three months, they went out two times a week to ice shows, to hear Pedro Vargas, the great interpreter of Mexican songs, Marequita Flores, the Spanish dancer, Marta Eggerth, the famous singer of exotic symphonic melodies, and Tatiana Leskova, the Russian ballerina, dancing Scheherazade by Rimsky-Korsakov. These artists were internationally known, and since gambling was legal in Brazil, the casinos offered the public the best and the greatest to entice their patronage. These opportunities to see such famous acts enlivened their days. Often they took friends with them, and Laura now was Arizle's periodic guest. Laura seemed to have stopped judging her sister.

Rameda and Arizle lived in a world of fantasy and light. Despite the beauty of their surroundings, Rameda from time to time detected her sad eyes, gazing at an invisible horizon. He did not ask her what she was thinking; instead, he respected her private thoughts. Arizle never forgot about Marcos and Leumas. She constantly wished Marcos could be with her, seeing the spectacular and glorious shows. That Marcos would adore them, she had no doubt. Happiness was never complete, she remembered from her readings. Would she ever find complete happiness? Would anyone? In the midst of glamour and beauty, her reflections were philosophical and fundamentally about searching for answers about life and about herself. No one knew her thoughts. Would these thoughts be the only real secrets she was to keep for herself? The rest of her life seemed to be the topic of conversation among her friends, acquaintances and relatives. She lived in sin, and that was the subject of their idle nights.

Laura came to visit her and liked how she had decorated the apartment. She was coming around from her rigid ways of thinking and had started to go out with Arizle and the group of friends Arizle had met at the Baile do Teatro Municipal. Life for Arizle was busy, with many evenings out. She had less time to think of Marcos and Leumas as often as she used to, but she continued to call them every week. Francisca was warmer towards her, for she felt that Arizle was a good woman trapped in a situation from which she could not escape. Arizle's choices had been made for her by her father, and it was time for her to take hold of her own life and try to find some happiness, if it was at all possible for anyone to encounter it. Francisca had not herself found happiness, but she admired Dona Arizle for trying desperately to discover it and for not giving up easily. Francisca had no education, but she had natural common sense and practical experience. She liked Dona Arizle for her tenderness and empathy.

Their apartment was beautifully decorated, due to Arizle's refined taste. She had chosen tones of beige, cinnamon and nutmeg for the drapes in the living room. Navy, beige and brick-colored cushions accented the two champagne loveseats they had bought at a store in Ipanema Beach. She bought fresh flowers every week to decorate the dining room and the coffee table between the sofas. Rameda was proud of the home she had put together for them, and he wished he could convince his father to visit them and witness how happy he was, how beautiful everything looked, how good a cook she was and how much she enjoyed reading and learning. Rameda was happy with her, but his father's reactions to learning about their living together 'in sin' concerned him. His father had no idea of the situation, and Rameda was afraid that his father would disinherit him if he found out. How would he then take care of Arizle in the manner he wanted? Arizle and Rameda both had problems and barriers to overcome. Arizle knew that life was a journey from her books on ancient Indian and Chinese philosophy. This awareness should have brought her a little more serenity, but it did not. She felt overwhelmed by decisions. Rameda did not talk to her about his father or his family. He avoided the subject, for he knew that she had enough on her mind.

The days passed, and the birth of the baby was nearing. She was very big, and she did not want to be seen at social events any longer. She was uncomfortable sitting and many times uncomfortable standing. Elza had recommended a maternity shop, and Arizle had purchased beautiful outfits. She did not eat much, but she looked heavy and felt very unappealing. Rameda did all the shopping now and had engaged a daily maid to come and help her. Arizle liked her independence and in such a small environment, she wished she did not need help and could be alone. Mirta, the day cleaning lady, came every day of the week, because Rameda did not want her to be alone.

Rameda was truly troubled by his father's expected reaction once he knew the truth about his love for Arizle. He had to tell his father that he was living with Arizle and that she was going to give birth to his child. He fretted with the thought of confronting his father and mother. He was concerned more with his father than with his mother. She was an unassuming woman who had lived all her life for her husband, children and grandchildren. She had no other ambitions but the ones of fulfilling her duties as a loyal, hard-working wife. The Pachêcos were Catholic, old-fashioned, family-oriented and hard-working.

Rameda was not sleeping well. He looked tired and preoccupied. He had made an appointment to talk to his father at his father's home. He told his father that he urgently needed to discuss an important subject with him and that it could not wait another week. On the following Sunday, Rameda left Arizle to visit his father arriving there at 8:00 a.m. The Danish guard dogs were still loose in the big garden. Rameda had been bitten by one of them one day when he had come home around three in the morning; therefore, he did not want to take chances, and waited for the gardener to come out, fetch the animals and put the dogs on a leash.

Rameda entered the home in which he had lived until he moved in with Arizle. The atmosphere was sad and gloomy. He had gotten used to rooms full of light, and now his father's home resembled an austere museum. He passed by the everyday dining area and followed the corridor to his father's office. His father was sitting in his chair and greeted Rameda cordially, but formally.

"What brings you here, Dr. Rameda?" he queried. Rameda was pale, and he had put his sweating hands in his pockets, for they were shaking badly; he did not want his father to see that he was a nervous wreck.

"Rameda," he asked, "are you all right? Rameda, calm down. You are going to have a heart attack the way you are behaving."

Rameda could not hide his nervousness any longer and finally blurted to his father, "Dad, I have been living with a married woman for the last five and a half months, and she is giving birth any day to my child." His father became very upset and told his son that neither he nor his woman was welcome in that house.

"But Father, she is giving birth to your grandchild soon!" Rameda protested.

His father answered, "Not my grandchild. I do not recognize any bastard grandchildren. We are a decent family, Rameda," he added. "How dare you leave your parents' home to go and live with a married woman! Are you out of your mind? Do not go back to the office Monday, unless you leave this woman and come back to your parent's home. I thought," he declared, "that you had better sense. What future does this child have? You know very well that by law this child is the property of the man to whom this woman is married."

His father's statements paralyzed Rameda. When he was able to move his legs again, Rameda left the room and went outside to the garden. He sat by the fountain, without listening to the running water or seeing anything in front of him. He felt destroyed by his father's insulting and harsh words. He did not know what to think or what to do.

After deep thought, he went to the telephone and phoned Leumas at his home.

He said to Leumas, "Come and get your wife, because my father just fired me, and Arizle is better off with you. Arizle needs a father for her child who can legally register it. The child will be a bastard without a father." Leumas was astounded by Rameda's words. He asked him where Arizle was at that moment, and

Rameda answered that she ought to be at the apartment.

"You have no character. The first difficult obstacle that appears in your path and you act like a stupid, cowardly madman!" Leumas reprimanded him before slamming down the phone.

Leumas told Marcos he was going to pick up Arizle, because she would be coming back to live with them, and he also told Marcos to put on his shoes, because he was going with him to fetch Arizle. Marcos jumped out of his chair and put on his shoes in seconds. Leumas and Marcos went downstairs and walked to the garage. Leumas started the car, not saying much. He was upset and did not want to sound irrational.

It took them twenty minutes to make the trip. He parked his car, entered the building followed by Marcos, and took the elevator to the second floor. He rang the doorbell. Arizle opened the door and started to cry. Leumas told her what had transpired and ordered her to take only the items she had brought into the relationship with Rameda. She did not need any fancy clothes; what she needed was a loving father for her baby. He was going to be this father. He told her Rameda had changed his mind, apparently after telling his father about Arizle and the baby. Arizle gathered her clothes, sobbing the entire time. Leumas told her to stop crying or the baby was going to be born a nervous child. Arizle blew her nose in her handkerchief and tried to dry her tears, but she could not stop. Leumas went into the kitchen, looked for a glass, filled it with cold water and sugar and gave it to Arizle to drink. After she drank it, she regained her composure, picked up her suitcase, tossed her keys on the bed and left with Marcos and Leumas.

In the car, Marcos searched for Arizle's hand. Finding it, he kissed it and then climbed into her lap, throwing his arms around her. She started to cry again, saying that at least one good thing had come out of this calamity—she might have regained Marcos's love. Marcos cried along with her, hanging on tightly to her hand.

After the car was parked in the garage, Arizle got out and went into the living room with Marcos. He still held her hand tightly, and nothing would persuade him to let go. Marcos took Arizle into his room and showed her all the plays he had written, all the sculptures made out of wood blocks and all the paintings he had made for the last five months. Marcos gave his mother a notebook full of poems he had written. Arizle hugged him for a long time and told him that she had missed him terribly and that she was happy that he could find strength within himself to forgive her for her weaknesses, faults and sins. Marcos and Arizle read to each other for many hours. Leumas sat in a chair by Marcos's bedroom door and listened to the reading session as if he had missed seeing Marcos and Arizle enjoying each other's physical and intellectual company.

Arizle was uncomfortable, but she did not want to interrupt her time with Marcos. Her feet were swelling, and Leumas insisted that on Monday she should visit the doctor. She agreed with Leumas, kissing his head and thanking him for coming to rescue her from loneliness, rejection and confusion.

The next day, Leumas called his office, letting them know that he had an emergency at home and would not be in. He waited patiently for Arizle and Marcos to finish their breakfast and told Marcos that, after driving him to school, he was going to take his mother to the gynecologist. Marcos interrupted him and reminded him that obstetricians, not gynecologists, delivered babies. Leumas smiled and reassured Marcos that he was absolutely right, but this doctor did both. Marcos picked up his briefcase and took his mother's hand, leading her to the garage. Arizle was heavy and was walking slowly and carefully. Marcos opened the door for her and made sure that she was comfortable sitting in the back. Leumas dropped Marcos at school and proceeded to the doctor's office.

When the doctor saw Leumas in the waiting room, he was surprised to see a different man claiming the baby's paternity. Arizle did not make any comment; she was there to solve the problem of the swelling in her legs and feet, not to solve her personal problems. The doctor examined her and said that the baby could come any day now. He prescribed a diuretic and suggested that she stay in bed as much as she could, for it was essential that she rest. Leumas was anxious to know if she was all right, for she looked pale, tired and despondent.

When she returned to the waiting room, Leumas got up to offer her his arm. How would she ever repay him for his unconditional love, the type of love that one expects only from a dedicated and responsible mother? Leumas was the mother and the father she had lost. She kissed his hand in front of the nurses, who watched his care and tenderness toward her. He looked at the nurses, smiled and shook his head, as if to say that he did not deserve her thanks.

Leumas drove home carefully, so as not to bounce the car around too much. She seemed to be in pain, but she assured him that she was just sad, not hurting physically.

"My soul hurts," she exclaimed tiredly.

Leumas stopped at the drugstore and bought her prescription, while she waited in the car. When they arrived home, Leumas helped her change and get into a light nightgown. She slipped under the covers, while he went to the kitchen to fetch a glass of water for her to take her pills. She was mentally exhausted, and she could not conceive of Rameda acting in this manner. He was scared, she thought, but he should at least be with her when his baby was born.

The following morning, Arizle's water broke at eight-thirty, so Leumas did not go to work, and Marcos had no one to take him to school. Marcos and Leumas helped her downstairs and supported her under her arms as she walked, bowed with contractions, toward the garage. The motor was running, and as soon as she was installed in the back seat with Marcos by her side, Leumas drove to the closest hospital in Meyer, a nearby suburb.

Arizle was met by a nurse and helped into a waiting wheelchair. Leumas had called the hospital, advising them that a patient about to give birth needed a wheelchair to go to the delivery room. The nurse took Arizle to a private room where a doctor was going to examine her and decide whether it was time to go into the delivery room. After a brief look, the doctor decided to send her to be prepared for the birth. The baby's head was showing. Arizle was in great pain.

Leumas and Marcos waited outside, anxious and scared. They were pacing back and forth and did not want to sit. Somehow, by pacing they felt they were doing something, and it was not so hard to wait. Around eleven o'clock, the doctor came out and told them that Arizle had given birth to a baby boy who weighed thirteen pounds and five ounces and was perfectly healthy. Leumas asked to see Arizle and take

Marcos with him, and the doctor accompanied them to the recovery room where Arizle was. She had been given anesthesia for an episiotomy, so she was quite sleepy. She opened her eyes momentarily and then closed them again. She was safe and sound, and Leumas was happy with his new son. Marcos looked at the baby boy and smiled.

"He looks so small," Marcos remarked. Leumas looked at Marcos, touching his blond head in a fatherly way. Arizle stayed in the maternity ward for five days. She asked Leumas what she should call her new son, and Leumas replied that it was entirely up to her. She then asked Marcos, who answered, "Ricardo." Arizle liked Marcos's choice and named him Ricardo Somar. Leumas registered him as his son, which by law he was.

Arizle was devastated that Rameda did not even call. Granted, how could he know? However, he could have called to check on her, but he did not. Leumas knew that Arizle's visit was not going to be of a permanent nature. Arizle needed support and love, and he would always love her and give to her when she needed it. Marcos was happy with his brother, except for the time his mother spent away from him, taking care of Ricardo.

Leumas bought a crib for Ricardo while Arizle and the baby were at the hospital. He also surprised Arizle with diapers, baby soap, talc and a baby's layette, which Laura assisted him in choosing. Arizle was very grateful for Leumas's generosity, and she knew in her heart that he was her guardian angel. He watched the baby so she could sleep, fed the infant and sang songs to lull him to sleep.

Marcos was less patient with Ricardo's crying sessions. Ricardo had changed Marcos's routine with his mother and that was a concern to him. Arizle slept during the day so that at night she could watch the baby and ensure that Leumas and Marcos would have a peaceful night. On weekends, Arizle involved Marcos in Ricardo's life, enlisting him in doing several tasks for his brother. Marcos enjoyed helping Arizle with Ricardo. When Ricardo went to sleep, Arizle would try to read with Marcos, but she was so tired she would fall asleep. Marcos did not like the feeling of being in second place. He was not ready to share his mother with anyone. Arizle explained to Marcos that when he was a baby, he had received the same attention Ricardo was getting now. Marcos became more willing to share her with Ricardo as time went by.

Arizle still expected Rameda to call every day. She thought of Rameda constantly, and the thought of never seeing him again was taking a toll on her. She was very sad and desperate. Leumas observed her in silence and he never mentioned Rameda's name to her, because he knew it would too painful for her to talk about him. Leumas fell in love with Ricardo. He could not do enough for the little baby, who adored being in his arms and seemed to recognize him whenever he went to watch him in the crib. Arizle took Ricardo outside in the early morning sun. Ricardo was very alert, and he seemed to love to be carried and placed on his stomach on a towel that was spread out on the grass.

The days were going by fast, and Ricardo was gaining weight. He looked more lively and was more demanding of attention. Francisca also liked holding him, but Arizle did not want him to become a crybaby every time he was not being held, so she kept him in his crib or in the playpen that Arizle had received as a baby gift from Laura. Laura told all her friends that her sister had had a baby boy. She loved babies and came to visit them often. Arizle still wondered why Rameda had not called. She was convinced that he had learned about Ricardo, and she was very anxious and felt desperately alone without his love and his presence. Ricardo was two months old when Rameda finally called and came to see Arizle. Arizle suspected that Leumas had phoned him and told him a few truths about himself—how stupid he had been in running away from his responsibilities and not being with Arizle when she bore his son. Leumas never mentioned a phone call to Rameda, and Rameda made no mention of his various arguments with his father, whose health was deteriorating with each passing day. Rameda had engaged in numerous discussions with his father. Seu Pachêco was tired of arguing with his son about Arizle and their future together.

One day, for health reasons, Seu Pachêco decided to retire from the business and leave it up to the direction of his four sons. He had built an empire, with seven large ranches close to Rio de Janeiro, the meat packing plant, and numerous acres of land surrounding the slaughterhouse. Also, he had built the Castelo do Rio, a building whose prominent location resembled that of the Empire State Building in New York. He had worked hard and honorably all his life, and he had been loyal to his wife and nine children. His three thousand employees loved him, and his leadership practices had been revolutionary for his times. He had given his sons and daughters the best educational opportunities, and his daughters had married well—one to a well-known count and the others to doctors and lawyers from traditional families. He knew he had performed good deeds during his long and regimented life.

Rameda did not lie to his father. Seu Pachêco had observed how thin and gaunt Rameda had become in the last two months since his breakup with Arizle. He rested his case; if Rameda wanted to throw away his life, he should do it. He was too tired and sick to continue his persuasive tactics with his son. Arizle or her children would never be welcomed in his house. Rameda did not have to see his father every day any longer, and what his father's eyes did not see would not hurt his heart.

Leumas was home when Rameda arrived to visit Arizle and see his son for the first time. Leumas made it very clear to Rameda that Arizle was not a prostitute or an abandoned woman. Leumas assured Rameda that she had a home and that his son had a father— Leumas. Neither one wanted anything from Rameda except to be loved and cherished by him, and a commitment from him to protect and ensure their safety Arizle was silent. She was amazed at how Leumas had the courage to tell Rameda off, as if he were his father. Rameda had tears in his eyes when he saw Arizle. She had returned to her normal figure, and she looked as attractive as ever. Arizle wanted to run to Rameda's arms, but the hurt she had experienced by his rejection of her and his son caused her to be very formal and reserved. After all, he had abandoned her.

Rameda told them both what had happened. Leumas did not accept any excuses that Rameda offered. Leumas told him that no one should concern him more than his son and his wife. Leumas said that even though they were not married in the eyes of the law, they were married in the eyes of God. That, according to Leumas was the only consent Rameda needed, not his father's or his mother's approval. Rameda should be mature enough to not have to ask

133

his mother and father for permission to assume responsibilities he had contracted when he asked Arizle to move in with him. Rameda got on his knees and promised Arizle that he would never leave her again. He promised, as God was his witness, that he would never willingly abandon his family—only if death intervened.

Leumas left them alone in the living room. Rameda asked Arizle to forgive him once again, and said she would never be sorry if she gave him a second chance. Arizle listened to his words, but she was not very moved by his promises. She was afraid to trust him again. He assured Arizle that she was absolutely right to be suspicious of his statements, for he had failed her as a man, as a husband and as the father of their son. Arizle stood motionless. She did not have anything to say to him, except that she had missed him terribly. Also, she made clear to him that she was not going to forsake her son Marcos and the friendship of a man like Leumas for Rameda, and she needed some assurance that he was sure that this was what he really wanted. Never again, she told him, would she live with him, until she was sure that he was making a deliberate decision because of his true need for her and his love for her and his son.

Rameda continued to plead with her to give him another chance. She finally agreed to go and live with him, but first she needed to talk to Marcos and Leumas. Rameda kissed her hand respectfully and told her that he had seen a piece of land for sale and that he wanted to buy it for her and build a house to her specifications. However, he assured her, this was not his way of convincing her to be with him as his wife in the eyes of God; this was his way to tell her that his mind was made up.

Rameda said, "The land and house will be purchased in your name. I want you and Ricardo, and I will take Marcos to live with us, if he wants to come. Dr. Leumas can visit us anytime he wants. He will be my friend as well as yours. I have grown to respect him as much or more than I respect my own father."

As he left, Rameda told her that he would call her the next day and would come to pick her up with her two sons the moment she agreed to go.

"The apartment is still there, just as you left it," he told her. "I stayed in the apartment all this time and never went back to my father's home. I truly suffered," he asserted. "There were nights when I did not sleep at all, thinking of you, but after what I did, I did not have the nerve to call you. I picked up the phone many times only to replace the receiver two seconds later, wondering if you hated me and if I would ever see you again. The only time I was able to sleep was when I traveled for my father, buying cattle for the slaughterhouse, and spent the whole day on horseback, going from pasture to pasture counting steers. Those nights I slept better, because I was totally exhausted from riding for miles at a time. When I was in Rio, I could not sleep a full night; I woke up every two hours thinking about you."

"I love you, Arizle," revealed Rameda. "I have never loved anyone like I love you; it is a frightening experience to love someone this much. My family is not very demonstrative. I never saw my father kiss my mother on the lips. I do not remember hearing my father tell my mother in front of us children that he loved her. Their relationship has always been a formal one in front of us children. It is a real miracle that they had nine children. We must have been brought into their home by a stork that felt sorry for them," he added. Arizle laughed at him; she knew he was sincere and honest.

He left, and she went back to Ricardo and Leumas. Marcos had gone to visit his grandparents and his uncles. Leumas was holding Ricardo in his arms. He had changed him and he was trying to sing him a lullaby. Arizle could see how much love Leumas felt for Ricardo. He loved Marcos, but for some reason with Ricardo, he felt more at liberty to show his affection. Ricardo seemed to love Leumas as well. What would happen to Leumas and Marcos when she left them once again? Would Marcos hate her? Would Leumas visit them? She had no answers for her questions. Only time would tell. She was not very patient with what she did not know. Marcos had seemed much happier since her return. It would be so difficult to leave her darling Marcos. Her life was a series of paradoxes of which she seemed unable to rid herself. Was she ever going to be happy? Was she destined never to find peace and serenity? Her stomach tightened and she felt queasy, thinking about the road ahead.

Leumas said nothing to stop her from leaving. Her happiness, he had decided a long time ago, was more important than anything else. He would not make her stay. It was obvious to him that she loved Rameda and that she would only be happy with him. She would say goodbye to him once again. This time, he would cry, for he had become very attached to Ricardo. He could not explain why he felt such affection for the little boy who was not even his natural son, but he sensed that Ricardo and he would become lasting friends.

Arizle and Leumas had a long and serious talk before she left. She asked him to promise her that he would come to have lunch every Sunday that he could. He also promised her that he would bring Marcos to the house that Rameda was going to build for her. Arizle told Leumas that he would always be her best friend and that he was the only man she knew who would risk his life to save her or Ricardo. She said she could not live without his friendship and could not leave without knowing that he would not abandon their friendship. Leumas promised her that he would always be there for her until death–hers or his. He knew that he would never marry again as long as she lived, but he did not tell her so. He knew that leaving them was very difficult and painful for her.

Rameda picked her up the next day. This time she had two suitcases. Leumas insisted that she should leave Ricardo's crib at his house. Rameda, he assured her, would want to buy him a different crib. The playpen stayed behind as well. Marcos was at school when Arizle left. When they arrived at the apartment, everything was exactly as she had left it. Mirta, the maid he had found to assist her in her last month of pregnancy, was there as well. Rameda was sure that Arizle was going to need her to watch Ricardo. The apartment had a tiny maid's room with a door to the service entrance, and Mirta said she wanted to continue working for Arizle and help her with the baby.

Rameda asked Mirta to watch Ricardo and convinced Arizle that they should go out and buy Ricardo a crib. At a children's furnishings store they found a lovely bed for the baby that would last until he was three or four years old. Arizle bought sheets, blankets, and a cover for the bed's canopy. The bed was precious, but where were they going to put it? Now they needed a bigger apartment.

Rameda told Arizle that he had already talked to the landlord, and that a three-bedroom apartment with larger maid's quarters was about to be vacated on the third floor. Arizle was happy to know that Ricardo would have his own room, but she insisted that the maid sleep in with him when they went out. Arizle in no circumstances would leave Ricardo to sleep alone. She had lost two younger sisters, and she was afraid he could die without someone there to call an ambulance and hold him. Rameda wanted to please her, and he said she should make her own decisions about Ricardo's well-being and safety. Arizle also told Rameda that if they traveled together, Ricardo would stay with Leumas, not with Mirta or anyone else. Rameda agreed to that also.

They returned to the apartment, accompanied by a young boy who was pulling a two-wheeler with the baby bed on it. Arizle had two light packages and Rameda was carrying four heavy ones. Arizle put Ricardo's bed in their room until they moved into the three-bedroom apartment. She did not want Ricardo out of her sight. Ricardo did not want to be carried by Rameda, and he seemed to miss Leumas. Rameda was irritated by Ricardo's reactions to him, but he did not complain, for he had not been there when Ricardo was born, and Ricardo only felt secure with his mother. Rameda thought Ricardo was a beautiful child, but he was not very good with babies. He did not know what to say or to do to entertain them. He liked his son, but his big love was Arizle.

Two weeks later, they moved into their new apartment. Arizle prepared a beautiful nursery for Ricardo with all kinds of toys, a dresser, a comfortable chair, and his canopy bed. Mirta started sleeping there with Ricardo, and Ricardo became quite attached to her. Rameda did not really feel close to Ricardo until much later, when Ricardo could play ball with him. When Rameda was not able to catch the ball, Ricardo would call him diabo. It meant devil, and Rameda laughed whenever Ricardo called him by this name.

Rameda and Arizle made sure that Mirta had all she needed to be comfortable in her room. She was conscientious about watching Ricardo and took him for walks in the beautiful baby carriage Rameda had purchased. She was not a good cook, but Arizle did not mind teaching her. While they were in the kitchen, Ricardo was in the playpen, surrounded by his toys. Ricardo enjoyed playing by himself, and they both kept an eye on him.

Now Rameda and Arizle had their bedroom to themselves. Rameda loved sleeping curled with her. He loved being able to kiss her and make love to her without having her worry about Ricardo. Mirta was responsible and reliable, and Arizle could depend on her to keep Ricardo safe. Now she had more time to cater to Rameda, who loved having her company all to himself. They were happy together.

Leumas and Marcos had come to have lunch with them twice, but Marcos had not wanted to stay overnight, even though he had a bedroom set aside for him. He always went home with his father. While there, Leumas spent all his time playing with Ricardo. Marcos spent time with his mother, but Marcos knew that their relationship had changed forever. Arizle would never again read with him. His father seemed enchanted with Ricardo, and Marcos felt lonely and isolated. Leumas never intended to have his son feel in this manner, but Marcos had never really related to his father as he did to his mother. Marcos had become a loner. Arizle observed these changes in Marcos and talked to Leumas. Leumas knew something was not right, and he felt he was making an effort to be closer to him, but Marcos preferred to be left alone.

Arizle loved having them all near her on Sundays. She worried about Marcos, who did not have friends with whom he liked to play or spend time. She talked to Marcos about being more sociable, but Marcos wanted to be left alone. He loved his books, his music, his paintings, his sculptures, his writings and his moments of solitude. He did not seem to be enthusiastic about going out with his father or going to a movie with a friend. He had enjoyed Arizle's company and only hers, but that had ended. He knew it was going to be that way, but did not want to talk about it with Leumas or anybody else.

Rameda admired and respected Leumas more than his own father. They became close friends, for the two loved the same woman, even though only one possessed her body and heart. Leumas knew he possessed only her spirit. He knew that she trusted him implicitly, and that she loved him as a father and as a best friend. Leumas never asked Rameda for anything and Rameda never contributed any money towards Marcos's upbringing. Rameda was the one always in need of Leumas. When he traveled with Arizle, they took Ricardo to stay with Leumas and Marcos. When they needed someone to come and water the plants, it was Leumas they counted on to perform these tasks. Leumas was their guardian angel and their faithful friend.

Arizle and Rameda began to go out again to the theater at least once a week. She loved Procópio Ferreira, and all of Pedro Block's plays. Pedro Block was the Tennessee Williams of Brazil, and Arizle liked his down-to-earth satires about life and its vicissitudes.

She loved "Morre Um Gato Na China" ("A Cat Dies in China"), Block's parody about playwrights who write plays, create characters and then forget about them. She thought her life was just like that, with her parents bringing her into the world, and her father choosing her destiny and then forgetting about her.

11

Rameda and Arizle bought a piece of land consisting of four large lots. The lots were back to back, bordered by two streets and had two large, old colonial Portuguese homes built around 1910. There were many beautiful old trees, but some of them needed to be cut down to make room for the large home they were going to build in the center of the plot. Rameda and Arizle wanted lots of gardens around the house. Rameda contracted with Derene Engenharia, a well-known architectural firm, to design the home Arizle wanted. The house was done in the Californian style, with big double doors opening onto a large terrace. There were twelve spacious rooms. The two bathrooms were so large that they had a sitting room inside of them. The color scheme in Arizle's bathroom was maroon and beige. She called this color combination "pus and blood." Arizle arranged the bathtub so that it was adjacent to a large fish tank, maintained from the outside. Only a glass wall separated the tub from the aquarium. In those days, anything out of the ordinary was a big attraction and that bathroom was certainly magnificent. The floor was of beige marble with Rameda's and Arizle's initials inlaid in dark green and maroon marble.

The master bedroom was enormous. She had its end walls covered with mirrors and it made the room look even larger, like multiple bedrooms with the same furniture and colors. Ricardo's room was very large also, and his bathroom was done in light yellow. The house's large windows had wrought iron protective bars, which allowed them to be left open in the hot summer nights. There were three living rooms, a formal dining room and an informal dining area that bordered on a large kitchen. All rooms, including the guestroom, opened onto the terrace. It was a dazzling home. Ricardo was almost two years old when they moved into it.

Arizle went to auctions and purchased artwork, porcelain and art objects to decorate their home. Every room had a collection of beautiful pieces in Sèvres, Limoges, Dresden, Delft, Ginori, Capodimonte, and Bastos Filhos ceramics. The chandeliers were of Baccarat crystal. Every piece of furniture was an antique or had been made to order by a famous craftsman. Arizle had been born poor, but she had exquisite taste and a flair for decorating. She even built a library for her books and had them bound in green leather with her initials, A.S.

They had four sleep-in maids, a chef, a butler, a laundress, a cleaning man, a full time gardener and a chauffeur for Arizle. A dressmaker came every day to fix uniforms, sheets, pillowcases and towels. The servant quarters had five large bedrooms with three adjacent baths. The chef had his own room. The chauffeur, the laundress, the gardener and the dressmaker all worked during the day and went home at night. On the other side of the plot, they had a four-car garage built. The property was protected and made private by a high brick wall.

Arizle and Rameda decided to have a formal open house for their families and friends to celebrate their new home, and they invited one hundred guests. An elegant invitation was printed, displaying both their names. The residence and its grounds looked festive, with fresh flowers and lights illuminating all the lush foliage, beautiful flower beds and lawns. Arizle invited her father and his wife, her brother and his wife, Laura, who was still single, Rameda's parents, brothers, sisters and nephews. Arizle never heard from her father, stepmother or other relatives. They were angry and did not approve of Arizle's life. Relatives were among the first in line to disapprove anytime there was an opportunity to point out that Rameda and Arizle were flouting the law. The invitations were an item of gossip among the friends and relatives, for Rameda and Arizle had used both their names without shame. There was no being right in such a situation. They knew they could never please everyone.

Sixty guests attended the reception. Arizle was not sure whether they were real friends or whether their curiosity had prompted them to attend. Rameda's parents sent no acknowledgement and no flowers. Only one of Rameda's brothers and one sister with her husband and three sons attended. Arizle was happy that not all the members of the Pachêco family thought of her as the enemy. Arizle treated everyone with courtesy and respect. She was sure that they would leave her house with a different opinion of her. She was not some woman that Rameda had picked up in a bordello, as they frequently spoke of her. Her uncle, the vice president of Brazil, was there with his wife, and he was proud of his niece and nephew.

They had the party catered by the Confeitaria Colombo, the most traditional caterer in the city. The house servants assisted with serving the food. Tables were set up on the lawn and there was a large tent in case of rain. Arizle, though beautifully dressed, looked sad and dispirited. Rameda's eyes were always on her, hoping she was enjoying herself. He appeared happy to be with her, but there was something missing for him as well. Happiness was never complete, just as Lin Yutang had stated.

A professional photographer took candid pictures of the guests and some portrait pictures of the members of Rameda's family and Arizle's Uncle Antônio and Aunt Claudia. Their friendship meant a great deal to Arizle. She learned a lot from Aunt Claudia, who enjoyed her company and took Arizle on trips. Uncle Antônio was the vice president of Brazil at that time, a career politician of unsullied reputation who had been a senator and ambassador to several countries. His moral support was tremendously important to Arizle. She asked for his help many times and followed his advice whenever he gave her guidance. She respected him immensely. He never judged her for her actions. On the contrary, he seemed to support his favorite niece in her union with Rameda. He had acted as her lawyer in her legal separation from Leumas. He recommended that Rameda and Arizle fly to Uruguay, obtain a divorce and get married, even though it would not be recognized in Brazil.

Claudia, Antônio's wife, was a beautiful, slim woman. She dressed elegantly and with impeccable taste. She had traveled all over the world with her husband, and as the ambassador's wife, had learned much about different cultures. Any conversation with her was interesting, because of her knowledge of worldwide politics, and also because she had a dry sense of humor. Her advice was gospel for Arizle. Aunt Claudia spoke candidly to Rameda and told him that Arizle needed a diamond ring. She had a beautiful home, but no good jewelry to adorn her person and accent her outfits. Rameda responded to her prompting by later giving Arizle a four carat diamond ring. Arizle did not think she needed a diamond, but Aunt Claudia had made up Rameda's mind that a ring on Arizle's finger was of the essence.

Arizle was like a sponge for knowledge, and Claudia loved introducing her to elegant stores, good theaters, fine restaurants, and the best auction houses to find lovely objects for her home. Arizle loved to improve herself. She read books on how to walk, how to dress, how to entertain guests, and how to prepare for a party, among many other social pleasantries. Arizle respected Claudia and told all her friends how much she had learned from her aunt, who spent a lot of time with the niece she came to enjoy and cherish. Moreover, Aunt Claudia loved parties, lights and dancing, as did Arizle, and the two were nearly inseparable.

Arizle was fond of telling young people who were about to marry a piece of advice that she had learned from her aunt. Aunt Claudia believed that joy of living was most important attribute to seek in a life companion.

"It makes life for two easier to manage," she asserted with conviction.

One day during the Christmas season, while they were shopping at the Confeitaria Colombo, Aunt Claudia created quite a scene with an innocent, but awkwardly amusing remark she made. Arizle and Claudia were picking up a few last-minute items for a reception that she was holding for her husband that day. She had left a turkey roasting in the oven, and suddenly she remembered that she had forgotten to tell the cook to turn the oven off. She became frantic with the thought that the turkey would burn.

Out of the blue, Claudia screamed, "Your uncle's turkey is burning!" Unfortunately, perú, the word for turkey in Portuguese, is also the common term for a man's penis. Claudia did not realize how much she had raised her voice, and nearly everyone in the store heard her comment. Curious, all the men in the store began moving towards her, and Claudia, fearing the mob, retreated to the establishment's kitchen. The police had to be called to escort Claudia and Arizle to their waiting car. When the crowd saw the official vice-presidential license plates on the car, they laughed and jeered even more. Arizle never forgot this incident and it was a source of great embarrassment to Claudia for a long time. Antônio, Claudia's husband, tried to imagine his elegant and ladylike wife caught in this awkward situation. He howled with laughter.

Arizle was a lady in her gestures, her manner of dress, the way she comported herself and how she wore make-up. Aside from her natural poise, she was articulate, intelligent and able to laugh at her own foibles. There was, however, an air that separated her from any other woman. It was her tenderness, her simplicity and her presence as a real human being. She did not have the superior attitude of a woman born to wealth. On the contrary, she looked at life in a down-to-earth, unique way. No job or person was beneath her. She treated the trash man in the same manner that she treated someone in high authority. She felt humble whenever she watched the sun rise, the birds sing and the flowers grow. She felt humble before the great creations of God, and thankful for his mercy and forgiveness.

Ranchers who dealt with Rameda and his father also attended the party. Arizle became friends with Rosina Duarte, the wife of one of the ranchers. Rosina was of Lebanese descent, and doing business seemed to be in her blood. She was constantly buying and selling different products; however, she never made any money on any of her transactions. On the contrary, she gave away her products for she was a very generous woman. Rosina liked to go with Rameda and Arizle to many casino shows, theaters and on trips. Arizle knew that Rosina had a crush on Rameda, but Arizle was patient and understanding with her friend, for she, too, had been the subject of an arranged marriage to an older man. Also, Arizle knew that Rameda did not care for Rosina, and so she did not have to worry about their having an affair.

She treated all the ranchers and their wives like royalty, for she knew they were very important to Rameda's business. Even though they were unsophisticated and ate their fish with their knives instead of with their forks, she did not mind and never commented on it. They were genuine but simple folk, and she respected them.

The party went on until the wee hours. Arizle's and Rameda's feet ached and their voices were hoarse. They had talked to everyone, always together, always holding hands. Leumas had not come to the party. He had been invited, but decided that his presence would only create more problems for her. She had been rejected by society many times, but she told him that he should never stop coming to see her and always come to have lunch with them on Sundays. He spent Christmas and Easter with them, and on Leumas's birthday, she prepared a formal dinner for him. His friendship with her was loving and strong, and no gossip or insults would ever separate them. Rameda came to feel that his family was not complete without Leumas's presence.

Rameda and Arizle had said goodnight to the last guests, and finally they were alone. Arizle removed her high heels and sat down in the middle of the living room to massage her feet. Rameda sat down beside her and took over the chore. She loved it when he rubbed her feet, and in exchange for his thoughtfulness, she also massaged his feet. He sighed with pleasure and remarked that she had healing hands. They retired to the bathtub for a bubble bath together and then went to bed. They were too tired to make love, but never too exhausted to sleep wrapped in each other's arms.

They loved to entertain, loved parties and adored dancing. They had their own table at the Casino da Urca and they continued to attend all the shows featuring Jean Sablon, who had abandoned his contract in the United States to sing at Urca's famous Bar and Grill das Estrêlas. Arizle loved Mariquita Flores, the great Spanish dancer, and José Mojica, one of Hollywood's greatest voices. When they were not out for the evening, they were entertaining friends. Her dinners were simply magnificent. She loved preparing flower arrangements and making sure that everything was taken care of, down to the last detail. Everyone admired her originality in designing beautiful and elegant table settings.

Rameda and Arizle decided to follow Uncle Antônio's suggestion and get married in Uruguay. They left Ricardo with Leumas and flew to Montevideo for three nights. Leumas took a three-day vacation from his job and devoted his time to Ricardo, who was attached to him as if he were his real father. They flew Panair, a Brazilian airline that had many flights to adjacent countries. They arrived in Montevideo at noon, and after leaving their luggage in their room, they went to see a Justice of the Peace recommended by Uncle Antônio. The old gentleman was waiting for them and was delighted to marry them. They looked wonderful together. She was dressed in a moss green suit that Elsa had showed her when she last went to Imperial Modas. Rameda wore a brown gabardine suit with a beige shirt and a light blue silk tie. He took advantage of the occasion to give her a pair of diamond clips that Aunt Claudia had suggested he give her.

"The girl has no brooch," he recalled Claudia saying to him. Arizle laughed at her aunt's frankness.

They spent three nights honeymooning. Arizle had taken the time to read about the culture and geography of the country prior to traveling there, but she saw very little of Uruguay's capital and felt more ignorant when she left than when she had arrived. They called for room service for every meal except dinner. They made love every night and during the day, for there were no phones ringing and no worries about the children. She called Leumas from the hotel once to ask him whether he was tired of watching Ricardo and to ask about Marcos. The phone call was brief, for Rameda pulled her toward him and told her that he was also a child, and that she should take care of him. In the evenings they went out for dinner and dancing. This was Arizle's first time outside of Brazil, and she wanted to wear her lovely clothes. She never forgot that trip and always remembered how content she had felt in getting a marriage certificate. Peace and quiet did not last long though, for when they returned to Rio, life was again real, with obstacles to be surmounted.

They had been home for only a few hours and were starting to unpack, when Ricardo's nanny dropped the little boy in the bathtub. Leumas had just dropped Ricardo off, safe and sound, a few hours before, and Ricardo's nanny had decided to give him a bath. The little boy was already clean and really did not want to take a bath. The scene with the little boy screaming in pain was chaotic. Arizle tore off to the hospital, where the doctor confirmed her suspicion that Ricardo had broken his collarbone. After making sure the bone was in the correct position, the doctor put Ricardo in heavy upper body cast to immobilize it. In the heat of summer, the cast was very uncomfortable, and Ricardo cried with the itchy rash that he got from the cast. Arizle slept restlessly for several weeks, keeping Ricardo company, singing sweet melodies to calm her two-year-old son's crankiness and discomfort. The nanny was fired, because the other servants had observed similar situations in which she was not very responsible or patient with Ricardo.

Arizle never forgot the time at the hospital, pacing in the waiting room, hearing Ricardo scream with pain. She recalled dealing with Marco's earaches all night long when he was a baby. Her present anguish was worse. She was older and more mature, but she had not learned to gain more control of herself in emergencies. When it came to an emergency involving Leumas, Marcos, Ricardo or Rameda, she was a hopeless, incapable idiot.

Leumas came to visit Ricardo everyday after work. He told him stories and played with him, and Rameda often insisted that he stay for dinner. Leumas had difficulty leaving Ricardo, especially when Ricardo had his arms around his neck and his head on Leumas's shoulder. Rameda enjoyed watching the love that they had for each other.

After four weeks, Arizle took him back to the hospital. The doctors took new x-rays and determined that it would be all right to take off the cast. When they cut the cast open, Ricardo's neck and shoulder were red and raw from the rash. For more than two weeks, Ricardo could not wear any clothes on the upper part of his little body. Arizle was patient as she slowly and tenderly soothed the child's skin with medicinal lotions.

The accident brought Rameda and Leumas closer to one another. Rameda felt embarrassed that he could not express his concern for Ricardo in the same manner that Leumas was able to do. They talked about their different natures. Rameda loved his son dearly, but Leumas seemed almost to love the little boy as a mother would love. Rameda said that he did not know why he did not enjoy children in general, but he thought perhaps it was because he had been one of nine children and had never had received the attention that Ricardo received from Leumas or Arizle. He was not sure so much attention was healthy for a child.

Leumas put his hand on Rameda's shoulder and told him that there was no such thing as giving too much love to a child. He told Rameda that Ricardo was very sensitive and was going to need lots of love and close friends. Then Leumas became pensive and admitted that his relationship with his own son was inhibited, and that he had great difficulty demonstrating the great affection he has for him. With Ricardo, it was different. Leumas felt that Ricardo craved his affection and also returned it. He felt needed as a friend and as a mentor.

"My own son," he remarked sadly, "does not want my guidance or my interference in his life. Since his mother left, he has turned into a callous young man, aloof and sarcastic." Rameda realized for the first time that Leumas had transferred his love for Arizle to Ricardo. Rameda felt sympathy for this kind man, who had lost the love of the only woman he had ever wanted and was now facing the truth that his only son did not seem to need him or his love. As understanding dawned, Rameda was no longer jealous of Ricardo's friendship with Leumas. He knew Ricardo had filled a void in the life of the lonely being he had grown to love and consider his best friend.

12

rizle was pregnant again. She had been using the contraceptives and pills prescribed by her gynecologist, but they had not worked. She was desperate, for she knew Rameda did not want more children. She called her friend Rosina and told her about the situation. Rosina had no advice, but she told her friend that she had had three abortions. Arizle did not want to tell Rameda. She could just see the disapproval on his face, and she did not want to upset him. She had taken the pills and used the diaphragm. What had gone wrong? Even her doctor had been surprised by the results of his examination. She hated her body for betraying her and was angry with herself for not being able to control the situation.

When Rameda arrived home that evening, she burst into tears. She could not keep the secret any longer and sobbed out the news. His face lost its loving expression and became austere. She knew her only option was to have an abortion, or she would lose him. She cried alone in their room with the doors closed. Rameda wanted to talk to her, but the only talk she really wanted to hear from him was that he was happy that she was pregnant again. She never heard that from him, and she continued to hate herself for the next seven times that she got pregnant and had to have an abortion. Although repeating the procedure surely and inexorably damaged her health, she did not know what else to do to save her relationship with the man she adored.

Her first abortion was traumatic. She cried for days afterward, and could not reconcile her actions with the thought of Rameda's abandoning her once again. She felt like a criminal, a selfish woman who enjoyed the pleasure of sex, but could not prevent getting pregnant. She even asked for surgery to tie off her Fallopian tubes, a procedure not done unless it was a matter of life and death, but the doctor refused.

Arizle loved children, and she never forgave herself for not allowing them to be born as nature had intended. If she got pregnant despite precautions, she was convinced that it was because God wanted her to have more children. Her personality changed after these abortions. She lost the twinkle in her eyes. She was a woman and no longer a child.

Arizle was not happy with herself. The life of parties and dancing no longer held appeal for her. She wanted to occupy herself with something nobler; she founded an orphanage for girls. There was much need for such a place because there were many children who had been left alone in the world for one reason or another and had no place to go. There were daughters of tuberculosis patients, children of prostitutes who had gone to prison or of destitute families who had left their babies at the gates of rich people's homes.

She organized a group of people who were willing to invest in this philanthropic cause, and they purchased an old colonial home on a large piece of land in Jacarepaguá, a suburb of Rio de Janeiro. She got Derene to draw the plans to enlarge the old structure for free, got Rameda to pay for the changes, and with other donations of friends and strangers who liked the idea, she purchased beds, chairs, desks, tables and utensils for the orphanage. The orphanage was named after Saint Anthony, since Arizle had always loved the cheerfulness of the matchmaker saint.

The orphanage was an immediate success. She hired three women to run the facility and formed a board of directors from among the very important men in city politics. In two months they had over one hundred girls, aged one month to four years old. The girls learned skills such as cooking, planting a vegetable garden, sewing, singing and playing instruments. She hired two women to teach the older children how to read. As they became older, they were allowed to go to other schools to finish high school or learn business skills such as typing, bookkeeping, and stenography. The fees were paid by donations. Many girls who wanted to continue their studies received scholarships and attended a school to become teachers.

Orfanato Santo Antônio had a waiting list of more than forty children. People from all over the city came to the establishment to ask for a placement for someone they knew. Arizle went to the orphanage three times a week. When Ricardo was five years old, she took him also. She thought that the experience would be good for him, since he might learn the value of what he had at home. She worked hard training the older girls to clean the kitchen and making sure that all bathrooms were left spotless. The girls were also

157

responsible for making the beds and keeping the dormitory tidy. Arizle trained the women carefully who worked in the kitchen. She wanted the girls to eat well and have healthy food. Any time she discovered theft or the mistreatment of any girl, she would dismiss the person immediately. The Board of Directors and Arizle hired employees only after thorough scrutiny. Leumas became Chairman of the Board and Arizle asked a retired colonel to be the president. She was the director.

The girls loved her. Once in a while, she would bring them all to her home for the day, for a picnic or a special celebration. She also organized trips to the zoo, to the botanical gardens, and occasionally to a museum. She purchased a movie projector for the girls to watch classic movies and interesting documentaries. She was dynamic and energetic when she had a project to accomplish.

Rameda complained that she was spending too much time with the girls and that she was working too hard. He wanted her to expend some of her energies in designing a country house for them. She jumped at this opportunity and started looking for a piece of land in Petrópolis, a charming town about fifty-five kilometers from the city.

13

Petropolis was well-known for its magnificent multicolored hydrangeas and for the fact that it had been the location of the summer home of the Brazilian Emperor, Don Pedro II. All the families of means had a summer place either in Petropolis or Teresopolis. Only an hour and a half away, located in the mountains of the Serra do Mar, it had a temperature twenty to thirty degrees lower than that in Rio. Arizle loved the little town, the cobblestone streets, and the beautiful homes along the road with their opulent gardens jammed with flowers. In her opinion, Petropolis should have been named the City of the Sun. The sun was strong in the mountains, so warm and nurturing, and Arizle enjoyed lying on a blanket with the sun beating down on her body. She called it the enchanting land. Arizle loved the sun in Petropolis, and that alone was a good reason to build a country home there.

Rameda purchased a large piece of land right across from the Quitandinha Hotel, the largest and best hotel in South America. The hotel had exquisite grounds and a large lake with an outdoor swimming pool. Pedal boats shaped like geese and swans waited on the shore for guests to rent them for a ride among the woods which grew out of the water and were full of tropical birds and metallic blue, Morphos butterflies. There were carts for guests to ride or lovely paths for long walks to observe the various trees and small wild animals. There were many playgrounds for children, where they could spend the entire afternoon safe and happy. Ricardo was six years old and had started school. He would love spending his weekends and summer vacations in a home on the other side of the lake, across from the front of the Quitandinha Hotel. Ricardo was already planning on bringing his school friends and cousins to stay with him at the house when it was built. Ricardo was very sociable and enjoyed having lots of other children around him.

The hotel had sprung from very humble beginnings. A man called Rolas, a street vendor, who sold tripe, giblets and offal from a small, refrigerated truck, had built the hotel. As young man of seventeen, Rolas used to like to sit on a log in a lovely spot near what was then a small natural pond. Rolas daydreamed for long periods of time and he envisaged a spectacular hotel there. He got several people interested in his dream hotel and eventually persuaded them to invest in his dream so that he could achieve his goal. He became a very wealthy man. Rolas had come from the ghetto, but he possessed a natural intelligence and vision combined with drive and persistence.

Word of the hotel's reputation for excellence spread throughout the entire continent of South

America. His contractor hired the best architects and interior designers he could find to execute the architectural plans. A Hollywood set decorator planned the interior of the hotel. It had ten lounges with exquisite furniture, art objects and famous oil paintings. An indoor swimming pool could be seen from an enormous terrace with a giant cage that held exotic birds from the Amazonas State. Glass panels and murals depicting maritime scenes surrounded the swimming pool. Octopuses, rays and other fish looked so real that small children were fearful of going into the children's pool, adjacent to the large one, without an adult. On the level below the pool, there were twenty-four changing rooms.

The hotel had four restaurants and a restaurant solely for children. In this unique restaurant, small adults waited on the little tables that accommodated children of ages three through twelve. The entire setting looked like a scene from a cartoon for small children. The walls were painted with scenes from Snow White, Peter Rabbit, and The Wizard of Oz. Scenes from stories by Brazilian children's writer, Monteiro Lobato, also decorated the walls.

The guestrooms were spacious and the suites were spectacularly furnished. Three large conference centers and various ballrooms occupied an area of thousands of square feet. The huge ballrooms were used for some of the luxurious Carnaval balls. Gambling casinos offered the best shows outside of the Urca Casino in Rio de Janeiro. Famous touring ice skating companies used an ice skating rink for spectacular shows. During Carnaval season, the grounds of the hotel held thousands of parked cars and the roads were packed with limousines. The chauffeurs standing next to the cars and leaning against the long automobiles went around and around the hotel grounds. The sunsets behind the hotel made the water in the lake like an ice rink on fire. A man with a dream had created a monument to beauty and endless recreation. People who came to this hotel forgot their troubles and lived in a fairy tale.

Rameda purchased a large piece of land consisting of twelve adjacent lots. The land extended from the main highway to the road on the top of the mountain. Arizle thought the plot was ideal for a one-story home with large windows where the sun could shine through, warming a giant living room with a rustic fireplace. She sketched the drawings for a beautiful house and gave it to Valença Engenharia, an architect located in Petrópolis, to draw her crude drawings to scale.

Valença came back with her rudimentary drawings, showing the floor plan of an original and exquisite home. Arizle accepted them and they signed the contract to have the home built. The building of the house took almost a full year. Arizle went to the house as it was being built and slept on the floor of her master bedroom before the walls had windows. Ricardo and Rameda loved her ideas and her spirit of adventure. She would get up in the middle of the night and call both of them to come to an unfinished kitchen, where she cooked the most delicious fried potato omelet they had ever eaten. They would sit together and laugh at nothing really funny, but only because they were alive together and healthy. She knew how to make life interesting for any one she knew. Leumas came a few times to inspect the construction, wearing his suit and tie as usual. No one ever saw Leumas dressed in a sports outfit. He had never owned one. Arizle would make him remove his tie and jacket, but he would remain in his dress shirt, rolling up the sleeves at her request.

As time passed, the house finally began to look like a home. It had five baths, five bedrooms, a room with a wet bar, two kitchens, one with a gas stove and the other with a wood stove, two living rooms and a large dining room. Behind the house there were the maids' quarters with three bedrooms and two baths. In addition, she had a small house built for the caretaker couple who would look after the main house and gardens during their absence. Rameda wanted a small barn for one cow and a few pigs. Pretty soon there were chicken and duck pens, too.

Arizle could not wait to bring Leumas to see the finished house. Marcos had been to the house twice while it was in its first stages, but had not seen it with window frames, marble floors and doors. Marcos was in military school and came home only on weekends. She asked Leumas to come and see it, even though they had no furniture and the walls were being painted. After Leumas had toured her beautiful house, he took advantage of Marcos's absence to talk to his friend Arizle and voice his concerns. They sat down in temporary chairs on the side terrace to talk about Marcos.

Leumas was concerned about his son. His personality had taken a turn for the worse. He was snappish and acerbic, always making cynical remarks about life, family, love and any feeling that meant sacrifice or commitment. Leumas explained sadly that he had exhausted all his ideas on how to get the point across to Marcos that he did not have friends because he insulted and made fun of anyone who was not intelligent or well-read as he. His friends at the Colegio

Militar avoided doing things with him, for they did not want to be put down.

"They seemed to like me," Leumas explained, "but they could not endure Marcos's cynicism. I brought him up, doing everything in my power to teach him good values and be kind to him. I bought a new car to take him to school because he did not want to take commercial transportation such as the trolley. I do not know where I went wrong, Arizle," Leumas said resignedly. "I am ashamed to introduce him to my colleagues, for he always comes out with something derogatory about what I do or believe. Marcos should know better. He is extremely intelligent and had two good people as parents. Where did we go wrong?"

Leumas was disheartened by his son's attitude and had tears in his eyes. Arizle hugged him and said that she thought it was her fault, not his. She was the one who had abandoned Marcos, not Leumas. Arizle cried with Leumas and told him that he was the only man she had ever trusted, and that he had been a loyal and dedicated father while she had been the one to leave Marcos to live with another man.

"Marcos never forgave me," she exclaimed with a pained expression on her face. "Leumas," she asked tenderly, "What do you feel I should do to help you?"

"I do not know, Arizle," Leumas replied. "I wish I knew, but I do not." Rameda walked toward them and put his hands on Leumas's shoulders.

"What are you both so sad about?" Leumas responded that they were talking about Marcos. Rameda thought they should leave the young man alone; Marcos was fourteen and was going through tough times. Rameda added that he thought Marcos was a nice young man with good manners and whenever he came to visit them, Rameda enjoyed his company a great deal. "I feel he enjoys his mother's company the best, but that has always been the case, has it not?"

"Marcos loves to talk to Arizle," Rameda concluded. "I see them both conversing and laughing together. I see him hugging his mother and kissing her with affection. That is a sign that he forgave her more than she believes he did."

Rameda pulled Arizle up from the chair and suggested that the three of them walk to the top of the mountain to see the view. They walked slowly and when they arrived at the top, their house looked smaller and it was like seeing an aerial picture of the whole estate. They walked further up on the road to the other side of the mountain and sat down to watch the sun set. Arizle thought it was a lovely moment for a prayer. She asked them to pray with her and she started talking to God, asking Him to bless the poor, to give food to the hungry, to alleviate the pain of those at hospitals, to give joy to the elderly waiting to die, and to forgive them their sins. Rameda and Leumas had their eyes shut, and when they opened them, they thanked Arizle for the lovely words of peace and goodness and charity. They got up and started to walk down toward the estate. There was a spring on top of the mountain where little toads croaked, mainly when the sun was setting. Arizle said it was because they did not want to be in the dark. Leumas assured her that frogs and toads loved dark places.

Leumas and Rameda left early the following morning to go to work. Arizle stayed with the landscaping people, for she had laid out the garden she wanted with a complete list of bedding flowers. She ordered blue, pink, and purple hydrangeas. She had added a round terrace in front of the house, surrounded by a low, cast iron fence, and from that site the view of the hotel, the lake and the mountains behind the large building was dazzling. She wanted the house painted brick red and she named it Casa Vermelha. She spent three weeks in a row there sleeping on a mattress on the floor, for she wanted to make sure that every detail was done right. She staked the flowerbeds and the lawn lines with the gardeners and she watched them build the paths, stone by stone. She helped build a stairway from the upper part of the round terrace to its lower level. She intended to place a ping pong table on the lower level for the children and their friends to enjoy. In three weeks, ten men built a magnificent garden. Sod was nonexistent, and the lawns had to be planted one grass sprig at a time. After four weeks, the lawns were filling in and becoming green. The flowers had been planted and were growing and budding.

Dividing the dining room from one of the living rooms, Arizle had hung a swing, suspended from the ceiling by two steel cables. The swing served as a sofa and sat three people simultaneously. The floor was dark green marble with a white marble design. Only the bedrooms had parquet floors. The master bathroom floor was navy blue marble with fish inlaid in white marble. Each bathroom was of a different color, coordinating with the colors of the bedroom to which it belonged. Marcos and Leumas each had a private bedroom and bathroom. Ricardo's bedroom was near the master bedroom. The entrance hall had a river rock wall, which extended to one of the living rooms and formed a large fireplace. The external walls were all glass panels that could be opened to allow the sun to come into the living areas. The bedrooms all had picture windows for light and sun to illuminate them,

as well. Drapes covered all the windows and could be
closed for privacy. Arizle also had drapes made for the
living rooms, but she seldom drew them closed. She
liked to see the sunlight and feel the warmth of the
days. She worshiped light, clarity and brilliance.

Arizle purchased all of the household items at
Casa Daniel. She had designed the furniture had
given her drawings to Leandro Martins to build, long
before the walls were raised. She had it all in storage,
waiting for the house to be finished. For the niche in
the dining room, she had bought a pair of large Ginori
parrots, two large Capodimonte urns with lids, two
dark green Chinese ceramic statues, and two Sèvres
birds in a shade of light gray. At private auctions,
Arizle purchased paintings for the house and signed
lithographs for the guestrooms. She had a great flair
for interior design and she should have studied interior design and have made that her career. Rameda,
however, would have never agreed to that. The women
in his family volunteered their services to charitable
organizations, schools or hospitals, but did not work
for money.

On the fireplace mantel, she placed a pair of
Chinese birds of paradise in shades of red, green, yellow and white. The furniture was lacquered light yellow and the upholstery took its colors from the Chinese birds in pastel shades. The rug was Chinese, in
stronger colors of the same shades. The drapes were
white and had a thick lining with plastic between the
inner lining and the outer material. This was to help
guard against the damaging effects of the ultraviolet
rays, which were so strong in the mountains.

The bedroom furniture was built in for better
space utilization, except for the beds and bed tables.
Her bed was lacquered black with mauve satin on the

headboard. She had a large vanity table built in, which occupied an entire wall. From halfway up the wall to the ceiling there were large windows, and regardless of the season of the year, Arizle had lots of light and she could see the flowers in the flowerbeds.

The house was finished a few days before Christmas Day and Arizle talked to Leumas and they decided to spend Christmas in Petrópolis that year. Leumas came with Marcos, and she invited Rosina and two of Ricardo's friends to participate in the Christmas Eve dinner. The house looked gorgeous, and she had worked hard putting together Christmas ornaments made of dried leaves that she had hand-painted. These Christmas ornaments were so well-made and beautiful that Rameda invited his older brother to come with his son and daughter to see them. Rameda was proud of her creations, for she had outdone herself that time. His brother, who also had a beautiful home in the town of Petrópolis, came with his daughter. Arizle was always happy to receive them and always entertained them with courtesy and a willingness to please.

For Christmas Eve dinner, she cooked the turkey with the chef from the city house. They prepared chestnut puree to accompany the turkey and glazed peaches. The turkey was filled with a delicious farófa made with chopped boiled eggs, smoked ham and olives of different countries sautéed in butter with pieces of brown onions and fresh parsley. The sauce for the turkey had red wine and was browned by frying butter and cornstarch together until it was dark brown and then adding the juices left on the bottom of the pan. It was not gravy; it was a delicate French sauce she had found in one of her magazines.

Arizle did not usually have guests join the family for Christmas Eve unless they were poor or did not have a place to go. Otherwise, that evening was sacred and reserved only for family members such as Leumas, Marcos and occasionally, Coló, Antônio's sister, who was also very fond of Arizle.

Aunt Coló was funny and loved Marcos and Ricardo. She was also very fond of Leumas, whom she considered like a brother. Before everyone started to eat, Arizle said a lovely prayer; often her eloquent and emotional words brought tears to everyone's eyes. Rameda never said the prayer. He always explained that he could not speak like she did, and only she could say so many pretty words that also had a lot of deep meaning.

The dinner was served at 9:00 p.m. and everyone was elegantly dressed, except for Leumas, who wore his usual everyday business suit. The butler served the dinner dressed in a tuxedo, and all the dishes were served using French service. Desserts were extravagant, and Arizle made sure that everyone's preferences had been prepared. Ricardo loved Christmas. Santa Claus came early, and watching Ricardo's reactions to the sweet sound of the bell announcing Santa's presence was a memorable sight. Ricardo would get on his knees and thank Papai Noel with tears in his eyes. Arizle bought items for Ricardo that he thought were made in the sky. She chose little toys that were so delicate and original that Ricardo's opened widely in amazement. They were items that were never seen in stores, and no one knew where she had found them.

Numerous gifts were placed around the Christmas tree, freshly cut for the occasion. Christmas trees in Brazil had soft leaves and branches due to the high humidity. The only type of ornaments the branches were able to hold in place were pieces of cotton and tiny multi-colored lights. Arizle changed the design of the tree every year and it was never in the same place or shape. There were several gifts for all of the dinner guests. Employees ate dinner in their dining area, but ate the same foods that were served at Arizle's table. The employees received gifts of money, as well as personal gifts.

For Leumas and Marcos, she bought clothing such as shirts, ties, underwear, suits, sweaters and socks. She bought them leather wallets when she saw that the ones they carried had, as she put it, probably been bought from Adam and Eve themselves. They laughed and received everything with enthusiasm. Leumas never knew what to buy for her. He bought her French perfume and French soap. For Rameda she bought shirts with his monogram embroidered on the cuff, Bally shoes, and imported materials for him to have suits made by his Portuguese tailor. For Coló she bought a dress or gave her money inside a card. For Ricardo she bought toys, records and books. She gave everybody refined and expensive gifts. She received very few for herself, except from Rameda and Leumas. Christmas was a time to give much more than to receive, she remarked numerous times. She also sent gifts to her sister Laura and to her brother and his children.

On Christmas Day, she went to the orphanage to see the girls, who waited for her arrival singing songs of love and appreciation. She had bundles of gifts for all the girls and the staff. Her face was radiant, watching the children opening their gifts. She truly enjoyed their laughter and brief happiness. She wished they had caring parents, but some of them had spent eighteen years of their lives there without ever receiving a visit from a family member or distant relative.

They kissed her sleeves, her arms, her hands, and her skirt as if they were not going to see her again. She hugged them with tenderness, touched their faces and caressed their hair tenderly. They sat around her to hear her stories. Their eyes were big and shiny and they drank in every word she told them. She told them about Sabará, about Emilinha, Sá Barbara, the slaves, Sací Pererê and about João Sem Liberdade. When she left, the women in charge said that it took the girls a few hours to go back to their routine activities and normal behavior. Arizle would reply that she did not want to hear about the girls' normal behavior; instead, she wanted to hear about them behaving with joy and laughter. The ladies in charge were good people but ignorant, having had a limited education. They never understood what Arizle meant by that.

Arizle always left the children, telling herself how much she wished she could take them home with her. Leumas and Rameda consoled her by saying that the girls had all they needed to create a future for themselves, and Arizle should not worry about their being in an orphanage. These girls had room and board and a good education available to them. Some day, if they wanted, with their skills sharpened and good common sense, they would develop a place under the sun for themselves, just as Arizle had done. Arizle would say emphatically, "No, they will not make the same mistakes I made. Hopefully, they will have better sense."

Arizle, Rameda, Leumas and Ricardo traveled to Petrópolis often after that Christmas. Rosina came to visit Arizle sometimes four times a week. They would go shopping together, go to the movies, theater, fashion shows, tearooms, and would converse for hours. Rosina knew to bring her toothbrush in her handbag, for she claimed that being Arizle's friend was like living on a magic carpet—you never knew where you were going to be for the evening.

Many days during the week, Arizle waited for Ricardo and Rameda to come home from school and the office, and as soon as they arrived, they got in the car and went to sleep in Petrópolis, coming back early the next day. Rosina had a man friend with whom she was in love. Nestor, her husband, was twenty-five years older than she. When she married him at fifteen, she was already in love with this other man. She had no say in her marriage, for her parents contracted with Nêstor directly. This man lived in São Paulo and Rosina took frequent trips to that city until one day she came back brokenhearted, for the man had told her that he was marrying the daughter of a well-known doctor in the city. Rosina thought about committing suicide, but Arizle brought her back to her senses, telling her that she had four children to think about and above all, no one in the world deserved her anguish and death over a lost love. The only way to force Rosina to think of something else was to take her out of her household for a while. Arizle took Rosina on a one-week trip to Belo Horizonte, Sabará, Ouro Prêto and Congônhas do Campo. These cities in the state where Arizle had been born offered numerous museums and churches containing magnificent art. Arizle felt Rosina needed to get out of Rio and be forced to see and talk about other things. When they got back, Rosina had changed her mind about ending her life.

Arizle often treated her brother and sister-in-law to a trip. Whenever they had a big fight, Arizle had her chauffeur pick them up with the children and bring them all to the house in Tijuca. She talked to them as if she were a professional counselor, got them to reflect and find a way to achieve the harmony, that is needed when a couple, with five children, is acting foolishly. After she had forced them to make a truce, she would give them a check to go out of town and spend a few days on their own without the children. The children would stay with her and with her sister-in-law's brother. Other times, one of her cousins had problems with her husband, and Arizle got them to make a peace pact and sent them to São Paulo for a week. Arizle paid for all their expenses.

Arizle loved people, and one of her greatest pleasures was to see everyone living in harmonious relationships, see everyone excited about life and involved in a productive type of task. She spoke to couples very frankly, bringing in her personal experiences as examples of mistakes that they should not repeat, now that she had shared with them the consequences of her bad choices. She was non-judgmental, open-minded, and always focused on what made a person happy. Life was short, she thought, and people needed to enjoy every second of their existence. They knew they could count on her for advice, human warmth, understanding and forgiveness.

Since they had built the house in Petrópolis, Rameda had not traveled as much to the interior of Minas Gerais. Arizle had gone with him on many trips and had always left Ricardo with Leumas. Now that Ricardo was in school, Leumas stayed with him in her house instead of Ricardo going to Leumas's home. Marcos continued in military school and Leumas did not have to worry about Marcos staying alone with Francisca.

Arizle and Rameda left at four in the morning for their trips to Montes Claros and other areas where the ranchers lived. The chauffeur usually drove the car, for Arizle did not drive, and when they got to town and Rameda had to go horseback riding to look at the herds of steers, she could be driven to picturesque places or to visit with the ranchers' wives, if she wanted.

On one of their trips, Arizle experienced a very unusual incident. Rameda had left Arizle at a hotel and gone to meet with his rancher friends. Arizle, not having anything else to do, decided to walk to the church in the square in the center of town. When she entered the church, she heard the heartfelt cry of a woman. She could not see the woman from the place where she was, so she decided to go around the altar to the back of the church, from which the wailing was coming. She found a woman at the feet of the statue of Saint Anthony, crying in total desperation. Arizle bent down and touched the woman's head tenderly and said kindly.

"Please let me help you. Do not cry. Tell me what I need to do." The woman got up, raised her skirt and showed Arizle her leg. It was full of cancer and the smell was unbearable.

The woman said, crying, "I owe the landlord for four months of rent, for I cannot work and cannot make money. The landlord told me he was going to evict me and throw me out on the streets. I have no place to go. I am desperate."

Arizle led her to bench in the church, sat her down and asked, "How much is the amount that you owe your landlord?"

The woman answered, "One hundred and twenty cruzeiros."

Arizle opened her handbag and inside she found the exact amount the woman needed. She gave the money to the woman, who started to cry out in a frenzy, "Miracle, miracle, miracle!" The priest came running from the back of the church. Arizle could not tell the priest anything, for she was puzzled by the woman's shouting. Pretty soon, several women and children entered the church to find out about the shouting. When the woman calmed down, she explained that she had had a dream from Saint Anthony the night before, who told her to go to church, because a woman from far away was going to help her. Arizle was scared by the woman's account. She left the church after everyone applauded her and went back to the hotel.

The next day, when Arizle went out, everyone pointed her out, calling her the lady of the miracle. Arizle was embarrassed and went back to the hotel, phoned the house of the rancher closest to town, and explained to the rancher's wife, what had happened. The rancher's wife phoned every person that she knew for donations to help the woman in the church. Arizle and this rancher's wife obtained three thousand cruzeiros, donations from all the other ranchers in the region that paid for the woman's rent for the whole year, plus gave her food and medication money.

Arizle denied being involved in any miracle. She attributed having the right amount of money the woman needed as a mere coincidence. When Rameda came back that evening, he apologized to Arizle for not leaving her with any money before he left for the day. Arizle told him the story and cried, thanking Saint Anthony for enabling her to help someone in need. Arizle never asked the woman's name. That in her opinion, was the only true charitable incident she had been involved with in her life.

There were other trips, but no other sojourn was as fascinating as that one, even though there were other moments of strange happenings for which Arizle had no plausible explanations. Three months later, Rameda and Arizle went back to the hinterland. The remote region was scarcely populated and they rode in their car driven by the chauffeur for miles without seeing a single human being or a single shack. Night fell on them. The sky was gorgeous. Arizle had never seen so many stars as she was witnessing that night. She rode in front with the chauffeur and Ricardo and Rameda were in the back seat. Heaven was so magnificent that Arizle had the urge to pray.

She turned to the back seat and said to Rameda and Ricardo, "Let us pray together and thank God for giving us such an incredible sight to admire." In ecstasy, Arizle started praying to God for all the dazzling stars, the peacefulness, the woods, the animals in it and the three human beings being driven by a good man, the driver of the car.

When she finished her conversation with God, everyone saw two red taillights, as if there were a truck ahead on the road. The dust was blinding them, and Arizle asked the chauffeur to accelerate and pass the truck. The driver stepped on the gas, trying to pass the truck. The faster they drove, the more dust they experienced. The red lights continued to be seen ahead, but no other vehicle was in sight.

Suddenly, Arizle shouted at the driver, "Stop this car." He slammed on the brakes, causing Arizle to strike her head against the dashboard, and Ricardo and Rameda to fall on the floor between the front and back seats. With the car stopped and the motor off,

Rameda and the chauffeur got out and walked ahead. Within twelve feet of the car, a bridge had collapsed, and the precipice in front of them was two hundred feet deep. Had the car not stopped, they would have perished. Arizle and Ricardo shook with fear.

Arizle was never able to come up with a rational explanation as to why she had shouted for the driver to stop. Rameda told friends this story over the years without finding any reason for them not to have died that night. Rameda claimed that Dr. Leumas was the only person that he knew who could explain what happened, but Leumas never tried to explain what had occurred in that magnificent night in the woodlands of the interior he loved and cherished. Leumas was the one who knew it had been a spiritual occurrence. No one, according to him, should look for an answer.

"Thank God, people. Do not try to rationalize it," he said bluntly.

Two years later, Arizle went to Buenos Aires with her Aunt Claudia. This was her second trip outside of Brazil. She was euphoric with the prospect of meeting Evita Perón. They were going to visit the Casa Rosada and Arizle could not wait to meet Evita, whom she admired greatly. They stayed at the Hotel Lancaster, near Calle Florida.

Arizle spent the first day distracted by her aunt's activities, but on the third day she hardly could stand being away from Rameda, Ricardo, Leumas and Marcos. She missed her home and Rameda's arms. She called him, crying and telling him that she did not know if she could bear being separated from them all for a whole week. Rameda told her to enjoy herself, to go shopping and buy some beautiful outfits, to enjoy her aunt's company and to forget about her family. They were all well, he assured her. Arizle replied that she was a foolish woman who loved her family more than anything else in the world. She would try. She assured him that she would try. Rameda laughed at her childish ways. He called Dr. Leumas, who was not surprised that the Arizle that he knew, the strongest woman he had met, was at the same time the most fragile. Rameda and Leumas loved her, each in his own way, but there was no doubt she was loved.

Evita was a lovely woman, well-dressed, with dark lustrous hair, and exquisite jewelry. She had delicate mannerisms, and laughed as she talked about the beauty of Argentina and its people. Claudia and Arizle had tea with her in the Casa Rosada one afternoon. Arizle was nervous about meeting the wife of the president of Argentina, but Señora Perón was down-to-earth and did not display any air of the grand dame. On the contrary, she was a simple woman who had not forgotten her poor beginnings. She talked of her husband with reverence and displayed much love for the workers of Argentina, who according to her, kept Argentina economically strong. She suggested some plays for Claudia and Arizle to see and told them where to buy the most beautiful hats in her country. They spent two hours with her, and she had the presidential car take Claudia and Arizle back to their hotel.

Arizle was concerned about the political situation in the country and she sensed an undercurrent of distress and the signs that revolution was soon to come. During that week she prayed for peace. The week passed faster than she wanted to admit, and the day to go back to her country arrived. She was delighted to step on Brazilian soil once again. She hugged Rameda and kissed him many times and then hugged him again for a long time and kissed Ricardo numerous times. When she arrived at home, all the servants waited for her with a bouquet of flowers from her garden. She brought gifts for everyone and bought nothing for herself. For Rameda she bought two bolts of material for silk shantung suits, and for Ricardo she bought a small crystal bottle full of tiny candies. Ricardo kept that lovely bottle with great fondness. Leumas got a sweater and a jacket and Marcos received a sport coat and slacks. For each of her employees she had a special souvenir.

Arizle was very enchanted with Evita's simplicity and charm. When Arizle went back to Brazil, she read an article in *O Cruzeiro*, a magazine with the same reputation in Brazil as *Life* magazine has in the United States. Arizle was terribly upset about an article, which called Evita a cheap prostitute whose only political interest was to steal the country's wealth. Just a few days before, Arizle had read about Perón's arrest and she was concerned about Evita. She wrote a letter to the director of *A Noite*, the second most important newspaper in the country.

> To Representative Leonel Brizola, Executive Director of the newspaper *A Noite*:
>
> Gentlemen:
>
> I speak without the endorsement of Brazilian women, but I am certain that all of them who read the report in *O Cruzeiro* will feel the disgust I experienced. Our lack of kindness toward Mrs. Perón is unnecessary and unfair. You recently visited Argentina, and you have already forgotten the hospitality and the courteous reception, as well as all the attention that the country's people and the Peróns showed

179

you. Reporters, you should not forget the generous feelings which are characteristic of our race, the empathy that we as a nation display toward those who suffer. You must be well-acquainted with the fact that pain does not choose an address. We all have to experience it despite our unwillingness to receive it at our door. The Perón family must be experiencing tremendous anxiety. We must respect Sra. Perón's pain. I am not talking about her anguish per se, for I know that for a strong person like her, the irremediable is remedy in itself. You are behaving as if you saw someone hurt, desperate, and bleeding and you chose to do nothing except slap this person's face. Is her suffering not enough for you?

I lament deeply what you have written in your article, for I am proud of my fellow countrymen and your words bring me dismay and shame. I have visited two other countries outside of Brazil. My husband has visited twenty countries outside of Brazil, and he concurs with me that there is no other people in this world that is more generous than ours, kinder than ours, warmer than ours.

Your mothers, young men, must be indirectly responsible for this news, for it is at home with our mothers that we learn to respect others and their situations in life. It is with our mothers that we also learn to forgive others for their mistakes. I am not an admirer of the Argentinean form of government, but I like and respect Argentina, its people and Evita. In my heart and in the heart of the Brazilians that feel and think, Sra. Perón has a large place for her moral value and the humbleness with which she accepts her suffering.

Tell her instead that we thank her for her example and courage. I am sure that if we understand her, strangers that we are, Argentineans will never forget her. Write her a letter of apology for she needs to receive it. You can only write those terrible words again if you have never experienced pain or you do not have any conception of its depth. I pray to God that God gives you the strength to admit that you made a mistake in writing this despicable, defiant and insulting article about Sra. Perón.

Let Sra. Perón know that your apology is from all of us, including all the Brazilian women who are sending her their affection and solidarity.

I want to continue to be proud of being born a Brazilian.

Yours truly,
Arizle S. Pachêco

Arizle never forgot Evita. She went back once again with her aunt a year later, after the revolution had ended, and Perón was back in power. She visited with Evita once again. Arizle thought that like her, Sra. Perón had learned that goodness does not exist in the world, but only inside of oneself. Evita's attempt to assist the people of her country had been interpreted as simply a demagogue's move to gain popularity among the blue-collar workers in order to win their vote. Arizle felt that Sra. Perón was ambitious, but did not possess the blind ambition of which she had been accused. Arizle felt that power did not bring happiness, it only brought more responsibility upon the person that had the power. It was the last time she was to see the woman whom she respected and with whom she had always felt a sense of kinship.

14

Arizle reflected on the reasons why she and Leumas had decided to place Marcos in military school in the first place. They thought that type of educational institution would help teach him the value of discipline and remind him about the need to make a commitment. Arizle and Leumas had found that the school had excellent teachers, and they thought that, afterward, Marcos would be well-prepared to take the eliminatory exam and enter any university of his choice.

After Arizle left, Marcos began to get up late, sleep during the day and spend his nights writing poetry, novels and plays; he had no set time to do anything. Francisca cooked dinner, and Leumas would eat alone, for Marcos had gone to the library and forgotten about the rest of the world. He had become a recluse, a loner among his books, his writings, and his artistic work, and he rarely left his room. He did not have or want friends. His sedentary existence had contributed to a serious weight gain, and Leumas and Arizle were extremely concerned about Marcos's health and mental state.

Arizle criticized Leumas for giving in to Marcos, for being his servant and not demanding that Marcos assume responsibility for his actions. Arizle remembered Leumas telling her about a typical occurrence between him and Marcos. Leumas had taken the streetcar with Marcos to accompany him to school. When Marcos arrived, he realized that he did not have his student I.D. card. The school did not allow students to attend classes without their identification cards, so Marcos made his father go all the way back to the house on the streetcar to fetch his student I.D. card for him, while Marcos waited for his father at the gate of the school.

Arizle was very upset with Leumas for not teaching his son responsibility. She thought Leumas should have told him to go back and get his own identification. There were many other occasions when Leumas did something special for Marcos, and yet Marcos did not show any gratitude or much respect for his father. It was as if Marcos viewed his father as a weakling for behaving so compassionately toward Arizle and for being so accommodating.

Arizle and Leumas spoke frankly with one another about Marcos's behavior, and after long deliberation on what would be the best way to help Marcos, they decided that military school would probably be the best vehicle to transmit the value of discipline to him. In their opinion, Marcos needed to learn time management, self-respect, discipline, obedience and responsibility. Leumas seemed to want to compensate for the fact that Arizle had left Marcos. Arizle, on the other hand, suffered from deep guilt and blamed herself for Marcos's harsh and unsympathetic personality. They tried to think of other options, other boarding schools, of Marcos going to live with her and Rameda, but the only option that made sense to both of them was the strict discipline of military school.

The school had an outstanding reputation and was located not too far from Leumas's home. They thought it would be good for Marcos to participate in the military drills, to march miles at a time, and to exercise with his fellow cadets, while learning civility and attention to duty. The professors, who were captains, colonels and generals, were demanding and had excellent reputations as educators. Upon graduation, Marcos would be prepared with superior skills to enter any public university, if he did not want to continue in the armed forces.

Marcos had to take an entrance exam in order to be accepted at the Colégio Militar. He earned superior scores and had no need for a "godfather" to assist him in being selected. He had made Arizle and Leumas proud. Arizle told Marcos that he, more than anyone else, should be proud of his knowledge. The Colégio Anglo Americano had prepared him well, but he had been born with intelligence and he should thank God for it. According to Arizle, lack of intelligence was the greatest tragedy that could befall someone, not poverty. With intelligence, she believed, one could go through adversity and come out victorious.

Marcos agreed to start military school, despite the fact that he just wanted to be left alone to his reading and writing. He was thirteen years old and had finished eighth grade at the American school. Arizle helped Leumas assemble the uniforms, boots and other gear, and all the necessities a young man would need for comfort in boarding school.

Marcos started school in March. As a beginning student, he had to go through cadet initiation. The established students usually made the freshmen dress as women and dance and sing with heavy make-up on their faces. However, that year, they had gone over-board by having the new students put their hands against the wall, while other students threw knives between their fingers. Arizle found out about the hazing and was incensed. She called the school and asked to talk to the officer in charge. Without mincing words, she told him that they could play all the pranks they wanted on her son, but they had better never think of removing even so much as a drop of blood from him, or she would turn their lives into a living hell. The school would have to face a lawsuit as well.

On weekends, Marcos would go home and visit Arizle, Rameda and Ricardo. Leumas came to lunch almost every Sunday. Marcos's disposition improved a little. Many times he came home with blisters on his feet and hands, and Arizle would tenderly nurse his wounds. She adored her son, but Marcos, though less caustic, still felt that his mother really did not love him.

One evening, she received a phone call from Marcos, telling her that he had been suspended for three days. Marcos had been caught reading after lights out. He claimed that he was not sleepy the night before, and he had pulled his bed near the corri-dor door where there was a light on, so that he could read a book. The officer patrolling the area caught him reading and turned him in, and the captain in charge suspended him for breaking the rules. After Arizle heard Marcos's account of what had happened, she called the captain in charge and got his side of the story. Arizle told the captain that she was ashamed of her son for not obeying orders and that he had been most kind in only suspending Marcos for three days. The captain was astounded. He was expecting Marcos's mother to reproach him for this severe punishment, yet he had heard just the opposite. Everyone in the school found out about Arizle's call to the captain. The captain called Marcos at home the next day and told him that he had a mother who was honorable, and because of her phone call to him supporting his actions, he was reducing Marcos's punishment by two days and allowing him to return to classes. Marcos was very angry with Arizle for being on the captain's side, and he did not visit Arizle for several weekends after the incident.

After several weeks without hearing from her son, Arizle sent him a note.

> My little man,
>
> You are becoming a strong and handsome young man and you are my pride. I want to see you soon because I bought a sport shirt and pants for you to wear to accompany your brother to the theater next weekend. Will you please do this for him? He wants to show off his big brother. His classmates will be there and he wants everyone to meet you.
>
> Remember that you hold a large place in your mother's heart and it was in thinking about your pleasure that I made these purchases for you. Call me with your answer soon because your brother is waiting anxiously for your reply.

Receive, son, the pure and tender
love of one who adores you.

Your Mother

Marcos did not bother to call; he just showed up
an hour before Ricardo had to leave for the theater.
Leumas was there to take Ricardo since they had not
heard from Marcos. Ricardo was beside himself with
joy when he saw Marcos. He hugged his brother and
thanked him for coming to take him. Marcos hugged
his mother tightly and left a pile of books with her. He
left holding Ricardo's hand. The chauffeur drove them
to the matinee performance and picked them up when
the show ended. Marcos went back to Arizle's home
and he seemed to have forgotten about how angry he
had been with Arizle over what had happened weeks
before.

Marcos graduated from military school with
honors, and Arizle went on stage to assist the director
of the school in placing a medal on Marcos's uniform
lapel. The general introduced her as the mother of the
most cultured student the school had seen in many
years.

At that, Marcos turned to him and joked, "Only
if it is the culture of potatoes." Arizle was embarrassed by Marcos's comment, but she quickly added
that her son enjoyed both humor and debate with an
equally intelligent and cultured man like the general.
Fortunately, the general ignored Marcos's comment.
Leumas later told his son that his comment had not
been funny. Marcos answered that he was sorry that
his father did not have his sense of humor.

Marcos at seventeen made the decision not to
make a career out of the armed forces. He showed no
interest in going to college, either. What he wanted to

do was to go to live in the United States, but for that, he needed the permission of his parents. Arizle was firmly against his going to live in a foreign country away from his family. She told him that she would not give the consent he needed. It had to be signed by both parents in order for him to obtain a passport. Arizle suggested that he should attend university in Brazil and then make a decision about whether he wanted to go to live in North America. She also told him that since his father was not wealthy and could not support him in a foreign country, he should be prepared with a university degree or a trade of his choice before leaving his country. He needed to equip himself to survive financially in any place in the world in which he chose to live. Marcos was very angry with his mother for trying to control his life, especially since she had not allowed anybody else to control hers.

Since Marcos did not want to go to a university, Arizle thought that he should learn about real life by working for the railroad system for which Leumas worked as an executive. She wrote about her concerns.

> My son,
>
> One thing I thank you for, and that is the fact that you do not pretend to be what you are not with me. You speak about studies with your father as if you were really interested in pursuing them. I wanted you to work in the shops side by side with the blue-collar workers, for I wanted you to observe life up close. I thought it would be a good opportunity for you to see how others suffer, what their pain is like, and what their struggle is to

obtain the bread and butter of each day. I wanted you to learn that great joy comes from very insignificant things. Your father wanted you to be spared from hard work that would develop calluses on your hands, and he ended up by cultivating and nurturing idleness in you. He spoiled his son by protecting him too much. As a result, despite your eighteen years of life, you are still acting like a child.

You criticize your father and he suffers in silence from your arrogance and contempt. I do not blame you for being angry with me, but please do not mistreat your father, because he has always supported you, right or wrong. He adores you and does not deserve your indifference and your scorn.

With extreme affection,
Your Mother

Arizle's efforts to get Marcos to face reality and learn that people needed to work and to be productive were in vain. She wanted to see her son with greasy hands, tired from an honest day of hard work. Leumas, however, disagreed with Arizle, saying that such an environment was not the right place for Marcos. Marcos instead became a private tutor in math, grammar, writing, and anything else students needed to learn. He made enough money so that he did not have to ask Leumas to buy books for him to read, but he never made enough money to become financially independent. He bought books, classical music recordings and materials for his sculpting, modeling and painting. Marcos never bought a present for his father or his mother.

One day he called Arizle and said, "I am leaving and you cannot stop me. I am twenty-one and will do what I damn well please." Arizle was bewildered by Marcos's call.

He left for the United States and stayed there for the next ten years, angry with his mother, who had made him wait to be twenty-one years old before he could leave Brazil without her signature giving him permission. He never understood that she did not want to lose him. Marcos only came home twice in ten years. Leumas visited him twice, and supported his son in the United States for all those years. Marcos fathered two children, but never got married and never finished college.

Arizle thought of Marcos every single day. Everything she ate that Marcos liked made her think of him and cry in sadness. Arizle's life changed with Marcos's departure. It was as if she had lost part of herself. She wrote him constantly, but he either did not answer or wrote harshly critical and complaining letters in return. Marcos never took the time to truly get to know his mother. Ricardo, on the other hand, understood and welcomed the fact that his mother knew him better than anyone else.

Ricardo was eight years younger than Marcos. Though shy and reserved like Rameda, he liked to be surrounded by friends. He worshipped and admired his older brother, who could do no wrong as far as he was concerned. He admired his brother's intelligence and talent, and he loved going with him to the movies, to parties or swimming at the pool at Quitandinha. Marcos, being older, looked at Ricardo as a child and felt that he did not want to be his babysitter. Nevertheless, Marcos agreed to take Ricardo to children's activities from time to time.

While in Petropolis one day, Ricardo and Marcos went boating without Arizle's permission. Marcos took Ricardo in a rowboat to a distant woodland lake, beyond the bridge that separated it from the main lake. Ricardo was afraid to go there, but Marcos laughed at him, saying that there were no monsters in the other lake of which to be afraid.

Marcos rowed slowly. That part of the lake was dark and spooky, for tall trees densely surrounded it. Ricardo was feeling strange and fearful. He was suddenly afraid that his brother had taken him to this place to drown him. He did not know why he was thinking such a frightful thought and experiencing such a horrible sensation. Ricardo gripped the side of the boat with both hands and started to cry. Marcos got the oars tangled up in the dense weeds in the dark waters, but was finally able to free them, continuing to row slowly toward the trees on the other side of the lake. The vegetation was so dense around the margin of the lake that there was no shore on which to step out of the boat. Ricardo pleaded with his brother to turn around and go back, almost wailing in fear. Marcos told Ricardo to stop that nonsense at once and behave like a man. Ricardo was still afraid and kept insisting that Marcos turn around and go back. Marcos stubbornly refused, but eventually gave in and agreed to turn the boat around return to the other lake.

Ricardo was silent except for an occasional dry sob on the way back to the wooden pier, where hotel employees helped guests with the docking of the boats. When Ricardo finally felt his feet were on secure ground, he was subdued the rest of the day. He was shocked by the thoughts he had entertained. Why had he felt that way? Surely his brother would never harm him. He never mentioned that strange premonition to anyone. As time went by, Ricardo tried to forget the incident at the lake, and he felt guilty about having had such suspicions about Marcos.

Ricardo had not inherited his brother's aptitude for knowledge. He had to work hard at school to obtain good grades. He remembered and told his classmates frequently that Marcos, his brother, never had to study at home. By attending classes Marcos learned what he needed to know to take tests and pass the exams with the highest grades. Ricardo loved his brother immensely, despite the fact that he knew he could never be like Marcos or develop his intellect.

Ricardo had been born with Arizle's malocclusion, but it did not show on Ricardo until he was four years old. Arizle wanted to have her son's lower bite corrected while he was a small child; however, the techniques to correct the slight malocclusion were not yet developed in Brazil. She took Ricardo to an orthodontist, who told her that the only thing she could do to help Ricardo was to have him use a device that he had developed. The doctor prescribed a jacket with straps that were attached to the side of the bed so that Ricardo could not turn on his belly to sleep. Ricardo was four and a half years old when he started to sleep with this uncomfortable, stiff jacket. On humid summer nights, the jacket caused a heat rash on Ricardo's chest. Ricardo endured the misery of the jacket for two years. His mother explained the advantages of sacrificing and wearing the jacket. He learned about self-discipline and perseverance at an early age. He never complained that he did not sleep well at night tied up to the sides of his bed. Unfortunately, the jacket turned out to be a futile exercise, for Ricardo's bite was only corrected with braces at a later date.

Ricardo wore braces for four years, beginning at the age of twelve. The dentist had wanted to wait for Ricardo's permanent teeth to erupt before he began treatment. Arizle many times asked Ricardo to forgive her for contributing the genes that caused him be born with this maladjustment of his lower teeth. Ricardo always laughed at his mother's apologies and reassured her that the braces were not unbearable, just a bit painful, and he did not mind having to wear them. He reminded Arizle that he was lucky they had the money to correct his bite, when many other children did not have the financial resources to have their teeth straightened. Arizle did not want Ricardo to ever suffer what she had gone through when other children laughed at her crooked teeth. Ricardo's braces were finally removed before he went to study opera in Milan in the summer of 1958. He loved opera, but his passion was in a different field. Despite his fine tenor voice, he had medicine on his mind. He wanted to become a plastic surgeon.

Marcos experimented with magic when he was a teenager. He often asked Ricardo to concentrate and help him practice his ability to read minds. Ricardo did not mind helping his brother, and his request made Ricardo feel important. Marcos would pick up a pack of cards, asking Ricardo to shuffle them thoroughly. After Ricardo had mixed them up, Marcos would ask Ricardo to choose one card and concentrate on it, while Marcos tried to guess which card it was. Ricardo always told his brother that his guess was correct, even though Marcos never guessed them right. Ricardo wanted his brother to feel powerful, and he was happy when Marcos was happy. He adored his brother and the fact that he thought that Marcos was ten times more intelligent than he was did not make him feel inferior. On the contrary, Ricardo admired his brother, even though he detected the differences in personality between them. His mother had taught him that different was not necessarily better. It was just different. Therefore, he understood his brother's idiosyncrasies and accepted him.

Like Marcos, Ricardo enjoyed reading, but he also enjoyed playing with his friends. Ricardo loved being surrounded by people, by activity, by friends. In the afternoon, after he had done his homework, he would go to the front gate of his house to see if there were other children playing in the neighborhood. Ricardo had several friends on the street where he lived and he enjoyed bringing them inside his garden to play hide and seek or other games. Fernando, Marly, Margarida, Reginaldo and Lucio were his companions for bicycle rides around the block, roller-skating or just chatting about school. They lived in apartment buildings across the street.

Arizle encouraged Ricardo to maintain friendships with those children. Ricardo also liked playing with a young black man who lived near Leumas's home. Often Leumas invited Afonso to play with Ricardo in his home, and Ricardo also played with Afonso at his home. Arizle wanted Ricardo to have all kinds of friends and understand at an early age that not everyone came from a rich family.

Ricardo felt secure in the company of his brother, for he knew his brother always made a good impression on people. When Ricardo went swimming with his brother, he loved to see how the girls wanted to be near Marcos. Marcos always felt they were too pushy and he had no interest in them; besides, they were too young for him.

Ricardo was left with Leumas and Marcos when Arizle went to São Paulo with Rameda. Ricardo was naughty and got into trouble with his brother, who spanked him a couple of times while Leumas was at work. Once, while Arizle had gone to São Paulo, Leumas and Marcos came to stay at her house and watch Ricardo. One afternoon, Ricardo obtained a clay pipe filled with tobacco and decided to smoke it on the top of the gate in the garage area. Ricardo was smoking his pipe while a bunch of girls watched him from the street when suddenly, he saw Marcos coming toward him. He was trying to get down from the gate in a hurry, when a nail sticking out of the gate pierced his knee. After Marcos cleaned the wound and placed a Band-Aid on it, Marcos spanked Ricardo, hanging him upside down on the clothesline outdoors. Ricardo complained to his mother later on over the phone that Marcos had spanked him. Arizle had recently received a letter from Marcos and took the occasion of her reply to mention the incident.

> My darling,
>
> Do not doubt that you are loved like the prince royal. I love you very much. We will discuss the ideas for your book when I return.
>
> Be patient with your brother and do not spank him; leave the spankings for your own children. The right to spank is reserved to the parents. Your letter made me happy.
>
> I kiss you, my love. See you soon,
> Mother

Ricardo had a beautiful voice and loved to play the piano and to dance. He was very affectionate towards Arizle and Rameda, and he and Rameda had become very close. Ricardo began feeling a deep love for his father when Arizle told him what Rameda had done to give Ricardo the Pachêco family name. His close relationship with Leumas had no bearing on how much he loved his father. He saw Leumas as his best friend and almost as a second mother.

Ricardo enjoyed going to the movies on Sundays with Leumas. Leumas religiously picked him up at 9:30 a.m. to go to the early session. Ricardo eagerly waited for Leumas at the gate of his home and ran to him when he saw Leumas turn the corner of the street. They went to the house to let Arizle and Rameda know that Leumas was there and to give them a hug. Leumas did not have a car during those years, and he used commercial transportation. He never explained why he had sold his car, but Arizle knew that he was supporting his father and two of his brothers and was assisting a niece who had had a child out of wedlock. He was also a contributor to Arizle's orphanage and another orphanage that he had started for boys.

Ricardo and Leumas left the house holding hands, a commonplace custom in Brazil. Teenager or not, Ricardo loved going out holding hands with Leumas. Ricardo liked cartoons and comedies. The show consisted of Tom and Jerry cartoons and comedies with Laurel and Hardy. Leumas bought candy for Ricardo to eat at the movie. Between Ricardo's home and the movie, Leumas greeted at least six different people. He was known and knew many people himself. He always introduced Ricardo as his godson. Ricardo loved being with Leumas.

At half past noon, they left the movie house, walking back to Ricardo's home. Lunch was at 1:00 p.m. on Sundays. The chef was off and Arizle cooked lunch for everyone. What a treat it was. Her black beans were out of this world and her rice was delicious as well. She always surprised her family with a new dish. For dessert, she had a tray of pastries that was devoured forthwith by her three men, who looked at the occasion as a special one. Sometimes Leumas and Ricardo were late returning for lunch, because the movie had taken longer, but Arizle was not sympathetic to their delay and scolded them both for being so late. She regarded meals as a sacred time for the family to be together and chat with each other. She asked them to be on time. When the next time came and they were once again late, she would repeat her sermon while they listened to her quietly. Leumas thought that it was better just to hear her complaint without trying to explain that they could not possibly leave the movie before it ended.

Leumas took Ricardo to the zoo, to museums and to birthday parties, and he was present at every piano recital in which Ricardo was one of the performers. Arizle never went to watch Ricardo play in recitals. The only time she attended, she became so nervous during Ricardo's performance that she felt that she was going to have a heart attack causing her to wait outside. The same thing happened when Ricardo received a silver medal at the end of the year at school. Her hands shook so much and her legs were so wobbly when they called her and Marcos's name to go up on stage, that she only went that once. On every subsequent occasion, she sent Leumas to do the honors. She stayed in her seat with Rameda, applauding with pride. Yet, Arizle could take the orchestra microphone during parties at her house and talk to all of the the attendees in a humorous and playful manner. When it came to her family members having a positive or negative moment, she was an absolute wreck.

As a teenager, Ricardo loved to spend his summer vacations with his cousins in the little town of Barbacena in Minas Gerais. He played hide and seek in the woods, lay on the grass watching the clouds passing by and rode horses from the orchard where his cousins lived to the little town of Tocos. Ricardo also loved to ride with his cousins at night when the moon was big, round and white, and the fields were silver with moonlight.

Ricardo helped his cousins sweep the stable, milk the cows and take the cans of milk into town. The milk was transported on a cart pulled by two steers. After finishing their chores, they could ride in the cart on the winding road that went up and down the hills and through the fields of rose farms. The noise of the wooden wheels creaking against the bearings of the cart became a nostalgic sound for Ricardo. Long after he had gone back to Rio, he continued to listen in his mind to his cousins' laughter and the squeaking of the cart's wheels.

Arizle commemorated all of Ricardo's birthdays. After they had moved into their first home, she hired a circus to perform for Ricardo and his friends. Every year the children in the neighborhood waited with great anticipation to receive an invitation to Ricardo's party. The owner of the circus was a retired professional circus artist, and his family doubled as the performers. He was the clown. His wife was a wonderful contortionist, and his eight children participated in different acts, which included dogs, parrots and other trained animals. Arizle aided the poor family and even had some business cards made for them and distributed them to all her friends. She also became the godmother of the family's youngest child, Flora.

In those days both the children and their parents were invited to a child's birthday party. There was a large table where the children sat to eat candy, pastries, homemade cupcakes, and drink soda or punch. Guests brought presents, and the children would all run to the honoree's room to watch the birthday boy open the gifts and place it on top of the bed for all to see. Arizle made sure that Ricardo read the cards first, thanked the child and then placed the gift on the bed. Ricardo treasured every gift he received. He showed as much enthusiasm for a pencil as he did for an expensive gift.

After the circus performance, they would eat and go to play in the grounds of the house. As Ricardo grew up, Arizle gave dance teas for Ricardo and his friends, and later on she held beautiful balls with orchestras and large crowds. Men dressed in tuxedos and women in gorgeous evening gowns attended these functions. Ricardo loved dancing, and he was the first one on the dancing floor and the last to leave.

Rameda had gone to Catholic school and believed Ricardo should do the same. The Catholic schools had the money to hire good teachers, and students received an excellent, well-rounded education. Ricardo was placed in Catholic boarding school for a year and in a Catholic day school for four years. Arizle and Rameda went to visit Ricardo every weekend, since he was only allowed to go home once a month if his average was a "B" or better. Arizle always took fruit and cookies to Ricardo whenever she visited him. Leumas also went to visit him a few times.

Ricardo was quite homesick, and the priest in charge of the school told Arizle that Ricardo cried when the sun set every evening, thinking of his home and his mother. Like Marcos, Ricardo adored being with his mother. Arizle did not want to deprive Ricardo of his family, but decided he should finish the year in boarding school. She knew it was good for him to learn some independence.

The following year, they decided that Ricardo would be a day student, attending school from 7:30 a.m. to 5:30 p.m., but sleeping at home. Rameda and Arizle also decided to travel to Europe for three months, and they wanted Ricardo to accompany them. Ricardo was twelve and they thought he would enjoy and benefit from visiting new cultures and countries. Ricardo took a three-month leave of absence from his school and left with his parents for Porto, Portugal on the Italian liner Conte Biancamano. The priests were not very sympathetic about a child's missing school, not even if he was learning a great deal by visiting nine foreign countries. Ricardo had lost a half-year of school by the time they all came back from their three-month-long sojourn, and the school authorities made him repeat the entire year.

They had a wonderful time in Europe. Rameda purchased a nine-passenger Chrysler New Yorker in Lisbon. They had taken their chauffeur with them, and he drove them through all the countries they visited. Arizle loved Portugal and Switzerland. Rameda loved France and Germany. Ricardo loved Venice, Paris, London and Lisbon. He took back a collection of stuffed animals, one from each city he visited.

The chauffeur had family in Portugal and Rameda, Ricardo and Arizle became very fond of them. They stayed with the chauffeur's sister for four days in her house in a little village north of the city of Porto. Everyone, including Ricardo, drank the wine from the family's cellar. Barrels of wine lined the walls, offering different flavors and different vintages. Ricardo saw wine being made, and he was curious whether the people had washed their feet before smashing the grapes in the large tanks. Rameda answered that they probably had not, and this thought caused Ricardo to avoid wine for the whole trip.

Arizle found a governess for Ricardo in Paris, and Ricardo was taken to the Opera House, the Bois de Boulogne, museums and all the points of interest. There were other Brazilian children with their families in Europe at that time, but Ricardo stayed with his French governess and practiced his French. Arizle had given him a private tutor for several years and Ricardo spoke French fluently.

While in Paris Arizle visited many historic sites and museums and shopped for furnishings for her two houses. She went to the best fashion designers in Paris and even had a mannequin made in her image. The sales women at Carven, Lanvin and Jacques Fath told her that they could send her swatches of fabric for her to choose from, since they now had her figure, and they could make any dress she desired.

Arizle bought beautiful things for herself, but her enthusiasm was for decorative items for her homes. She bought umbrellas, two chaises longues, Limoges china, a set of crystal, and a gold-plated sterling silver service for twenty-four. Arizle bought many gifts for Leumas and Marcos. Ricardo missed Leumas a lot and wrote to him everyday. Arizle also missed her country and her home. She could not even hear the Portuguese language spoken or see a Brazilian flag without crying. Traveling was wonderful, but being home was better.

Arizle wrote Leumas frequently as well, for they had left him in charge of the remodeling work she wanted done before her return. Rameda had hired the masons, carpenters and painters from the slaughter-house business to do the work, and Leumas was the architect and engineer in charge. Arizle kept writing to him and asking him about all the repairs. Leumas kept replying and telling her about the progress of the work. He wanted everything to be just as she had ordered. When Arizle returned, she was very happy with Leumas's efforts and the workers' craftsmanship.

The day the Andes reached port in Rio de Janeiro, Arizle was the happiest person in the world. She was so happy to be back in her homeland, where the people were the kindest in the world. She hugged everyone waiting for her at the pier. She hugged Leumas, crying with joy. He tried to tell her that her house looked beautiful, but all she wanted was to have him near her. Rameda embraced his friend, as well. Leumas's hair was getting gray, he noticed, and he appeared quite anxious, having spent many months making sure that everything had been arranged and executed as Arizle had wished.

They had taken many photographs during their trip, and Ricardo had two slide shows for his friends. He was especially excited to show them the celebrations of Bastille Day. Arizle and Rameda invited their friends for cocktails and showed them the photographs of the beautiful trip they had taken.

15

A year after they went to Europe, Rameda and Arizle purchased one hundred and twenty meters of private beach by the Araruama Lake, between the towns of Araruama and Iguaba Grande. The lake was about forty kilometers long and ten kilometers wide and was situated between a sandbank and the Atlantic. Its salt content was quite high and it was said that no one could drown in the lake, since one could float without even trying. They once again bought several contiguous lots, and the land extended from the beachfront to the dirt road which ran behind the property. The place was quite secluded and scarcely populated, so it was the ideal place for serene relaxation. The murmur of the waves slapping the shore was quite soothing. There was a small island near the shore, which lent itself to nude sunbathing. The land itself was arid, covered with low shrubs and a few large trees. Rameda arranged for several trucks full of topsoil to be brought in so that Arizle could have fruit trees and plant flower and vegetable gardens.

Arizle wanted to build the house on the sand, only ten feet from the lakeshore. She designed a large front terrace surrounded by a ground cover whose flowers bloomed all year around. She envisioned the house in the shape of a giant barge. She sketched a model showing varnished wood planking on the exterior and other walls. The house had five bedrooms and four baths, a large living room and a dining room with a table that seated twenty-four people. All the bedrooms faced the ocean and had picture windows. Arizle's room had a large, sliding glass door which went the length of the bedroom and allowed her to bring the outdoors right inside.

The kitchen was spacious, with both a gas range and a wood burning one. There was a large built-in refrigerator, which was powered by the house's own generator. There was no fresh water supply; so they had a cistern, which collected rainwater from the roof. There were also two other small guesthouses, each incorporating a master bedroom, a full bath and a small kitchen. All the floors were parquet except for the bathrooms and kitchen, which were paved with slabs of marble. The bathroom fixtures were chocolate brown, cinnamon, nutmeg, beige and black. Their colors coordinated with the color of the drapes and the bedspreads. Each room had two double beds. Arizle's room was the only one in which there was a king-sized bed. Her room was mauve with green accents.

Construction of the main house was finished in six months. The construction crew built the servant quarters and the two guesthouses soon thereafter. Arizle named the house Baton Rouge, after the place where Marcos had gone to live in the United States.

The cabanas she named Casa Louisi and Casa Ana. Together the two words formed the name of the state where Marcos lived. Marcos was always present in her mind and heart.

Arizle never spent a single day without thinking of Marcos. She often blamed herself for having lost control on that summer weekend in Petropolis when she and Marcos had a terrible argument. She preferred to think of the incident as a distasteful misunderstanding, but it had been a moment with tragic consequences.

Just before Marcos had decided that he was going to the United States despite his mother's opposition, they had another painful argument. The discussion had started while they were in the car, being driven by Raul, the chauffeur. They had both kept themselves in control while in the car, but as they arrived at the house and entered the hall door, Marcos told his mother that he thought she was a selfish woman who had abandoned him to do what she wanted. He went on to say that she had always done what she wanted without any concern for anybody else's feelings and that she was nothing other than a cheap prostitute. At that, Arizle slapped him so hard that she cut her finger on one of the gold prongs that held the diamond securely in place on her ring.

When she saw the blood on her finger, she cried, "With this blood I curse you, my son!" She ran to her bedroom, locked herself inside and cried the whole afternoon. Rameda tried to go to her, but she wanted to remain alone.

Marcos was taken aback by her reaction, and he staggered out of the house and climbed to the top of the mountain to be alone. He spent the whole afternoon walking through the mountains and the forest behind the lake. Ricardo did not know whom to go to or what to say. He was quite anxious and eager for his brother and mother to call a truce. He went outside in the garden and hid behind some trees to think about what he could do to get Marcos and Arizle on speaking terms again. He knew how much Marcos had hurt his mother with this insult, for that was the term others had called her when they had harshly judged her for her actions.

Marcos returned to the house at dusk. He had obviously been crying, for his face was red and swollen. Ricardo was in his room, praying for something to happen which would restore family harmony. Later, Ricardo heard from Rameda that Marcos had apologized weakly to his mother and that she had told him that the curse she had directed at him should have been directed at herself.

Neither Marcos nor Arizle ever forgot that dreadful incident. Arizle used it as an example of a weak moment and lack of control on her part. Arizle always admitted her faults when the example could help others. Ricardo remembered the incident for the rest of his life. Slapping someone's face became a sign of deep shame and irrational anger to him.

Arizle threw herself into decorating Baton Rouge with her usual fervor. The furnishings were rustic, comfortable and attractive. She found many maritime objects in auctions, including a chandelier for the dining room that had once been the helm of a ship. Arizle bought it and had the fixture made by Casa Daniel. She purchased attractive lithographs of lake and ocean scenes for the living room and dining room. The living room had two wicker sofas and a boat with a heavy glass top for a coffee table. All the rooms had boat lights mounted in the walls. The noise of the waves outside and the décor gave one the distinct sensation of being on a ship, even to the point of some of the guests feeling seasick.

There was no need for air conditioning, because the breeze from the nearby lake and ocean kept the house temperature pleasant most of the time. From her bed, Arizle could see the waves breaking on the sand beach. The house was practical, functional and very original. It was not a luxurious place, but it was a house which guests never wanted to leave.

The year the house was completed, they spent Christmas in Iguaba Grande. Christmas was the hottest day of the year, right in the heart of summer, and Arizle prepared the most exotic Christmas her family ever saw. She had a luau and they all felt like they had been transported to Hawaii. Leumas drove with Rameda from Rio de Janeiro and stayed for the whole week. Two of Marcos's friends had come to stay, and Ricardo had invited two of his friends. Arizle asked Leumas if he wanted to bring a lady friend with him, but he answered emphatically that not only he did not have one, he did not need one. Arizle also invited her cardiologist and his wife and her regular doctor and his wife. Ricardo's friends also brought their parents, so there was a houseful of guests.

Leumas slept in Ricardo's room, and the young man was delighted to share with his best friend. The two of them went swimming at night after everyone had gone to sleep. Leumas did not own a bathing suit and had to use one of Rameda's. He did not want anyone to see him in swimming trunks, and going to the beach at night was just right for him.

Christmas Day was delightful. Arizle had paid for a palm-thatched hut to be built on the west side of the house, just like the ones in Hawaii. The shack was built around a thick tree trunk, which served as the support for an umbrella-shaped roof. A wide counter encircled the column, making an ideal table for a buffet lunch or dinner.

The butlers, dressed in Hawaiian shirts and white slacks, helped with the serving, and Arizle hired a band to play Hawaiian music during the luncheon. She had made the table centerpiece herself, from palm leaves and coconuts. She had cork trays made for the guests, so that after helping themselves to roast pork, rice, farofa and shrimp mayonnaise, they could place their plates on the cork tray and eat while in the water. For desert, she had the butlers serve fresh pineapple, watermelon, different flavors of sherbet, and fruit tortes.

There were no waves that day. The sky was thinly overcast and the lake looked like a green mirror. The weather was hot and ideal for swimming. Everyone had a lot of fun playing games, fishing, and bicycling on back roads leading to the small fishing village of Iguaba Grande. No one ever forgot that Christmas.

The guests went back to Rio de Janeiro before New Year's Eve, because they wanted to spend that evening with their families. Only Leumas and Coló stayed with Arizle, Rameda and Ricardo the whole week. Rameda drove everyone to the other side of the lake and they went to see the ocean beach that ran for endless kilometers along the coast. Ricardo and Leumas had a marvelous time walking on the beach and collecting all kinds of shells.

The other side of Araruama Lake had the most ravishing beach in the world in Arizle's opinion. Praia de Veneza was a real paradise. The temperature of the water was quite warm, and the lake was shallow enough that people could walk for five hundred meters with water no higher than their waists. The water was so clear that they could even see small fish swimming over their feet.

Arizle prepared a picnic, and everybody ate and took a nap on straw mats while listening to the soft rhythm of the waves and the wind blowing in the casuarina leaves. These leaves sang in a low hum that soothed all one's cares. There, Arizle felt at peace with herself. She commented that Marcos would have enjoyed being there with them all.

Again, Marcos was always present, despite his physical absence. Leumas always claimed that Marcos had no idea of the love Arizle had for him. Leumas wrote Marcos once a week, but Marcos only responded every two to three months, and sometimes he went for a whole year without writing. Leumas loved being with Arizle, Rameda and Ricardo in Iguaba or Petropolis. He spent his birthdays with them, and Arizle always had a traditional formal dinner waiting for him with gifts and cards. She always had a letter for him thanking him for being her friend and accepting her as she was.

They were Leumas's family. His father and mother were getting old, and he had little in common with his brothers and sisters. He went to visit his parents every week, sometimes twice a week, even though they lived with two of his brothers who had never married. His mother had gone blind. He was patient and kind to her. Every time he went to see her, he fed her dinner. Ricardo liked to visit them with Leumas and he called them vovô and vovó, grandmother and grandfather. Arizle and Rameda felt that their family gatherings were not complete if Leumas was not present.

Arizle liked her lakeside home for its restorative atmosphere. She often took long walks on the beach wearing a large straw hat and dark glasses. She drank in the intense colors of nature and noticed small things too, such as the rows of thick foam the waves left as they broke on the sandy beach of the lake. Arizle took Ricardo and Rameda with her on these long strolls. They looked at every shell and snail they saw. Arizle knew that these moments of deep communion with nature were peaceful and regenerating for Rameda, too.

They decided to dynamite the beach in front of their property. While the other side of the lake had sandy beaches, their side was covered with boulders and there was only a small area in which they could swim without cutting the soles of their feet on the sharp stones. Boating was also impossible because of the large boulders that jutted up from the bottom. The explosives opened a very large area in the water for swimming and snorkeling. It was such a good idea that their neighbors decided to do the same. Then all the neighbors went together and hired a group of youngsters to clear away the stone fragments left in the water.

After the beach was cleaned and there were no more big rocks in the water, Rameda purchased a speedboat for water skiing. Ricardo loved to go water skiing with his friends. Arizle watched their prowess from the terrace off her bedroom. The boys often went fishing in the evening for shrimp, for the stones that had remained in the water had large shrimp underneath them.

Arizle loved to watch the moon as it rose over the horizon across from the house, and its reflection on the water looked like a large, holy Eucharist on top of a golden chalice. She was often moved to pray for humanity while watching this gorgeous representation of God's beneficence. When there was no moon, the profuse stars twinkled brightly, especially when Rameda would turn off all the lights in the house. Then they would move the mattresses onto the terrace and sleep there until the sun peeped over the blue horizon and kissed the waves, the land and their sleeping forms.

Arizle spent many a Carnaval at this house, crowded with guests as if it were a hotel. She cooked and served three meals a day with the help of the couple who were the caretakers. Though she could not cook, the wife helped by washing the dishes, peeling vegetables and washing the lettuce for the salad. Their city chef and the butler often went to the beach house with them for long weekends or when they had too many guests.

During Carnaval, however, everyone's servants disappeared for the three days, and homeowners had to be the chef, maid and butler, as well as host and hostess. Arizle's solution was to serve simplified meals and outdoor buffets. Everyone helped himself, and then after the meal, took his plate to the kitchen to be washed. Arizle was an excellent cook. While they were in Paris, she had taken a course in preparing sauces at the École Cordon Bleu. She always had music, either from a live band or the latest Carnaval hits on the record player, and the guests often danced while eating. Those three Carnaval days were spent dancing, singing, eating and building wonderful friendships that would last for over twenty years.

Whenever Arizle and Rameda did not have guests or the only guests were a few of Ricardo's friends, they worked on the property, planting the vegetable garden, pruning the fruit trees and showing the caretaker how to build vegetable planters that retained the soil moisture. They planted corn, spinach, sweet potatoes, squash and pumpkins. Arizle loved to put her hands in the rich, dark soil. She was delighted to observe the little organisms that lived and grew and moved in it. They also raised animals and kept pets. Raul, their chauffeur, liked rabbits and they encouraged him to raise and sell them to neighbors. Ricardo would take in abandoned dogs he found, feed them and search for new owners for the pets. Rameda even purchased a pair of pigs from France. Arizle could never bring herself to slaughter either of them, and eventually they both died of old age. She admitted being a hypocrite, for she certainly enjoyed eating pork; however, she could not bear the thought of seeing those two killed, since they had become pets and she was very attached to them.

They installed two hammocks under the branches of a grove of old trees near the shore. Rameda and Leumas loved to take naps after lunch, even though they did not normally have the habit of sleeping during the day. The noise of the waves lapping against the shore was relaxing and made them feel tranquil and content. Guests also felt the calm ambience of the place. People would come with all sorts of deep concerns and worries and leave without a care in the world, amazed at the change in their outlook.

Arizle became interested in helping the inhabitants of the local village whenever she could. One of the young men from Iguaba Grande had become one of Ricardo's close friends. When he finished high school, Rameda gave him a job in the office while he attended law school. This young man became a lawyer, thanks to his own efforts and Rameda's and Arizle's guidance, support and motivation. The young man considered Arizle almost as a second mother. She had a way with children and teenagers. She treated them with respect. She also spoke frankly with them and they admired her practical advice and knowledge. She often wondered why it was that many complete strangers treated her like a mother and Marcos, her own flesh and blood, did not. She was reminded of her mother's old saying that "a saint in one's own home does not perform any miracles."

Arizle worried about Marcos all the time. She wanted him so much to want her as his mother. She did not mention the subject to Leumas any more, for she did not want him to get depressed. One Monday when she returned to Rio from a weekend at the beach, she found a letter from Marcos telling her that he wanted to visit, but did not have funds for the ticket. Immediately, she phoned Leumas, told him the news and gave him the money to buy a round-trip ticket for Marcos. She spent four weeks preparing for his visit. She told Ricardo that while his brother was in Rio, she was going to give him all her attention, for he lived abroad and needed to feel important and wanted. Ricardo understood and asked her how he should behave toward his brother. Arizle answered that he only had to be himself, for it was very obvious that he adored his brother.

When Marcos arrived, he was dressed like a vagrant, without socks, and smoking cigarettes—a habit that his parents did not approve of. He was so thin and aged looking that her eyes filled with tears when she saw the deep worry lines he had developed between his eyes and his hairline. He looked tired and unwell. She made appointments for him to go to the

doctor for a check-up, called the dentist, and purchased multiple vitamins with iron for him to take
every day. Arizle did everything in her power to make
him feel needed, loved and welcomed. She had all the
foods he liked cooked and the wines that he loved
served. She bought him clothes—shirts, slacks, a
sport jacket and new shoes. She planned a big party
for him and invited all his old friends from military
school. Ricardo invited his friends and asked them to
bring young women to meet Marcos. Arizle also asked
her friends to find new young women to attend the
dance. Marcos appeared relaxed, but his personality
had not changed much. On the contrary, his four-year
absence had caused him to become more withdrawn
and caustic than he had ever been. Ricardo was embarrassed to introduce Marcos to his friends' girl-
friends.

Seeing him off at the airport was devastating for
Leumas and Arizle. Ricardo begged him not to go
away again, but Marcos laughed and responded as if
Ricardo was silly and naïve to be so attached to his
family. Arizle wrote Marcos a long letter after he left.
She never mailed it, though, for fear that he would
sever all ties with his family after reading it.

The letter spoke from her bruised heart. She felt
more guilt than ever for having been the one to leave
him behind first. She had given him the example.
Why was she so surprised that he would abandon his
family now? She spent time in her bedroom, crying
and writing.

Marcos,
Never look back; never justify. Develop the self-control that is never too late
to be learned. What is the secret of the

perfect life? Is it a balanced way of living? Conscious and deliberate, the time has arrived: you must rearrange your life.

A majority of great men had tough beginnings. You did not have these difficulties; the difficulty is in you. In your youth, we imposed the majority of decisions on you, but after you are twenty-one years of age, you are expected to take responsibility to work to survive and to develop self-dignity. You were not obliged, nor forced to do it. You, like Don Quixote, went in search of windmills; you did not listen or hear what we had to say. You made mistakes, but you gained experience. Do not fight the dragon that is your hurt pride and your foolish vanity any longer. To lose is also to win, when we know how to lose.

It is important for you to fight to tame your dilettante brain, which is empty and snobbish. You cannot allow yourself the luxury of being a father's boy all your life. You must struggle; you must formulate a good plan, not scattered and foolish ideas as you have now. You must make a plan for your future, for your own self-respect and economic liberation.

You should not have written the letter to your old classmate about your father, criticizing his work. Your father is a great man who has been sacrificing himself in every way in order to support you in America. You had your answer when he told you that he needed to work to make a living and he did not have time to become wealthy in the manner you wanted. You sounded ignorant in everything that you told your friend about your father. You have taken psychology, but you have not put what you have learned into practice. You wanted to do well, but you did not reach your goal. Theory, theory and more theory! You sounded so foolish, so immature. You carried high the flag of independence, but you did not build independence by your own efforts.

While I perceived the empty-headed futility in exercising your lips so that you could kiss women better, I was saddened by your actions, for a twenty-four-year-old man should have more serious things on his mind. When you arrived at the airport, we were overtaken by nostalgia, and we were so very happy to see you. We spoke of how much we missed you and how much you meant to us. You, instead, talked about the women you had met and the perfume bottles you had bought them so that they would not forget you. These were conversations for you and me at some other time, but not in the presence of others, who though they did not make any comments, despised you for your frivolous prattle.

People always despise the weak; it is a human instinct. As you despise others, so will they despise you for your weaknesses. You thought you were so strong and turned away from us. I built a country home by the serene and peaceful lake, expecting to receive the young man who had gone to study abroad, who had loved solitude before he left. What a surprise I had! You were a wild colt, sarcastic, without control, drinking too much, and silly. Your only concern was women. You treated Ricardo and his female friends with contempt, forgetting that they had learned to love and respect you through your brother and mother's perceptions of you. One of your school friends was shocked with your acrimonious remarks. He told me that he had always admired you, but that he was now disillusioned with you; he said you only talked about ridiculous things. He did not tell us the nature of the ridiculous comments you made, but I can well imagine. You have become stupefied with the discovery of sex. My poor son! This is the weak side of human beings and only brings us disillusionment. I speak to you with the voice of experience. You were an introvert. All your interests were around you, for you and for your imagination and fantasy. The well-balanced personality is neither an introvert nor an extrovert, but a combination of both.

When you satisfied your fantasy to leave your country, you did not think of your parents. You did not need them— they were the ones who needed a son. We give and we receive. However, you only want to receive. We would give you more

if you also gave us the satisfaction of fulfilling your duties, studying, progressing
and learning. You gave us nothing but
pain. I do not write you everyday because
I do not know what to say to you. I do not
know you anymore.

I was against your departure for
America. I was against the car your father
bought you and your move to live outside
of the university dormitory. I was against
studies without a goal or a career in mind.
Also, I was against the piano and music
studies. You should learn them as an
avocation, not to follow a music career. I
was against your moving into an apartment of your own and the large collection
of records you purchased. A young man
who has a mediocre semester of studies
does not have time to listen to records.

I am wrong in everything. Your father supports everything you want. His
love for you blinds him to reason. When I
told him not to let you do those things, he
was against me and for you. He defended
you like the tiger does his cub.

I feel sorry for your father. He has
high blood pressure and he had a slight
stroke that paralyzed his lower lip. Thank
God the stroke did not leave him with a
handicap; we rescued him in time. He has
been very sad and full of anguish, but he
did not want to say anything to anyone.
This anxiety is what caused his heart condition. He has become a walking shadow

compared to his old self; he has little enthusiasm and looks like a broken man.

I know many mothers of youngsters who live in America and receive ten to twenty pages from their sons and daughters per week in which their children relate all the news. You seldom write unless you need something. Your brother prayed for you, admiring you as he always has, while I suffered in silence, not knowing what to say to you.

I ask you please not to mention parapsychology to us. This study did not help you with your errors. How can you want to teach concepts that you are yet to learn?

Do not speak about being a translator. This is not a career; this is only part-time work to supplement a full-time job. Tell your father that you will finish a master's degree in something that will enable you to get a job and give you economic freedom. The career of your choice will give you self-esteem and self-confidence and will allow you to become a responsible, contributing citizen. I feel that you should be here near us; it is never too late to learn. I do not think that you wasted your time in America, as long as you use the experience gained while there to recognize the greatness of your soul. To err is human, but to persist in the error only brings a waste of time and energy. Come back and love your father, who was blinded by your actions and by the immense love he dedicates to you.

I have not lost my faith in you. You possess large reserves; it only depends on you. My son, it is necessary that you become the engineer, not the passenger, on your train of life; a man of action, not a dreamer; a participant in life's struggles, not a spectator. It is time to bring equilibrium into your life, into your personality, so that you can maintain the reserves of goodness that I know exist in you. This opportunity will be a fountain of energy that you never realized existed in you. It will be a fountain of new ideas, new aptitude, new career, new conquest—at last a new beginning in your life.

If until now the concern was to develop new knowledge, it is now the time to develop internal equilibrium. The parapsychological knowledge can come later, after financial independence gained by you. Nothing makes us feel better than that which we do by our own efforts, and with the assurance that our actions will not cause others to lose respect for us.

Develop in yourself the complementary side of what you have developed up to now. Search, my son. Search not externally, but in yourself, for the strength for which you have desperately searched elsewhere. To own a car or hundreds of records is wonderful, but more meaningful if bought with your own money. Do you see yourself as self-sufficient?

Let us have the pleasure of assisting you to rediscover yourself. The well-balanced spirit is flexible. In the same way the body needs exercise to maintain itself, the spirit needs positive stimuli to expand and grow. You must be able to interrupt an activity so that you can initiate another, focusing on the extent of your possibilities. Enjoy parapsychology, if you so desire, but do not allow it to dominate you entirely. Make it a hobby for moments of leisure. Control your instincts. You were a child, now you are a man. Change your way of thinking. Try to understand that this will rejuvenate your body and your mind. You should face your errors with honesty and openness.

To a certain extent, we always depend on each other, for we depend on the affection, friendship, and the love of our fellowman. However, you should not become a financial burden on others. It is our responsibility to help you, but it is also your responsibility to help yourself. Without discipline and will power to change, nothing changes. I ask you to value yourself and to recognize that in you there is a potential waiting for you to free it. Let go of the windmill. Come back to the ones that really love you,

Your parents

Arizle did not understand Marcos's love for the occult. While in America, Marcos had become involved with Aleister Crowley's followers. They followed the motto of Thelema: "Do what thou wilt shall be the whole of the law." It was not parapsychology, but Crowley's teachings, which were to change Marcos's outlook on life, his family and himself forever.

As time passed, Arizle could not stand his silence. She wanted to see her son again. Three years had gone by and she missed him greatly. She talked to Rameda, who suggested that she ask Leumas to help. Again, Arizle gave him the money to buy Marcos a round-trip ticket, and Leumas asked Marcos to come and see his mother again. Leumas did not want to tell Arizle that Marcos had not changed, but he believed in miracles and this visit could be the source of a miracle.

Arizle planned Marcos's stay in Rio de Janeiro just as she had the last time. She prayed to God to help Marcos forgive her and be united with his family once and for all. Arizle prepared all three houses for Marcos's visit as well as Leumas's home where, she knew, he would want to stay. She wanted him to feel at home, to receive all the attention and be reassured that he was loved and that his parents missed him. She also wanted him to realize that his brother looked up to him as an example of notable intelligence, worldly culture and extensive talent. She went to the flower market downtown and bought magnificent gladiolas, roses, zinnias, and green foliage to place in all the vases and table containers. She had prepared all the pastries and tortes that he liked, placed the fruits he enjoyed on platters in the refrigerator, and other foods he adored were ready for him to eat. She was so happy that her joy was contagious. Every servant waited for Marcos's arrival with equal anticipation. Arizle had the houses looking like it was her wedding day. Leumas and Rameda were laughing for no reason with her joy and enthusiasm.

One early morning he arrived. They all went to the airport to fetch him. His thoughts seemed to be on his life and his friends in the United States. He was indifferent to everyone around him. His father was saddened, watching him looking at everyone with disdain.

A party was scheduled to take place during his stay. All his colleagues from the Colegio Militar were invited. Marcos invited his friends, asking them to bring additional young ladies. Arizle hired a band to play all the new Brazilian dance songs and American dance music as well. The party was planned with his enjoyment in mind, and Arizle wanted him to have an opportunity to see his friends.

Marcos stayed aloof from all her preparations, and the party did not seem to bring him close to his family. He now had his own ideas and philosophy of life, and they were quite different from the ideas of his family and the culture of his native country. Arizle saw him as not completely American but no longer Brazilian.

She never mentioned anything to him about her observations. She wanted to tell him her impressions of him before he went back, but she did not want to make him unhappy during the few days they had together. It had been over two years since she last hugged him. She was hurt that all the things that she had so lovingly prepared for him did not seem to have any value or meaning for him. The little nothings of affection that for him were meaningless had been given to him with tenderness that had come from the heart and had been repressed during his absence. She wanted to tell him that she expected to see him become mature, with more control over his actions and words. Instead, Arizle saw him as a child, who could not control himself and who enjoyed abusing his family and being unreasonably disagreeable with everyone.

Whenever Leumas, old and tired, would start talking, Marcos contradicted him harshly, treating him like a child; yet Marcos himself was the one acting juvenilely, not seeing his boundaries or respecting friends and visitors. Whenever they were driving and Leumas called his attention to the landscape or some other feature, Marcos would tell him to shut up and concentrate on the road. His father would become quiet and then would try to make a joke to hide his embarrassment. Marcos made a very bad impression on everyone and Arizle felt that it was better to withhold her criticism.

Ricardo also was wrong in everything he did; nothing he did pleased Marcos. When Ricardo told him that he had told his friends that Marcos was a kind man, Marcos disagreed, telling him that he was wrong, for he was neither kind nor wanted to be kind. Marcos also criticized Ricardo because he wanted to stay near his parents. Arizle assured Marcos that she had never prohibited Ricardo from going anywhere, and said that maybe Ricardo wanted to take advantage of their company.

When Arizle mentioned to Marcos that she had lost her mother too young, Marcos told her that the best thing her mother had done for her was to die early. Arizle was shocked by his answer and she thought that perhaps he was trying to tell her that her sons would be better off if she died early as well. Arizle was horrified and that prompted her to ask herself what she had done to him that caused him to dislike her so intensely.

They all avoided chatting with him about their daily routine, for he made it very clear that he was not interested in hearing such trivialities. Arizle tried to explain to him that he should be interested in their lives, for they were his parents. Also, she told him that if he wanted to become a writer, he would do well to develop his ability to listen, so that he could write more accurately about people.

"It is not sufficient to just to write a book," she told him. "It is important to have the power to transmit what one wants to say from the depths of one's soul. For that to happen, my son, it is important to hear and to understand, so that you can judge and analyze the feelings of others and then you will understand their hearts and minds."

Arizle wanted to tell him that one could only teach others when one was capable of self-control and was himself noble and worthy. Arizle and Leumas had wanted him to graduate from college, but they had never forced him to choose a particular profession. They just wanted him to be in the position of being able to earn his own living. After that, they felt, he would be free to search for his truth. Arizle always thought that borrowing money from friends or relatives left a sour taste in one's mouth long after the debt was repaid. Marcos had lost all those years, spending his father's savings, without giving any return on Leumas's investment.

The mystery that surrounded him was frightening to her. She really did not know where he lived and who his friends were. Was he hiding something from them? Arizle's friends and Leumas's family laughed at them when they could not say what he was studying so far away. Arizle told them that he had gone to study a field that was not available to him in Brazil.

When they asked her what that field was, she told them it was nuclear physics. She just could not tell them that her son had espoused Crowley's cult, a sect so secret that very little was known about it.

She ached when she thought about all she had wanted to say to him, but had refrained from saying. She regretted not telling him that he had lost everyone's respect and that only his mother, father and his brother remained loyal to him. Those three believed in him despite everything.

A month after his return to the United States, she could contain her silence no longer. She wrote to him:

Marcos-

The day, my son, that you will be able to do not what you want, but what you do not want—this day, my son, you will be a strong man! Your instructor, Crowley, seems to be able to do anything he wants because he is independent. I understand he is married and has children. Observe his life at home and you will no doubt see how autocratic he is. I do not think others obey him because of his leadership, but because he is a despot. You told me he is a German who, although not a Jew, had been held prisoner in a concentration camp. How is that possible? If he possesses so many "dark powers" as you claim he does, how could his life have been so horrible and out of his control? Why was he imprisoned? Do not believe everything people tell you; believe in God and yourself, not in a man who claims to have replaced God with himself. Do not follow an accused Satanist. Study and work, Marcos, for you are twenty-nine years old. Work will make you productive and you will develop more self-respect and become self-reliant.

Every one suffers and struggles and it tears me apart to see you suffering more than anyone else. Like Don Quixote in search of the windmill, you pursue your dreams without a plan or a destination. My heart breaks when I see you sad, offended, vulnerable and lost. Forgive me, my son; my words are harsh and they may sound to you like a beating, but sometimes a beating can be an expression of love. I will make you sad and unhappy with what I am writing to you, but hearing other people's opinions of you hurt me immensely and would hurt you even more. I know what my son is capable of achieving. I know my son is not an insane human being. I know my son is capable of deep love.

Arizle wanted him to build a future and she wanted to help him, but he had to stop inflicting pain on all of them first. In Marcos's view, his father was a weak man because he was kind, his brother was foolish because he was honest, Rameda was an idiot because he had gone to visit the chauffeur Raul's family in Portugal, Arizle was an opportunist who took advantage of everyone. Everyone was stupid in his opinion. To shield herself from his letters, she did not write to him for the next two years. She placed all his letters in a box in her closet. On top of the letters that were insulting, cold and indifferent, she placed a lovely letter he had sent her years before. Her silence almost killed her. She hoped that in two years he would acquire maturity and learn on his own that he had to choose a different direction for his life. During these two years his progress was nil.

Arizle continued to cry when she thought about Marcos. She prayed to God to help him come back to his family. She asked God to give him a family of his own. She thought that maybe he would take responsibility for himself if he were forced to protect and educate his own children. Nothing changed Marcos; he had made the decision to follow what he thought would bring him the only happiness he needed in life.

Marcos's ideas about living in America could have started with his school, Colégio Anglo Americano. Arizle spent a great part of her life wondering why Marcos had joined the Thelema society. Had he not gone to the United States, would he have had contact with the sect? Had he stayed in Rio de Janeiro, would his destiny have been different? Had she stayed with Leumas, would he not have felt abandoned and thus not needed to join a group where he felt wanted? Ricardo knew that she often thought of Marcos and his life. Ricardo wanted to be instrumental in uniting his brother with his mother, but he did not know how, and he felt like he had contributed to their separation.

Letters that Marcos wrote to his mother in 1941 were 180 degrees different than the letters he wrote her in subsequent years. His early letters conveyed that he trusted her, that he adored her, and that she was the best mother in the world; he sounded like a concerned son for in 1943 Arizle was traveling frequently to São Paulo, to Aguas da Prata, Caxambú, and São Lourenço to improve digestive problems that had plagued her all of her life.

Whenever her pains were overwhelming and her morale was low, Marcos would write to her to cheer her up. He told her he knew how she was worried about losing her health, and that he also knew how she suffered with the gossip about her reputation. She was a great soul, he wrote her. Nothing could conquer her or destroy her. He believed she had a strong spirit. He also said that Rameda's family members, as well as the outsiders who judged her, were not deserving of her friendship.

"Smile on your exterior and laugh in your interior," he reminded her. "Do not feel sorry for them." Did she feel sorry for the mother that moans as she gives birth to the child that will be the joy of her heart, he asked Arizle. The world, he told her, was going through a spiritual rebirth that he felt was gigantic. It would take time, he reminded her, but men that are blind would eventually be able to see and then they would recognize her value.

They had lifted each other's spirits continuously. She trusted, respected and revered his advice. They were close friends, one supporting the other, and they found strength in each other's convictions and analysis of life. They had been extraordinary friends.

She continued to go mineral spas. He knew that she was in pain and in need of rest. He told her to take long walks in the early morning, as walking fortified the muscles in the walls of the intestines, helped the digestive organs and forced the lungs to work harder.

"Do not remain in your room in the hotel amid the four walls," he wrote. "Do not worry about your skin; when you come back to Rio de Janeiro, your skin should not look like you crawled out from under a rock! Get a little sun on your face and body. Early sun is better for your health and skin." He occasionally ended his letter by saying something in Latin, such as, "filius tuus te salutat," which translates into "your son greets you."

They wrote and exchanged ideas about films, books, and articles; they always had a lot to talk about. After Marcos left for America, Arizle lost her intellectual companion. They had enjoyed discussing Tolstoy, Dostoevsky, and Thorne Smith. She knew that he loved Tostoy, who they both thought explored ideas to the end and always shared with the reader his conclusions about life. Dostoevsky excited the reader and placed one in a state of great speculative thought, but then left one with a sense of nihilism and emptiness. Marcos and Arizle agreed that Dostoevsky's characters neither knew what they wanted nor were conscious of what they did.

Marcos had still never been with a woman by age twenty-one. He told Arizle that it was not a matter of virtue, but it was lack of opportunity. He added that he could not go and pay a prostitute, for he considered it impious—a desecration of all women and of himself. He did not think something so sacred should be a commercial exchange. He found sex to be the root of the being; men, he thought, did not mind losing intelligence, but did not want to lose their virility.

Marcos had many philosophies about love and sex. He condemned men that had fathered children and abandoned them. He thought that love was the union between two souls, cemented by the bodies. He believed love was a sublime feeling capable of making men feel like gods. It was fire in the flesh, and it was inspiration and desire; it was blood and soul. He also wanted the tenderness of love that everyone desired, yet few had found. He believed that some of the great lovers, such as Romeo and Juliet, Heloise and Abelard, Antony and Cleopatra, had found such tenderness in each other; however, all these characters had sealed their union with blood. Perhaps later on his turn for love would come, and he would be happier. At least he vowed that he would try.

Marcos thought Leumas wanted him to be a colonel with medals hanging from his chest, since he had sent him to military school. Leumas was more concerned with Marco's developing a career to fall back on, if necessary. Marcos thought, erroneously, that his father never had any interest in the symphonies, the ballets, the plays, the novels or the poetry that he wrote. His father loved him deeply, but his actions were the opposite of love in Marcos's mind. Marcos viewed his father's dispassionate engineer's nature as disinterest in his accomplishments. He forgot that he had never shown an interest in his father's drawings of bridges, viaducts and tunnels. They simply had different interests.

Marcos had once believed that the only human being who understood him was his mother. Her approval and her support were vital to his positive frame of mind. As time passed and Marcos experienced other influences, he argued more and more with his father and mother. Marcos claimed that Leumas and Arizle had brought him up to be a free-spirited, independent man, but that now they both wanted to reverse the process by trying to keep him near them, persuading him to leave his Thelema beliefs of making one's actions the law, and to do something else with his life. He wrote his mother that she had to lose him in order to gain him. Leumas, he claimed, did not accept that this loss needed to occur, and didn't want to lose him even temporarily.

In 1952, a year before Marcos's abandonment of his country of birth in exchange for a life in America, Leumas and Marcos went to Europe together. Even though they had good moments, Marcos felt driven to do his own thing and not to include his father, who he thought always wanted to control him and force him to accept his ideas. Marcos ended up going to Germany by himself, against Leumas's wishes.

Marcos told Arizle that Leumas did not want him to go to live in the United States, and that if his father wanted war, he would get war. "I will be the general," Marcos sneered, throwing his father's adage back in his face. There was nothing Leumas could do; upon his return to Brazil, he would leave for America. He had made the decision, and no one was going to persuade him to the contrary.

The tone of Marcos's letters changed, starting in 1955. He became an aggressor then, without any specific reason. When Arizle had left him, she had understood his initial harsh reactions. After so many years, after they seemed to have arrived at some understanding, his new harsh tone seemed unjust and unreasonable. His offensive and scathing language hurt her. Arizle wondered what could have happened. Marcos was not the same man. He had left his country and his family to gain some independence, but he had ended up repudiating everything for which they stood.

16

Seven years after Arizle's first trip to Europe, she decided to go back again for another visit. Ricardo and Arizle went together for the first two weeks, and then Rameda met them in Paris at a later date. They departed on the *Louis Loumiére*, a French liner with excellent accommodations and French cuisine. Ricardo was eighteen and enjoyed this trip much more than the first one in 1951; however, because he was nauseated for the first two days, they took their meals in their suite. Arizle missed Rameda from the moment the ship left the port. She took several books to read during the nine days at sea before they docked in Cherbourg, France.

Ricardo wrote his father from the ship after he could finally stand and walk to the deck without being seasick.

Dear Dad,

I am standing on the deck, believe it or not. I was a big burden and source of worry for Mother. She was so concerned about me that she thought about having us stay in São Salvador until my sickness passed. We thought about you, alone on a Sunday, and we wondered what you were doing.

Dad, you are a great man and role model. As I mature and gain more experience and begin to observe other fathers, I am reassured by your character and admire your qualities more and more. You might not be perfect, but be assured that you and Mother are perfect parents and simply adoring creatures. I believe that God created you two to be together, and I am the lucky one, for I have you as my parents.

Today, we had lunch by the swimming pool while the ship's speakers played Tchaikovsky's "Nutcracker Suite." I thought about you and how happy Mother and I were being on the ship. Mother said that, although our life is pleasurable, it does not guarantee real satisfaction, but she also said that your life is a good life that includes satisfaction. I believe she wanted to remind me that a life full of fun and amusement is not always a good life. In real life one has to face obstacles with serenity and strength as you do. You wrote us that while we enjoyed the fruits of your efforts, you were working diligently.

Dad, accept the certitude that we love you deeply and we wish you were here with us. You are the one that had all the right to be here; instead you stayed back to close a large contract so that you can give us more. God bless you, Dad, and keep you always my father, for mother's joy.

Your son,
Ricardo

Service for Arizle's suite was the responsibility of a British woman named Anne. Anne became a companion for Arizle in her moments of longing for Rameda's company. Like Arizle, Anne had left her husband behind. She had worked on the ship for four years, rarely seeing her beloved husband in London. Anne spent every off-duty hour she had talking to Arizle about the war and its hardship on families. Arizle found out that Anne's husband had been in the Auschwitz concentration camp. Anne liked French literature and she and Arizle talked about the different periods and famous writings.

One morning a different chambermaid assisted Arizle. Arizle asked about Anne, but the new stewardess seemed reluctant to answer Arizle's questions. Arizle called the Captain to find out what was happening and explained to him that she had become fond of Anne and wanted her to continue as her chambermaid. The Captain regretfully informed Arizle that Anne had received a telegram from London, saying that her husband had passed away the night before. Upon receiving the news, Anne had thrown herself overboard. The ship made a search during the night, but could not find any sign of her.

After receiving the Captain's tragic report, Arizle did not feel like participating in any of the ship's parties or activities for several days. After about three days, Ricardo had finally acclimated to the motion of the ship, and Arizle dressed up to accompany Ricardo to dinner. Ricardo felt so proud to be with his mother, whom he admired and respected. Arizle tried to keep Ricardo company until he found some friends of his own; then she spent her time on the deck reading and chatting with other couples while Ricardo was busy playing ping pong, going to the movies, swimming and dancing.

When the ship docked at the pier, Arizle was happy to be back on firm ground. They went to London for two days and then returned to France before taking the train to Venice. Arizle adored Venice. She loved the originality of the city surrounded by sea and crisscrossed by canals. She loved San Marco Square, the Basilica and the Palace of the Doges. Ricardo and she went shopping in the galleria around the San Marco Square. They stayed at the Royal Danielle Hotel facing the Grand Canal. In one of the shops she bought some lovely abalone shells in which to serve seafood. After visiting the Murano glass factory, they took the train to Milan.

In Milan, she took Ricardo to audition for a maestro at the Conservatorio Giuseppi Verdi. The maestro was impressed with Ricardo's fine tenor voice and encouraged Arizle to send him to Milan to study. Arizle was very proud of Ricardo for having this gift of music. Ricardo's vocal talent had been discovered by one of the priests in Catholic school. The monsignor, director of the school, had phoned Arizle to let her know that her son had one of the most beautiful voices he had heard in a student in many years. Arizle wanted proof that Ricardo's voice was worthy of an education in Milan, the center for study in operatic music. That day, she had her assurance from one of the masters. She phoned Rameda that same evening to let him know of Ricardo's ability. Before leaving Milan, Arizle looked for a Catholic pensione in which Ricardo could reside, in case he decided to ever come back and take voice lessons.

In Florence, Arizle and Ricardo visited art galleries and museums. Arizle missed Rameda and wrote him every night. She also wrote Leumas, whom she missed almost as much as Rameda. Leumas, once again, had been given instructions on more changes to be effected on the house in Rio during her absence. Leumas wrote her three times a week letting her know what had happened and how the changes looked. Rameda left these changes up to Leumas, and he kept himself busy with his business. He had bought out two of his brothers and he and his older brother were the only ones left in the company.

From Florence, Arizle and Ricardo took the train to Paris, where they were met by a familiar face, Madame Suzanne Janvier, the governess that Ricardo had when he was twelve. Arizle was delighted to see this lovely and cultured lady again, and Ricardo was overjoyed to see his old friend. They had dinner with Madame Janvier at the Plaza Athène, where they were staying, and the next day they went out to the Bois de Boulogne together.

In three more days Rameda would be arriving. Arizle could not wait to embrace him again. She thought of Anne and her committing suicide when she heard the news that her husband was dead. She could not imagine life without Rameda, Ricardo, Leumas and Marcos. She continued to think of Marcos despite the fact that now she rarely heard anything about him. She frequently prayed to God to allow her to die before they did, for life would be shallow and uninteresting without them.

Arizle was busied herself again by buying lovely things for her homes. She had gone to Carven, Jacques Fath and Lanvin, but had bought only two suits. She was much more interested in buying for her homes, for she felt everyone would enjoy whatever she purchased. At night they went to the theater with Suzanne Janvier. They saw "Tea and Sympathy" with Ingrid Bergman. Suzanne knew the stage manager and arranged for Arizle and Ricardo to visit Miss Bergman in her dressing room. This moment was extremely exciting for Ricardo, who got a large picture with a dedication from Miss Bergman.

Rameda finally arrived, and with good news. The contract he was expecting to close had been finalized and his company was going to sell meat to the Brazilian Army. Arizle was so happy to see him that she cried for joy. They hugged and kissed for a long time. Ricardo and Suzanne left to go to the opera to hear "Faust." When Ricardo came back, they were waiting for him to arrive, happy that they were together once more. Only Leumas and Marcos were not with them. Arizle once again reminded herself that happiness was never complete. She thanked God that everyone was healthy as far as she knew.

They stayed in Paris for another week, driving to Germany and Switzerland and going over the Simplon Pass to Italy. They drove through the lake region of Como, Maggiore and Lugano. Rameda had brought the chauffeur Raul back with him and they had rented a car in Paris. After touring the northern part of Italy, they went to Innsbruck and Salzburg and then returned to Switzerland. They spent three days in Geneva driving around the lake. They loved that region, with its enchanting castles, and original hotels that overlooked the blue lake surrounded by snow-covered peaks.

Arizle did not forget Leumas during her trips. She wrote to him frequently from every place she visited. She wrote him from Geneva, one of her favorite places.

Dearest Leumas,

My nostalgia is immense. I long for my house that I love so much, and its foundations, which I watched being built stone by stone. I long for my son, Marcos, who despite not understanding me and finding me stubborn, ungrateful and domineering, loves me and esteems me. I long for the sensation of being needed, for the sensation of affection that my home and my dogs give me. I long for those who love me despite the fact that they know about my transgressions and faults, just like you know, and yet, you love me. I cannot live without love around me. If I could be the happiest woman in the world you would know the happiest woman in the world, for I would not suffer with the rejections from my relatives and Rameda's family; no one would reach me with their scorn. I have not reached the state of mind in which love, friendship or affection is not needed. I ask God to teach me not to need anyone, to only count on me. Only then I will have peace.

Yesterday, I found out about the train disaster in Nova Iguaçú. I am anxious to know that you are all right and suffered no harm. I could not bear the thought of losing the only father I had in my life. My real father gave me life but you gave me happiness by renouncing every-thing that was dear to you. Forgive me for my sins. I have been settling them with high inter-est.

I only think of going back and seeing all the friendly faces: yours, Rosina's, our friends' and the servants'. My dogs, I love them also. They are loyal and they show me affection when I return from a trip. I hope you never die, at least not before I do. To lose you would be like losing a son, and a son can never be replaced. God give me patience; I need it. Since I came and made my own decision to come, I have to do the best I can until the end of it. I cannot see the Brazilian flag without crying. My country is really lovely. There is no place like home!

Receive fondest sentiments from this woman who treated you unfairly, but who is your friend despite everything,

Love,
Arizle

After a month and a half of sightseeing, they drove back to Paris where they returned the car. They were to receive some money that Leumas had wired them when they got back to the hotel in Paris. The money had not arrived, and Rameda was getting nerv-ous, for they had to leave by train to go to Lisbon. They were going to visit the chauffeur's family there and then meet the ship to go back to Brazil. They did not even have enough funds to pay their hotel bill. Rameda called Brazil to talk to Leumas several times and every time Leumas said he had wired the money as per his request. After Rameda inquired about the money in the hotel, they admitted making the mistake of giving the money to another guest in the hotel with the same surname. Rameda was frantic, for the guest who got the money erroneously had pocketed it and gone to Switzerland!

Rameda called Leumas again and asked him if he could stop payment on the money he had sent already and wire it to them again. Leumas however, said that there was no time to do this before they left for Lisbon. It was Bastille Day in France, and there was no commerce. Leumas was very concerned about them. What a predicament, Rameda thought. What could they do? How was he going to pay their hotel bill and get money for the rest of their trip? Arizle had the idea of going to the manager and offering to leave her jewels with them until the money arrived and the hotel would be paid, but the hotel manager told them that they were good customers and there was no need to leave any jewelry as security. Rameda could simply wire the money to them after they went back to Brazil. The manager asked Rameda if he needed any money to get to Lisbon, where he hoped to finally receive his funds by wire. Arizle and Rameda were surprised with the kindness of the manager and the trust he showed in them. The manager loaned Rameda all the money he needed, and they were able to get on the train to Lisbon.

They were relieved, but tired, when they finally got on their way and slept most of the way into Madrid. In Madrid they had to get off the train, because there was something wrong with it. All passengers were asked to change trains. Here was another obstacle. This time they did not have a visa to get off the train and enter Spanish territory on foot. The customs agent insisted to Arizle, who spoke Spanish fluently, that they needed the visas to walk on Spanish soil as they got out of the defective train and got onto the new train. Without the visas they were stuck on the defective train. It made no sense to them, but Arizle made a whispered suggestion, and Rameda nervously passed a large denomination peseta note discreetly to the inspector, who then expedited the visas, allowing them to continue their journey to Lisbon. When they got on the new train, they laughed together at their adventures.

Rameda was proud of his wife and told Ricardo, "Your mother is the most extraordinary woman I have ever met." Ricardo completely concurred. Raul did not want to be impertinent by getting into the conversation and putting in his two cents, but his thoughts agreed that Madame Pachêco was indeed extraordinary.

They arrived in Lisbon early in the morning. Rameda had made reservations at the Hotel D'Avila. When they arrived in the hotel the money Leumas had sent was waiting for them. Rameda went out with Raul and rented another Chrysler Imperial to take them to Porto and to the village where Raul's sister lived. They had a lovely time with Raul's family, who always made them feel at home, and Raul was very grateful to see his sister, nephews, and nieces.

They spent two days with them before returning to Lisbon to board the ship. Raul drove them to Lisbon and then went back to spend another week with his sister. He flew to Rio de Janeiro at the end of his vacation, and when Rameda, Arizle and Ricardo got to Rio, Raul was there waiting for them with Leumas and twenty family members and friends. The next morning, Rameda wired the money to the Paris hotel manager, along with his thanks. Arizle sent a beautiful gift to the manager's wife, a gold brooch with Brazilian tourmalines.

Rameda and Arizle returned to Europe two years later, taking Raul with them once again. This time they all flew to Paris, where Rameda rented a car. They toured for one month and then went to Milan to meet with Ricardo, who was there taking voice training. From Milan they drove to Paris, and they stayed at the same hotel. The manager brought his wife to their table one evening, so that she could thank them in person for the lovely gift Arizle had sent her. They found flowers in their room and a large basket with champagne, delicious cheeses, and fresh fruits, compliments of the manager.

This trip was the last time Arizle went to Europe. She had been feeling unwell, and the doctors told her that she had a gallbladder that did not function properly. The bile produced by the liver was not being expelled via the bile duct and had to be extracted through a tube instead. From time to time Arizle went to the mineral water spas to see if she could ameliorate her digestive system problem.

Arizle and went to Aguas da Prata for a ten-day treatment with mineral waters, which had the reputation of helping people with gallbladder problems. Arizle and Rameda went to the various mineral fountains four times a day. They walked through the parks where the medicinal springs were located and around the hotel grounds all the time. Arizle missed Leumas, Ricardo and Marcos a great deal. She wrote Leumas and Ricardo almost everyday. She did not write to Marcos, for he wanted nothing to do with his mother. Marcos's attitude contributed to her health problems. She was very troubled and felt responsible for his being disillusioned and uninterested in cultivating his father's friendship. She understood that Marcos was not the same person after he joined Crowley's sect; however, she spent her life blaming herself for his actions. The fact that he was unhappy about life and cynical about his family members worried her deeply.

In one of her letters from Aguas da Prata she wrote,

> Dear Leumas,
>
> Rameda had angina, but no fever. I was feeling fine, but I ate mangoes and pork sausages together and of course, the combination upset my stomach. Everything here is unattractive, but the mineral water is helping my gallbladder, and I want to be healthy again; only God knows how much I do. I have had a very good appetite. The hotel is mediocre, but the chef is good.
>
> I want to stay here until the end of the twenty-one days recommended by my doctor. Please write us. How is Francisca? Is your home being taken care of with zeal and responsibility? Any news about my home? Is everything all right? I am always asking you to do things for me. Forgive me please.
>
> We have been visiting the little towns near here in a horse and buggy. We also travel around by car. We eat, read and sleep. What else is there? I hope to become strong and calm.
>
> Did you have covers made for the car seats? Write us please.

How are Rosina Duarte and John, our beloved butler? Give them my regards. Please remind John to water my flowers with lots of water. The more water, the better. I am sending Belarmina ahead of us so that she can get the house ready for our arrival.

Receive our gratefulness; we are brothers and sisters in God. May God keep you always.

Please accept an embrace and my deepest affection.

Yours,
Arizle

Rameda loved Arizle in his own way. He never really understood why Arizle loved and worried so much about everything and everybody. Being a man, he had never taken any time to read books about women so that he would learn how to deal with them more successfully. Leumas was much more nurturing than Rameda. He took the time to listen to her with all his senses. Rameda listened to her with engineering logic, not human sympathy. Arizle, though strong, was vulnerable. Rameda tried to become more giving, more supportive as a friend and a companion, but he lacked her sensitivity. His family were survivors in a new country and had to be tough to fight their misfortunes. They had transmitted strength of character to Rameda, but had forgotten to give him a tender heart.

Arizle taught Rameda to give money to the poor in the streets. She taught him to pray for the ones who suffered in the hospitals, to feel sorry for the ones who were lonely, the ones who were sad, and the ones who were sick. Rameda never thought about these things until he began his relationship with Arizle. She taught him to touch and feel deeply the beauty of life.

Rameda had many internal conflicts from his family's rebuff of Arizle. He never reconciled completely the choice he had made and the consequences of it. His father's lack of support was a blow to him, and he felt like the prodigal son. He wanted his father's and his mother's support, appreciation and respect for Arizle. They died without showing it to him.

Arizle encouraged Ricardo to visit Rameda's parents despite their distant treatment of him. Ricardo went to visit his paternal grandmother as she waited for death to take her. She had cancer of the liver and was just skin and bone. One afternoon, Ricardo went to see her with his father. Arizle had asked Ricardo to kiss his grandmother and to show her affection and love, for this would probably be the last time he would ever see her. The old lady hugged Ricardo as he kissed her hand. Then she asked her eldest daughter to bring her jewelry box to her. When she had the box, she opened it with trembling hands, took a golden chain with a pendant containing two diamonds and a sapphire and gave it to Ricardo. Ricardo did not want to accept the present, but his father told him to take it as a remembrance of his grandmother. Ricardo thought the chain and pendant were beautiful, and they became sacred items to him.

The mind and soul of others are secret realms. They and only they know their thoughts and their feelings. Arizle had learned a great deal in life, and she understood that Rameda's mother had tried to ask Ricardo for his forgiveness and also to convey to Arizle, through her gift to Ricardo, that she should also forgive her. It was not too late. It was a moment of mutual forgiveness.

Rameda's father died of a weak heart and complications resulting from cancer. Seu Pachêco also showed Ricardo that he respected him. He treated his grandchildren all in the same manner. He gave them an envelope with money every Sunday morning when they came to visit him. Arizle sent Ricardo with Rameda, who preferred not to go, but went with him because Arizle insisted that a son should visit his father whenever he could. Arizle reminded Rameda that his father probably would not live much longer, and that Rameda needed to show the old gentleman that he loved him. She said that Rameda would feel guilty after his death if he did not take the time to visit while his father was living. After the elder Pachêcos passed away, Rameda was grateful to Arizle for insisting he visit them.

Arizle's father spent fourteen years without communicating with his daughter. Arizle always believed that gossip and news about her life passed along to him by her brother and sister had turned him against her. One early morning, Arizle received a phone call from her stepmother, saying that Cantarini Somar was dying and wanted to see her, Ricardo and Marcos before his death. Arizle asked Raul to take her to her father's home. Upon arriving, she ran to his bedside crying. They caressed each other's faces and kissed each other's cheeks with emotion. He asked her to please forgive him and his ignorance. She nodded her head, saying that she had nothing for which to forgive him.

He told her, whispering, "If your mother came back to life today, I would kiss the floor where she walked. A woman like her I never again saw or found. She was a real hero, an unsung one!"

Arizle went home to cook for her father, who wanted food prepared solely by her hands. Also, Cantarini Somar wanted to see his grandson and to meet Rameda. For the following two months, Arizle cooked or had cooked three meals for her father every day, which she not only delivered, but also fed him each spoonful with the patience and the tenderness of his deceased wife. Cantarini told Arizle many times that she looked and acted like her mother.

Arizle canceled all her appointments to take care of her father. She had to be very tactful in order not to anger her stepmother and thus create more problems for her dying father. She brought Rameda to meet him and Ricardo also went with her in the afternoons after school to visit his grandfather. Cantarini gave Ricardo his dark green Royal typewriter, an object he cherished very much. Unfortunately, Cantarini had forgotten that he had already designated the typewriter as a gift for one of his stepchildren. To prevent problems, Arizle asked Ricardo to return the typewriter to her stepmother without Cantarini's knowledge. Ricardo said that he could never give away the typewriter, since it was the only thing he had by which to remember his grandfather. Arizle solved the problem by buying a new dark green Royal typewriter and giving to her stepmother in lieu of the one given to Ricardo.

Arizle was with her father when he took his last breath. She was devastated. They had just gotten to know one another and feel a tremendous attachment to each other, and now he was gone. Arizle and Ricardo cried together for the final loss of a father and grandfather, who had been lost, found and lost again. Why is life so complex, Arizle wondered? Why can we not be together and live in harmony? Why only at death do we understand the meaning of forgiveness and love? Why do people spend so much time judging instead of understanding and accepting?

She never forgot him. She learned to focus on his strengths, his integrity as a husband, his honesty at work, his responsible ways to his boss as an employee, his handsome green eyes, face and his tender hands. The memories of his violent nature dissipated almost entirely. Yes, his hands had developed a soft touch. She felt his hands on her face for a long time. She had learned that in forgiveness there is healing and regeneration.

Ricardo watched sadly his mother age rapidly after her father's death. She led a regular life, making sure that her family was happy and always had lovely environments in which to live. She still prepared delicious desserts when the chef was off, but her eyes had become sad, and frequently he caught her looking at the horizon, frowning and lost in thought. Ricardo sensed that she was thinking of her father.

Two months later, Leumas had an accident. He was flying a glider when it suddenly went down. When she heard this news, she was totally distraught. She was told that an ambulance had taken him to the hospital and that he was alive, but in critical condition. Arizle was frantic. She told Raul to drive her to the hospital immediately. She flew into the hospital with one thought on her mind—to see Leumas. He was in surgery, for he had broken his back. She called Rameda, who came immediately to stay with her. Leumas's brothers also came to the hospital and were introduced to Rameda for the first time.

The surgery lasted four hours and then Leumas stayed in intensive care for the night. Arizle and

Rameda dozed in the chairs in the waiting room. By 5:30 the next morning Arizle had already drunk a cup of coffee and checked on Leumas several times. He was out of danger. They put him in a cast that completely covered his torso, and he had to keep it on for four months. In the second month, the heat and perspiration had created an itch that was unbearable. It nearly drove him crazy. Arizle made long sticks with a piece of sponge on the end to scratch Leumas's back for him.

Arizle took him to her house after he left the hospital and took care of him for a month. In the second month, he went back to work and insisted on taking the bus to work and back home. She wanted to have her chauffeur drive him, but he declined. Arizle went to visit him twice a week and spent an hour scratching his back with her invention. Ricardo was with him all the time. Ricardo developed his reading abilities reading *Popular Mechanics*, *Time* and the newspapers to Leumas. Ricardo also became an effective back scratcher. After six months, Leumas was able to resume his normal life. He flew gliders again without Arizle's knowledge. He had no fear of death. He believed that in death one found the eternal life of the spirit.

17

Arizle's health problems persisted for two straight years. She went to the doctor constantly and underwent bile removal once every two months. The doctors continued to advise her that her condition was due to the malfunction of her gallbladder. They attributed her illness to menopause, the many abortions she had undergone, stress, and her gallbladder. They said she had nothing to worry about as long as she emptied her gallbladder once every two months. Her doctor also told her to drink milk, but the more milk she drank, the sicker she became. For a woman who had rarely drunk a glass of wine and did not smoke or eat fried foods, her health should have been much better. In order for her to understand what was happening to her body, she decided to read medical books. She purchased all kinds of books on the gallbladder, bile accumulation in the blood, the liver, pancreas, and other organs. She pored over the medical books as if she were preparing to take medical board exams. She knew just as much as the doctors did, since they really did not know what she had. The doctors seemed unable to isolate her symptoms and observe them. They had been guessing for many months, actually for years, and seemed to know less and less with the passage of time.

Rameda thought they should move to Alto da Tijuca, where the climate was cooler and perhaps better for her health. She would be close to the forest, the sun and the flowers that she so loved. He bought a large piece of land in the forest of Tijuca and got her involved in designing and buying all that she needed for the building of the house. She wanted a Swiss chalet-style home. She designed it along the lines of the lovely chalets she had seen in Switzerland and Austria and was excited with her new home. The front wall of the living room was going to consist of double-pane glass windows that stretched from the floor to the ceiling. She was going to name the room "a window to the sun." Without the sun, there could be no life, intelligence would be stillborn, and flowers would never grow. She could not conceive of a world of darkness.

Rameda rented a house for her near the new building site, and she began buying bathroom fixtures, kitchen fixtures and furniture for her new home and storing them in a large garage. The new home took much of her attention, and everyone thought her health would improve, since she had something interesting to do, for many of her friends actually thought Arizle's illness was somewhat psychosomatic.

One day when Arizle got up in the morning, she had jaundice. She was also experiencing much pain in her back. She called her doctor and he told her to come to the office. She got dressed, and Raul drove her to the doctor's office in the city. Her doctor examined her and found nothing. Since he had no idea what to do, he suggested that she consult an endocrinologist. So, she went to the specialist. After examining her, he also did not find anything. Nevertheless, the jaundice was continuing and her severe back pains had not subsided. Rameda was very concerned and asked one of his brothers to recommend another doctor named Dr. Bernardo who had been the Pachêco family doctor for several years. He was a surgeon and he recommended exploratory surgery to pinpoint what the trouble might be. Arizle went to see him twice, for she thought he ought to have an idea based on her symptoms of what was causing her pain and jaundice. Both times he recommended surgery as a way to find out what was wrong. Arizle decided to go ahead with it.

The day before her surgery, she called Rameda, Ricardo and Leumas to her bedroom and told them she thought she had a tumor in the pancreas. They were shocked with her diagnosis, since she had no formal medical education, and they wanted to wait for the Dr. Bernardo's expert opinion before getting too concerned and upset.

Everyone went with her to the hospital. Claudia, her aunt, was very concerned and kept Ricardo company during surgery. Leumas and Rameda stayed at the hospital in the waiting room. Three hours later, the doctor came out and confirmed what Arizle had told her family the day before. She had a malignant tumor in the pancreas. Similar cancers had been linked to heavy smoking and to high intake of alcohol. Arizle had never smoked and had never overindulged in drinking. The doctors explained that the symptoms included a pain in the upper part of the abdomen, which often spread to the back. In most cases, Dr. Bernardo explained, the symptoms do not appear until the cancer is well advanced, often after it has metastasized to other organs, such as the liver and the lungs. Arizle's tumor was very large and could not be removed surgically without presenting a severe threat to her life. Veins were covering and wrapping the tumor, thus making its removal almost impossible without causing internal hemorrhaging. The prognosis was sobering. Arizle had but three to four months to live.

Rameda was desperate and discussed with Leumas whether to take Arizle to the United States for treatment. There, he thought, procedures were much more advanced and they could prolong her life. Arizle spent a few hours in the recovery room and then was taken to a private room. She had been resting for a while when the family went into her room. She had her eyes closed when the family entered, but she was listening to everything people said.

Claudia took a look at her and exclaimed, "Poor Arizle!"

Arizle heard her and later confronted Rameda about her true diagnosis. Rameda wanted to lie to her, but could not find the words to do so. They held each other tightly in a long embrace and cried together until she went back to sleep. Ricardo and Leumas waited in the visitor's lounge. Ricardo was devastated by the news. Leumas, although in control of his emotions, felt helpless. His heart had been broken for a second time in his life. He kept his eyes closed as if in prayer. He had his arms around Ricardo's shoulders. Their family would never be the same.

Leumas stayed with Ricardo in the lounge for several hours until Rameda came out and asked if they wanted to see Arizle again. Leumas and Ricardo went into the room, and there she was—a feeble little candle, a flickering light in the spreading darkness of their lives.

They hugged her and Leumas said, "Little Arizle, we shall fight the cancer with you. We will not let you down."

Arizle looked at Leumas and said, "You are all tired. Take Rameda and Ricardo home, Leumas."

Rameda immediately told her that he would not leave her. He asked the nurse to find him a chair where he could sit and be near her for the whole night. He was thankful that in Brazil, close family members are allowed to stay in the hospital with their loved ones.

Leumas left with Ricardo. Life had placed a chasm in their path, and he was confused and tormented, not knowing how to cross it. They did not know what to say or what to do. Leumas tried to cheer up Ricardo by telling him that his father was taking Arizle to New York City for treatment at the best cancer hospital in the world. Leumas was going to check the names of top doctors who he thought could save her life. He told Ricardo in detail what he was going to do the next day to save their Arizle. They had to ask her, and she had to agree to go, but he thought she was a fighter, and she would not hesitate to accept this suggestion.

Medicine in Brazil was behind the times. Only in São Paulo did they have a good hospital and some doctors with a little more prestige, but in the United States, they thought, she would certainly be helped. Leumas reminded Ricardo that hope would never die. It was like a flame and it had to be kept alive for her sake and everyone else's. Ricardo promised Leumas, his best friend, that he would stay optimistic toward his mother's health and would only make positive statements around her. Leumas hugged him and told him he was a wonderful young man, a caring son and a loving friend. Ricardo also told Leumas that he was his best friend and second mother, and that he loved him with all his heart.

Leumas tried to call Marcos that night, but could not locate him. Leumas sat at the table and wrote him a letter. He was going to send it express the next morning. After he finished writing, Leumas had some soup, took a shower and retired to the guest-room. Ricardo also had a shower and had a plate of soup, keeping Leumas company. The house seemed cold and sad. Ricardo did not want to be alone in his room and asked Leumas if he could sleep in the guest-room with him. He preferred to be with Leumas so they could talk some more about what they were going to do to help her. Leumas reassured Ricardo that they were going to take action and start the plans the next morning. They both eventually fell asleep from nervous exhaustion.

The servants were crying in the corners, and everyone seemed to be bewildered with the thought of losing her joy, her vivacious personality, and her humor. She was the sun in their lives; she brought warmth, light, hope, understanding, forgiveness, consolation and love.

"God had to be crazy to do such a thing to the most loving human being we know!" exclaimed Chico, her chef, clutching a rosary in left hand.

Leumas corrected Chico, "You should not make this statement, Chico! God did not have anything to do with Dona Arizle's illness. God is a merciful being who loves his children. Dona Arizle has been given a difficult task to perform. She will win," he asserted. "When she comes home," he ordered, "she should find you all happy to see her, not in despair or even sad. She needs to be reassured by your attitude that she will be cured. Anything else besides joy in seeing her, I will not allow!" Leumas was serious and his voice was firm. The servants dried their eyes, blew their noses and went to wash their hands and faces. Ricardo was surprised at Leumas's statement, but he knew Leumas was right.

After they had breakfast, they left for the hospital. When they entered Arizle's room, she was awake and greeted them with affection. She hugged them and told Leumas that she wanted to give him power of attorney to distribute her assets when the time came. Leumas looked at Rameda, but Rameda said that Arizle and he had discussed the matter prior to Leumas's arrival and that he, Rameda, did not want anything to do with that task. He was the one that had asked Arizle to give the power of attorney to Leumas. Leumas reminded Rameda that Arizle's assets had come from Rameda and that he thought Rameda should be the one to distribute them. Rameda insisted to Leumas that he wanted him to be the one to take care of those matters, and stated that he trusted him fully.

Ricardo overheard this discussion with pride in his heart for his father, mother and best friend. They were indeed an unusual family. Ricardo sat by the bed and took Arizle's hand. He told his mother that they were going to do everything in their power to get her cured. Leumas interrupted their conversation and asked Arizle if she would allow them to plan a trip for her to New York City so that she could visit the top pancreatic cancer specialists in the world. Arizle nodded her head, crying. Rameda immediately told her that she had to keep her faith and could not waver. Together, he declared, they would fight and win.

Arizle remained in the hospital for the remainder of the week, until she felt strong and rested enough to go home. Ricardo and Leumas came to the hospital everyday. While they stayed with her, Rameda went home, took a shower and went back to be with her. Rameda hardly left her bedside. He ran his office from the hospital and his home. He did not want to leave her alone, and as they held hands, Arizle beamed with the realization that Rameda had finally become the man she wanted him to be—sensitive, compassionate and tender. He was determined to make her well.

On the day Arizle went home, Leumas reminded all the servants that they should not cry in front of her. They waited for her at the door with bouquet of flowers, baskets of fruit and special cookies she liked. She hugged each one of them. They all looked happy to see her. Not one cried in her presence. After she retired to her bedroom, they went to their rooms and cried in private. Leumas knew they were crying and went there and tried to console them by letting them know that Dr. Rameda was taking her to the United States to be treated by great doctors. She was going to improve and get better. He thanked them for not crying in front of her. His voice cracked briefly, as if he himself could not contain his emotion, and he left them to their thoughts.

Arizle was feeling better, but was still in pain. The pain subsided slightly more when she was standing than when she was lying down. Rameda made sure that she stood up whenever she was able. He brought her meals, and told João, the butler, to prepare her trays with lacy doilies and not to forget to put a rosebud in the tiny vase on her tray. Chico made beef tea for her every day. She had fruit juices with vitamin B-12, calcium, and vitamin C. They were determined to get her to gain at least ten pounds. She had no appetite and struggled to eat even little portions. Rameda begged her to eat. He called the Confeitaria Colombo and ordered limas da Persia, a hybrid of two different types of oranges, for her. He sat by her bed and peeled the limas with such affection and care that anyone observing them would cry in sorrow for the man who wanted to see her well again. Nothing else mattered to Rameda. If he had committed sins in the past toward her, he redeemed himself completely and totally during Arizle's illness.

Leumas came to visit her three times a week. He tried to divide himself between his blind mother and Arizle. He always brought her something funny to raise her spirits. Ricardo asked him where he found those incredible gadgets.

He laughed and replied, "Around."

Arizle had signed the power of attorney for Leumas, as Rameda had wanted. Leumas was busy getting U.S. visas. He had purchased four roundtrip tickets, as per Rameda's instructions. Because Arizle was petrified of flying, Rameda, wanting to make her feel more secure during the flight, asked her personal doctor to accompany them.

Arizle was terrified, but she did not want to disappoint Rameda. Ricardo was going with them to cook and help with his mother. Leumas had finally contacted Marcos, who was ready to fly to New York to be with his mother as soon as Rameda sent him tickets. Marcos had two children with a woman who did not want to marry him. Arizle wanted to meet the woman and also meet her grandchildren for the first time. Rameda told Leumas to tell Marcos that he was sending tickets for him, his friend and the two children to visit Arizle in New York.

The day of departure arrived. Dr. Orlando, Arizle's physician, was to be seated in front of Arizle's seat in case she needed his help. Leumas kissed Arizle's head and hands. He told her not to worry, because he would take care of her houses. Arizle was weak and she had only gained three pounds. Leumas embraced Rameda, wishing him a good trip as they walked toward the plane with Arizle in a wheelchair. Ricardo hugged Leumas, and they boarded the plane.

As the plane took off, Arizle was praying with her eyes closed and gripping the arms of her seat with both hands. Her head was pressed back and her forehead perspired freely. Arizle did not want to give anybody any trouble, so she stayed as quiet and still as she could. It was Ricardo who scared them all. His pulse rate dropped precipitously, and his hands became distorted as if he had suffered a stroke. Rameda panicked, for he was not prepared for Ricardo to be the one in need of medical assistance. The doctor was able to give Ricardo an injection, however, and he got better in a few minutes.

Doctor Orlando took Arizle's blood pressure every hour. Arizle slept on and off for the twelve hours that they spent in the air. Rameda held her hand and changed the three small pillows underneath her head, helping her find a more comfortable position. Dinner was served, but Arizle did not eat anything. Rameda wanted to peel a piece of fruit for her, but she declined.

They had chosen to go to New York in late May, when the weather was warm, for they did not think she would survive the cold and the snow. Upon landing, they found Marcos and Jaime, Rameda's nephew, waiting for them. His nephew was one of the Brazilian president's advisors and was on official business in New York. Marcos had hired a limousine, at Rameda's request, to take her to the hotel. They went to the Sheraton Atlantic Hotel, where they had booked four rooms. On her second day at the hotel, Arizle wanted to write to Leumas.

My dearest Leumas,

I am dying not from cancer, but from homesickness for my country, my home, you, Leumas, my oranges, and my limas. I do not have too much hope that I will get well. I went to see a doctor named Parke today, and he feels that there is a possibility I will get better. Tomorrow, I will start the X-rays and a modern therapy called radioisotope.

I was shocked to see so many people at the hospital, like me, waiting to be treated. I, as you know, am very stupid, for I live both my pain and the pain of others. I suffer with my suffering brothers and sisters! My God, have mercy on your Arizle. I fear to become insane before they are able to cure my cancer. Other women told me that they come back every six months, and they have been doing much better.

Please, dearest Leumas, ask Saint Jude to guard and help me. Also, ask him to help all the ones who suffer more than I do.

I kiss your face, the face that I miss, while tears are rolling down my face. I

wish you were here with me, my greatest
friend.

We will be leaving this hotel tomorrow to go to an apartment. Tomorrow I
will write you again with the new address.

I see you, I kiss you, and I ask God
to bless you.

Please accept my tenderness and my
kind sentiments.

Yours,
Arizle

P.S. Hugs to João and Chico.

Two days later, they moved into an apartment at
the Hotel Navarro on Central Park South. There, they
rented two large, two-bedroom apartments. One
apartment was for Arizle, Rameda and Ricardo, and
the second apartment was for Marcos and Dr. Orlando. Each apartment had a complete kitchen. A few
minutes after they arrived, Ricardo went out to the
neighborhood grocery store and purchased ground
beef to make beef tea for his mother. He also purchased fruit, vegetables, olive oil and spices. While he
was shopping, Marcos and Rameda helped Arizle into
bed. Next, they asked her if she wanted them to draw
her a bath. Arizle agreed, and Marcos, who was very
strong, carried his mother in his arms to the tub.
Arizle stayed immersed in the warm water for twenty
minutes. Rameda kept throwing hot water on her
back and she reached for his hand and kissed it. They
said nothing to each other. Words could never express
the love and the dedication that Rameda felt for her. If
he could pick up a knife and cut his pancreas out and
give to her, he would have done it in a minute. She
stayed in the tub with her eyes closed, experiencing a

few minutes of peace without the excruciating pain that she lived with all the time. While Rameda was in the bathroom with her, Marcos tried to put away their clothes. Ricardo had returned from his shopping expedition and was preparing her food. He had purchased a rose and put it in a paper cup on her meal tray.

Rameda called for Marcos and Ricardo to help carry their mother back to her bed. Marcos told Ricardo that it was easier for him to do it alone, for he did not want to risk dropping her. Marcos carried her to bed while Ricardo pulled down the covers. After she was in bed, they propped her up with pillows, and Rameda told Ricardo that it was time to bring her food tray. She kissed Marcos's hand with gratitude. Marcos kissed her on her cheek and Rameda placed his hand softly on her head.

Ricardo had tears in his eyes, seeing Marcos help his mother with such patience and good will. Maybe they could achieve a truce and become closer now that she was so ill. Ricardo left the room because he could not control the profusion of his tears. Rameda was feeding Arizle when she asked for a glass of fruit juice. Ricardo heard and brought her apple juice. She touched his face in a caress of gratitude. Ricardo kissed her hands. Marcos came in and told them he was going to take a shower, change, and go out for a walk.

The hotel faced Central Park. The tree buds were just starting to open up into leaves, and there was a lot to see if Arizle had the strength to go to the window and see the park and the people in the street. But Arizle was not strong enough. The apartment had the two bedrooms, each with its own bath, plus a living room and dining room in an "L" shape. The kitchen was completely outfitted and there was a rear door for deliveries.

Ricardo discovered that the refrigerator was not working, and he called downstairs for the manager to send a repairman. The bell rang just five minutes later, and the man introduced himself as an engineer. Ricardo was impressed that they would send a graduate engineer to fix the refrigerator. Marcos laughed at Ricardo's comment and explained to him that repairmen were sometimes called engineers in America, not professionals as they were in Brazil.

Rameda went out with Ricardo, while Marcos stayed with his mother. Rameda thought it was good for them to have some privacy and discuss anything they felt like without his being around. When Rameda went outside of the hotel, he realized that the section of New York City was elegant and refined and had some nice stores. On the corner of Central Park South and the Avenue of Americas, Rameda saw a beautiful antique shop. He told Ricardo that he wanted to buy Arizle the small rooster he saw in the window display. Ricardo went in with him and Rameda bought Arizle a crystal rooster and a hen on a red wooden pedestal. He also bought her a beige linen tablecloth embroidered with brown thread. He wrote her a card and gave to her in the evening.

> My love,
> You have always been and will always be the person whom I loved in this life. I am happy because we will soon have you strong and healthy. I promise you that I will be for you the husband that I have not been in the past: I will be more

tender, more understanding, yours and only yours, with all my love.

I bought this tablecloth for our dinner on September 23, and the little rooster and chicken as a remembrance of our twenty-third anniversary.

Yours, and only yours, forever,

Rameda

He told Ricardo that it was very important to convey to her that they expected her to live for many years to come, and that the gift of the tablecloth would remind and assure her of that. Arizle named the rooster and hen Chôchô and Deidei. Anytime she liked an item, she had to give it a special, endearing name.

After Rameda and Ricardo left the antique shop, they turned the corner on Avenue of the Americas and found a grocery store, larger than the one Ricardo had been to before. They had all kinds of lovely fruit. Rameda bought many different varieties of them, telling Ricardo that freshly squeezed fruit was better for Arizle's health. He also purchased a juicer and a blender. They were back in less than two hours. As they entered the hotel, to their surprise, they saw Nat King Cole waiting for the elevator. Ricardo and Rameda were discreet and greeted him as if he were any other resident at the hotel. Later on Marcos found out that the singer also suffered from cancer and was going for therapy at Memorial Hospital—the same facility that Arizle would use. Rameda and Ricardo told Arizle that they had gone upstairs in the elevator with a celebrity. Ricardo was saddened by the fact that even a celebrity was nothing more than a human being in search of survival. This comment led to a conversation between Rameda and his son about the fragility of life, how it could end at any moment, and how small things were not really important. Life was so precarious, so precious and so ephemeral!

The next morning Marcos and Dr. Orlando went to the hospital to talk to Dr. Parke and Dr. Arenson. These doctors had examined Arizle to determine the dosage and the time period the treatment would require. Marcos and Dr. Orlando came back two hours later. They were very enthusiastic about the abilities and trustworthiness of the two oncologists. They were one of the top teams of doctors specializing in pancreatic cancer in the country. Marcos explained to his mother what they were going to do and took her in a taxi to the Memorial Hospital. Marcos went in with Arizle, for he needed to translate everything for her. He also needed to translate her questions from Portuguese to English. Marcos was a great help to her and everyone else, translating for everyone.

Arizle's radiation lasted for ten minutes. They placed her on a large table under a radiation therapy machine in a room that was specially designed to prevent radiation leakage. The machine sent X-rays in predetermined directions and amounts. Dr. Parke had marked the area to be radiated and told her the skin would become dark brown. Also, Dr. Parke had warned her of other unpleasant side effects, including fatigue, nausea and vomiting. She was already so weak that she did not think she could afford to lose more weight. Dr. Parke told her that after two to four hours, the nausea would subside, allowing her to eat.

Before making the decision to start with ionizing radiation, they had placed her in a scanner machine and looked at her whole body, specially her stomach, liver, intestines, gallbladder, pancreas and lungs. She liked both doctors, but preferred Dr. Arenson, who was tender and affectionate with her.

After four hours, they all came out with Marcos to talk to Rameda and Ricardo. They wanted to give her ionizing radiation treatments, and during this phase, she would be an outpatient. Later on, they might have to look at radioactive mustard, cobalt or other types of radiation, in which case she would have to stay at the hospital for a week or so longer. They explained that the tumor was large, and its removal was contraindicated. They had been able to detect no spread of cancer into the liver, but they had seen some evidence of metastasis in the stomach. They wanted to try X-rays and gamma rays and observe whether the tumor would shrink and cells in the affected stomach area would die.

When the time came for these other methods, they would get her a private room, for she would have to remain in isolation because of the radiation emanating from her body after the applications. Rameda would have to put on a special coat to visit her and he would not be able to stay in the room with her for too long. The other relatives would not be able to see her at all. Dr. Parke and Dr. Arenson explained that the hospital had hotel accommodations for relatives and friends who wanted to stay near the patient. Even though they could not see her, they would keep them informed. They wanted to start the ionizing radiation treatment the next day.

Marcos told Rameda that if Arizle went to the hospital for other radiation treatment, he would stay with Rameda in the hospital's guest quarters as long as he was needed. He put his arms around Rameda in a gesture of solidarity. Ricardo watched them together and enjoyed seeing how Marcos seemed to like Rameda. They said goodbye to the nurses and took a taxi back to the hotel. They reminded the nurses that Arizle would be back the next day, at 9:00 a.m. The taxi only carried four people, so Marcos and Dr. Orlando took a different taxi. At the hotel, Arizle was sitting in a chair in the foyer, waiting for Marcos to help her go upstairs. As soon as she saw Marcos, she began to get up on her own. The meeting with the two doctors had given her some hope, and she seemed a bit stronger. That evening she wrote Leumas and her servants.

> My dearest people,
> I feel a tremendous homesickness for you all. The longing for you is so strong that I see you entering my room here often. I miss Brazil very much, but I am a fool, am I not? Tomorrow I will start my saga. I miss you all very much. Please look after Dr. Leumas with the same affection with which you have looked after me.
>
> Yours truly,
> Arizle

While she was busy writing, Rameda also wrote a letter to his friend Leumas. Rameda seemed to get a lot of strength from Leumas's serenity and spirituality. He missed his friend. With him, he could share his true thoughts and perceptions.

> Dr. Leumas,
> The bank did not want to open a temporary checking account. I am going

to need more money, for little Arizle may need another surgery. I will ask the doctors tomorrow. If I do, will you send the dollars through the National City Bank on my behalf?

Marcos is well and he is helping us a great deal. He is an excellent companion. He has had some tough moments in his life, and I hope he will be able to change his lifestyle as well as his way of thinking.

Alice, his girlfriend (who I consider his wife, for she has two children by him), will come to visit Arizle with the two children. I rented an apartment for her and the children on the same floor where we are located. I sent for them, because I think Arizle will love to meet her grandchildren.

The flight on the Boeing was extraordinary for one who is healthy, but for Arizle, it was pure torment. Marcos and Jaime, my nephew, were waiting for us at the airport. Jaime also has been helpful to us. Tomorrow at noon, we will see Dr. Parke, who was Eva Perón's doctor. Marcos and Dr. Orlando will go to the Mayo Clinic to look for Dr. Augusto Fernandes. I feel that if they decide to operate on Arizle, the risk will be enormous, but there will be the hope that she may live a few more years relatively well.

I embrace you. My best regards to our servants. From your friend,
Rameda

While Arizle and Rameda wrote letters, Ricardo wrote Leumas, for he, too, was experiencing anxiety and he felt he needed to talk with his best friend.

My dearest friend,

Your letter is enchanting and I thank you, dearest friend. Tomorrow I will mail six letters, which I have started but have not been able to finish. Mother becomes very emotional when she reads your letters. Often she cries, cries and cries, falling asleep saying, "Leumas, Leumas, Leumas, my father and friend, come to give me your affection." Last night she slept very little, as she was very nervous because she was going to start the treatment today.

We left here at noon, as we will do for nineteen consecutive days. I am happy she has your friendship. Marcos sends you a hug. Take care of your health, my dearest friend.

Hugs and my love,
Ricardo

Arizle wrote Leumas every day. She had a need to communicate with him and she wanted him to know every detail of her life in New York. Life was less difficult with Leumas's support and understanding, and his devoted and big heart. Like Leumas, Arizle believed that hope could never die.

Rameda also wrote Leumas every day. Sometimes in his despair, he would write twice a day. When Arizle started to lose more weight, he panicked, and that day Ricardo saw him writing three times. He needed his friend's support. Arizle seemed to be getting worse. He could not bear the thought of losing her forever.

Following the radiation treatment, she was as sick as a dog. She could not eat; she vomited every bit of liquid and solids she tried to ingest. She was getting weaker, and yet she was hungry. Her hair and her eyelashes were starting to fall out. Her lips and skin felt dry and rough.

"How should one behave? What should one say?" cried out Rameda, locked in the bathroom and unable to hold back the tears.

Ricardo knocked on the door and when Rameda opened it, he hugged his father for a long time, whispering softly, "I know... I know."

Ricardo also did not know what to say or do; he was suffering from the same illness—hopelessness! Ricardo went out to Central Park. Alone on a bench, he thought of his mother, her love for life and her love for everything that existed. A poem that Marcos had written years before came to his mind.

Despair

Only he who some day in despair saw
The purest of his ideals destroyed,
Only he who felt love,
Will know what is a blasphemy!
He who met pain sometimes
And in desperation and in suffering

Became speechless
Only he who ran from life
And ran away from everything else
And he who then returned to life
Purifying in his own pain
Only he may have in his sensitive soul
The secret to love life with immense ardor.

18

Rameda was quite worried about Arizle's suffering and losing her strength because she could not eat. He had asked Marcos to call Dr. Parke and ask him if there was anything that she could take intravenously to help her with nutrition. He wrote Leumas that Arizle, besides being terribly nauseated, was afraid to eat, and as a result, she was not hungry. He told him that she continued to experience pain from the seven minutes of radiation that she had everyday at the Memorial Hospital. One application was below her stomach and the other was on her back at the same level. He told Leumas that they were hopeful that after seven applications, she would get better and the pain would subside, allowing her to eat a little better. She would have to undergo about twenty applications to get well. Every year, he said, she would have to return to the hospital for the same treatment. Dr. Parke said that he was against another surgery, because based on what the Brazilian surgeon wrote on his report, not even in America could the tumor be removed. Rameda assured Marcos that the Brazilian doctor had made the right decision in not trying to remove it.

Rameda was impressed with the fact that Dr. Parke and his associates had a complete clinic with laboratory, pharmacy and all kinds of medical equipment that occupied several floors. He was considered to be the best in the world and had treated several important heads of state and other celebrities. Since Arizle did not have any cancer in her liver, her prognosis was hopeful. Dr. Parke felt that the treatment would shrink the tumor and the cancer would recede, enabling Arizle to live much longer.

Arizle was very ill, but she did not forget to take care of everyone around her. She asked Rameda to order two suits for Marcos. Leumas, she explained to him could buy two kinds of fabric and take them to Rameda's tailor. She wanted them shipped to Marcos at the hotel when they were ready. Marcos was looking pretty shabby, for most of what little money he had went to Alice and the children. He had not been to a dentist in a long time, and Arizle wanted him to make an appointment while he was in New York for which she would pay.

Rameda knew that Arizle wanted to meet her grandchildren, for whom she had brought gifts, and also meet Alice, for whom she had brought a family heirloom as a gift. Rameda sent the tickets for Alice and the children to fly to New York from Baton Rouge. They arrived in the afternoon and Marcos brought them to see Arizle. The little boy had no manners. He was obnoxiously impertinent and he hit his sister, who was a sweet and neglected little girl. All of the parents' attention seemed to be for the boy. The little girl was personable, kissed everyone, smiled all the time and never cried. Everyone fell in love with Mara. Alice paid a lot of attention to her son, but no attention to her daughter. Alice was not particularly attractive, and she reminded everyone of Arizle's sister-in-law, casual and lazy. Marcos was sure that the boy was his son, but he was not convinced that the little girl was his child. Mara was not loved as much by her parents, so she did not take attention for granted. She had to work hard to get affection and she concentrated on behaving well, as if she understood that to be the magic with which she could win people's love and respect. Mara had developed a delightful personality and she charmed everyone who met her.

Alice put the children to bed around 11:00 p.m. and went out every night, leaving the children under the supervision of Dr. Orlando. She never came back before 3:00 or 4:00 in the morning. It was on one of those late nights out that she missed her plane going back to Baton Rouge. Arizle rarely saw her after she arrived, and the children were left unwashed and hungry. Marcos bathed them, changed their clothes and gave them their meals. On the day the children departed, Arizle asked Rameda to write to Leumas on her behalf. She dictated the letter while Rameda wrote her words.

> Dearest Leumas,
> Your grandchildren are returning today to Baton Rouge. Your grandson is handsome, but is a brat. Mara is enchanting, sweet, and tender. She gave affection to everyone and she walks like a little duck due to her chubby body. She is crazy about Rameda. You would enjoy her

tremendously. Alice will not hook Marcos.
She is not a good housekeeper.

Marcos has served us very much
and learned a lot in these last days. I
miss your goodness, your patience with us
and your faith.

How is your mother doing? Give her
a hug from me and thank your brothers
for the honey they sent me. Tell the girls
at the orphanage to pray for me. With
their innocence, God will hear them for
certain.

A big hug and a kiss from a war
refugee who loves you very much,

Arizle

Arizle spent her days lying in bed except for
those few moments when she could find the strength
to get up and sit in the sunlight for a few minutes or
so. Rameda was concerned that Arizle would not have
the strength to go to the hospital for the radiation
treatment. He wrote Leumas, asking him not to reply
to any medical news about Arizle in letters to him, for
he did not want to alarm her. Arizle lost eight pounds
after she arrived in New York. Rameda was extremely
concerned with her lack of food intake. He had asked
Marcos to see the doctor with a list of questions for the
doctor to answer. Rameda was frustrated, for if he
called the doctor, he was with a patient and could not
talk to him, and he could not reach anyone else to
whom he could ask about options for feeding his
Arizle. Marcos waited for four hours at the doctor's office and still did not bring back any answers to
Rameda's anguished questions.

The Brazilian Consul in New York was a kind woman who took a special interest in Arizle's illness. Claudia, Arizle's aunt, had given Rameda the consul's private number in case they needed her assistance. After talking to Arizle and Rameda a few times, she even sent the doctor from the consulate to visit Arizle. He was an American, but had lived in the northern part of Brazil where he learned Portuguese well. Rameda was relieved that he could communicate with this doctor directly without needing anyone to translate for him. The doctor was a good person who took an interest in Arizle and did not leave that evening without first prescribing vitamin B-12 for her. Arizle took the vitamins religiously and felt a little stronger.

While Alice was in New York, Marcos had to watch the children all the time and he neglected Arizle. Now that Alice was gone, Rameda asked him if he would go to the Mayo Clinic to talk to a Brazilian specialist about Arizle's condition. Rameda was still trying to obtain answers for his questions. He wanted to see his Arizle get well. On the day Arizle received her sixth application, she left the hospital radiation room and embraced him, crying and laughing at the same time. Dr. Parke had told her that her condition had improved and that the tumor had shrunk a little. Dr. Parke also told her that the nurses and doctors assigned to her case had told him that she was a very calm patient, very accommodating and eager to follow instructions.

"Poor Arizle," Rameda thought. She was making a tremendous effort to help the treatment. She suffered seeing other human beings with the same illness but it could not be avoided. She could see them passing by listlessly in the corridor, sad eyes cast downward, their faces drained of light and hope.

Arizle had kept away from people with this disease all her life, because she knew she was very sensitive. Every time she had come across a person with cancer, she had left the person and later was not able to fall asleep for a long time, thinking about the person's predicament. Seeing Arizle now in the same situation caused Rameda to feel as if his hands were tied and he could not do anything of importance to spare Arizle from the disease. Rameda prayed for Arizle to live many more years. Life without her would be intolerable for him.

Arizle received a blood transfusion on August 4. After the transfusion, she could hardly walk to the car and at night in the hotel, she developed a high fever. Rameda had no idea that the blood transfusion would have this side effect, and he was afraid that she might be experiencing anaphylactic shock, a life-threatening allergic reaction. He was panic-stricken, because Dr. Orlando was out for the night. It had been a waste of money to pay Dr. Orlando to accompany her, he thought. He was being irrational, though, for he knew Dr. Orlando had been brought along to appease Arizle's worries. He knew that having her doctor by her side would relieve some of her stress.

It was around 3:00 a.m. when the fever finally subsided and she was able to eat a little soup. Rameda awakened Ricardo, and he immediately got up to fix his mother some food. In the morning, she was much better. That morning, Marcos and Dr. Orlando went to meet with the Brazilian oncologist to whom Rameda wanted to talk about Arizle's situation. They came back, reassuring Rameda that Dr. Parke would have been his choice to treat Arizle. The Brazilian doctor felt that Arizle should improve with the radiation treatments. He had also assured Marcos that

Arizle was taking the maximum radiation that it was advisable to give to a patient in her condition. More radiation than that could destroy the healthy cells as well.

Rameda found out about another Brazilian doctor in New York. He asked Marcos to talk to the doctor, who was accompanying his father at the Memorial Hospital and was staying at a hotel on the Avenue of the Americas. The young doctor was apprehensive about his own father who had undergone an operation, having an anastomotic procedure performed, connecting his stomach and his gallbladder to his intestine. The surgery had been performed at the Mayo Clinic and Rameda wanted to know if that procedure had helped his father. Rameda wanted to talk to every doctor he could find, and he wanted to learn anything he could from them.

Some days Arizle felt better and on others, she felt worse. One morning when she woke up, she felt like she was really improving and feeling better. The next day was to be her eighth radiation treatment. The day was getting closer and closer when she could return to her beloved country.

Three more days went by, and now Arizle was weak again. She could no longer walk from the taxi to the hospital without assistance from two people. Once in the entrance, she was placed in a wheelchair and rolled to the room where the radiotherapy was applied. On the day she received her twelfth treatment, Rameda told her that after the nineteenth application, she would have to stay in the hospital two days for a procedure in which the doctors would intravenously inject radionuclide in minute doses. She had to stay by herself because of the radiation effect on others.

Rameda was extremely concerned about Arizle staying alone in the hospital.

On August 13, Rameda wrote Leumas, telling him about Arizle having to be alone in the hospital. Also, he mentioned that only five radiation applications remained and that after she finished the treatment, she should feel better. He told Leumas that he was scared. He wanted to be with her all the time, but he recognized that she would receive much better medical assistance at the hospital, and they could feed her intravenously.

On August 18, Arizle finished her applications. Dr. Parke asked her to be at the hospital Sunday evening, for he wanted to start a new treatment on Monday. Also, he said that he was going to give her radioactive mustard together with the intravenous radionuclide. Arizle was concerned about being alone at night, but Rameda hired a nurse to stay with her. Rameda and Ricardo moved into the hospital with Arizle. They took two rooms with connecting doors on the third floor. This hospital was called Doctors' Hospital and had floors that functioned as a hotel. Arizle was on the fourth floor and they were on the floor below. Marcos stayed at the Hotel Navarro in his apartment, since Rameda had paid for the apartment until August 30.

Arizle's condition had deteriorated greatly with the treatment. She looked pale despite the blood transfusions and the intravenous glucose solutions they were giving her, but she was not vomiting as often. After the two days of radioactive treatment, the doctors wanted her to walk to the park across the street from the hospital, but she could not stand, much less walk. Rameda again wrote several questions for Marcos to translate and give to the doctors to answer. The doctors as usual, were very busy and responded with monosyllables. Rameda was not happy that the doctors did not try to communicate with him and let him know what they were observing in Arizle. The nurses were very kind, and the interns checked the medication and dosage any time they were going to administer a pill or an injection to Arizle. Rameda knew that they were very responsible and meticulous in relation to her medication. Those days at the hospital were quite traumatic. Rameda met parents with children who had deadly brain cancer and old people with cancer of the liver. He had learned with Arizle to feel for other people, and he had never before realized how life was precious, and how hundreds of people were fighting just to live an extra day. This experience in the hospital had given him a new perspective on life. He spent his days talking to different people with the help of Ricardo, who spoke French and English well. This new dimension to his life made him realize how much Arizle had taught him during the twenty years that they had been together.

Arizle stayed at the hospital for four more days after her treatment finished. After she was released from the hospital, they went back to the Hotel Navarro for a few days. She was eating better now that she had finished her treatments, but she was still in pain and extremely weak. Rameda was pretty exhausted himself. He had been in a room with her all the time, only leaving for brief purchases at the grocery store. Ricardo had cooked in the middle of the night for his mother with patience and devotion. His hands were rough and full of cuts from peeling vegetables and dried out from washing her clothes and doing the dishes. Ricardo did not feel like less of a man for doing these chores because he was helping the parents he adored.

Arizle, however, poor Arizle, Rameda sighed, was the one that deserved pity. No other human being would have endured what she went through for that month and been so humble, accommodating with doctors, and affectionate and kind with the nurses. Arizle thanked the doctors for everything they did for her and she made good-hearted excuses for what they had not done. She asked Ricardo to buy presents for the nurses and treated them as if they were the patients. Arizle had prayed numerous times for her mother's spirit to help her. She thought of her mother's sweetness and asked God constantly for Him to give her strength to be the same way. God had heard her prayers. All the nurses on her floor went to hug her goodbye. Leaving the hospital was an emotional moment for Arizle. She could not afford to feel emotional, but she cried while telling them that God would repay them for their patience and good care of the patients in pain.

During these last days after her release from the hospital, Marcos carried her to Central Park, where she lay on the grass on top of a blanket for a couple of hours in the shade. Rameda and Ricardo went for a walk in the park, leaving Arizle and Marcos alone. Marcos's fingers trembled as he stroked her hair.

Despite her condition, she was still trying tactfully to convince him to go back to Brazil, where he could try to enter the diplomatic service. That, she thought, was an ideal goal for him to consider seriously. He spoke four languages, and was very intelligent, well-read and cultured. She wrote Leumas and asked him to please not mention religion to Marcos any more and not treat him as if he were a child.

Arizle suggested to Leumas that he should move out of his house and rent or buy an apartment near public transportation. Leumas's home was on a hill, and Leumas had to go up a steep incline to get to his door. She told Leumas that while she was talking to Marcos about becoming a diplomat, Marcos had wanted to know if his father had moved into a nice house. Arizle told him that his father had a lovely house with a well-furnished room waiting for him. Arizle, knowing that what she had told Marcos was not completely true, wrote to Leumas that she had some money in the bank of her own and that she was going to give it to him so that he could move into a nicer home before Marcos returned. Poor Arizle, she believed that Marcos was finally going home!

Leumas had been sending money to Alice and the children every month. Marcos did not support his family—Leumas did. Arizle did not think much of Alice's methods of raising her children. They did not have a set time to eat or to sleep. Alice was not meticulous with their cleanliness, either. When Alice first arrived to meet her, Arizle had given her a ring with a deep blue aquamarine set in platinum. The ring had three small diamonds on each side and was dazzling. Arizle had broken up her aquamarine matching set when she gave Alice the gift. After Arizle got to know Alice better, she realized that the woman was going to sell the ring at the first opportunity. Alice did not have any idea of the heirloom value of the gift she had received from Arizle. Alice was a simpleminded woman, who had led a life of parties and fun with very little or no responsibility. Soon, Arizle realized why Marcos had not married her. Marcos had commented to Ricardo one afternoon while they waited for Arizle at the hospital that had Alice been like his mother, he would have married her. Ricardo did not ask him to explain what he meant. Ricardo knew what he meant.

It was only a few weeks before that, Arizle thought Marcos had made the decision to return to Brazil, but the day they talked about his future in the park, he seemed to be once again strongly bound by the dogma of the secret society in which he believed. She sensed that she had lost him again.

Saying goodbye to her son was another moment of great emotion. Ricardo cried, observing his mother hug Marcos. She pleaded with Marcos not to forget her. She asked him to accept and love his father, for he was one of the best men she had ever met. She also asked him to forgive her for her sins. Finally, she reminded him that she had always loved him deeply and that she would never stop loving him, not even after her death and that he should do the same for his children. She also knew that she would never see him again. Marcos remained silent.

Marcos went back to Baton Rouge after he said goodbye to his mother at the airport. He would never see her again. The rest of the family left New York on a Boeing jet. Arizle had missed her country. In her moments of depression, she had written to Leumas that she did not want to die in New York. She wanted to go back to Rio de Janeiro and be with her loved ones. She asked Leumas not to tell anyone when she was returning, for she did not want anyone to see her in the way she looked. She was just bones, covered by a thin layer of skin.

Rameda paid extra for a special bed on the plane that at least allowed Arizle to lie down, resting for those hours. Dr. Arenson prescribed some pills, which helped her relax during the flight. Dr. Orlando had left two days before, so during this trip Rameda and Ricardo were on duty.

On the plane she was able to rest for a while. Rameda stayed near her during the whole trip. He never ate dinner, for he did not want her to see him eating when it was such an ordeal for her to eat anything. Ricardo did not have any problems with the trip. He slept off and on, waking up from time to time to check on his mother. Ricardo would look at his mother and go back to dozing restlessly.

They finally arrived at Rio's international airport in the early morning. Arizle left the aircraft on a wheelchair. When she was wheeled onto Brazilian ground, she started to cry. She wanted to fall to the ground and kiss the soil that she loved so much, but she did not have the strength, and Rameda did not want her to kiss the dirty ground anyway. Customs expedited their inspection of the luggage and stamped their passports quickly. Seeing and hugging Leumas was wonderful. She even hugged Raul who had tears in his eyes when he saw she was so weak, so fragile and pale.

Leumas told her that she now had to look ahead and get better. She promised him that she would do her best. They helped her into the car and Raul drove them carefully home. They were all happy to be home at last. In the thrill of seeing Leumas, she had forgotten about her pain. She felt that she had been given a miracle, for there had been days on which she thought she would never again see Leumas, her country and her home.

When she was carried inside the house, all of her servants were there to greet her. The laundress and the dressmaker were there, as well as the chambermaid, the butler and her chef. The gardener and the outdoors cleaning man were watching her with a smile. They had purchased a large bouquet of red roses for her. João had placed them in a vase in her bedroom. She was touched by their warm reception and happy to be home. She kissed the roses as she went by in the direction of her bed. Rameda and Ricardo were supporting her with João's help. She was home, and even though the pain was still strong, she felt calmer and more able to handle it.

While in New York, she had not taken any homeopathic pills. She asked Rameda to call Dr. Hermogenes and ask him to prescribe some medication for her pain. She explained to Rameda that she felt she needed something to assist with the healing of her tissues that had been burned by the radiation treatments. Dr. Hermogenes prescribed homeopathic tablets, and she took them religiously, but her pain persisted.

Arizle had been back for nearly three weeks when Rameda decided to call Dr. Augusto Fernandes, the most famous surgeon in Brazil for him to examine her. They had talked to him while they were in New York City, while he was at the Parke Medical Group, enjoying some additional medical training. They certainly did not want to consult the doctor who had operated on her before. Dr. Fernandes informed them that had Dr. Bernardo done the anastomosis then, it would not have been necessary to go through another surgery at this point in her illness. Dr. Fernandes asked Rameda to bring her to his office where he had the equipment to examine her more thoroughly. He confirmed after four days of tests that the cancer was spreading again. He told Rameda that she needed another blood transfusion. He found her very weak and asked her to consider having an anastomosis connecting her esophagus directly to her intestine. The surgery would allow her to bypass the blockage and eat more easily. Rameda did not know what to think. He had thought she was going to get better, but all that treatment had been palliative, and she knew it now. They left the doctor's office shattered and in silence. Rameda held hands with her, and he tried very hard not to show her his sorrow.

Dr. Fernandes set up the date for her operation. She went to the hospital in an ambulance two days before her surgery. At the hospital they gave her injections of B-12, multiple vitamins and glucose for forty-eight hours. Her blood pressure was normal and Doctor Cardoso, Fernandes's assistant, went to see her in her room. When he arrived, he saw her dancing with Rameda. She had asked Ricardo to sing "Dancing Cheek to Cheek," and supported firmly by Rameda, she leaned against him and danced dreamily, just as they had danced toward the end of the Carnaval ball where they had first met. Dr. Fernandes stopped at her door and pretended he was not yet ready to go into the room. Ricardo had his back to the door and did not see him. Ricardo never forgot those few seconds between his mother and his father. He wished he had a camera to take a picture of the two of them together.

The surgery went without problems despite her thinness. She looked like a soft wind might blow her way if she were not held down. She went back to her room after six hours in intensive care. Ricardo was waiting with Claudia, Rameda and Leumas. They did not know what to say to each other while they waited for her to return. As soon as they saw her on a cart being rolled toward the door of her room, they began to speak normally as if they had no doubt she was going to be able to eat and get stronger.

The next twenty-four hours were difficult and they had a big scare. She developed a high fever and the doctors could not bring it down. Rameda picked her up with Leumas and took her into the bathtub. He drew a tepid bath and immersed her in the water, splashing it on her body, trying to bring her fever down, a treatment that hospital doctors would not have considered because of its homeopathic, home remedy nature. Ricardo went out and bought a small bottle of rubbing alcohol, and they put it on the water in the tub. With this bath, her temperature went down immediately. They repeated this three times that night without the nurses knowing. The next morning, her temperature was normal. She had a good, soft breakfast and felt much stronger.

The private apartment in that hospital was spacious, with two bedrooms and a full bath. The hospital was an expensive private one, and was located in Gavea, a barrio in Rio surrounded by tropical forests and lovely mountains. Arizle stayed there for a week.

After Arizle recuperated a bit and felt stronger, she planned to write to Dr. Arenson at the Parke Medical Clinic. She had sent his wife a gorgeous amethyst ring, once again breaking up a complete jewelry set. He had sent her a thank you letter asking her to write him.

My good friend Dr. Arenson:
I am answering your letter inquiring about me. I decided not to go to São Paulo for my surgery. I decided to stay in Rio de Janeiro and have the procedure done in my city, because Dr. Fernandes travels every year outside Brazil to learn about and keep up with innovations in his field.

He is the best surgeon we have in Brazil, and he reminds me of you, for like you, he is kind and has an enchanting personality.

It has been several days since I had the surgery, but I still have difficulty eating. I feel my digestion is slow despite the fact that I try to get a little exercise. Every afternoon I experience a burning in my stomach and the back pain, as well. I think there is no solution for my problem. The Brazilian doctors do not tell their patients the truth. I thought when I left New York and you told me that you would see me next June, that I had the possibility to live at least a year more. I felt so happy! My tumor I suppose is growing. There is not anything else to try for my cancer. I have always known that money has no value without good health.

It is very sad to die after your children have grown up and you have more of an opportunity to rest your heart and enjoy life a little more. I am forty-four and I am going to die! I cannot even eat the foods I enjoyed in my youth. My good Dr. Arenson, angel of the healing rays and thunder, please write me. I will reimburse you for all the expenses you have incurred on my behalf. I enjoy it when you call me or send me telegrams. Please do not forget to write me. Send us letters please.

Do not thank me for the ring I sent your wife. I am the one who needs to thank you for all your kindness and care toward me.   I will be sending her a matching amethyst brooch.

Give my best regard to Dr. Parke. Please accept my eternal gratitude to all the Americans, nurses, patients at the Memorial Hospital, the taxi drivers and every soul who treated me with kindness and affection. I remember them all. God bless America! May God preserve you in perfect health.

Sincerely,

Arizle Pachêco

P.S. Could you prescribe a medication for the pain at the end, a medication that is not morphine?

19

One morning Arizle called Rameda and told him that she did not want to die in the house she was leaving to Ricardo. She did not want him to keep his mother's dying moments in any room of the house. She wanted him to love the house and only have pleasant and joyful memories of it. Some day, she added, he would live in it with his wife and children.

Rameda understood her request and immediately called around to see if there were any homes for rent in the Alto da Boa Vista, the neighborhood where he had purchased the land for her to build her fourth home. A broker he knew found a beautiful stone castle in the mountains that overlooked the seashore of Barra da Tijuca. He could rent it by the month, because the family patriarch had died, and the children were litigating to decide who would get what. While they resolved their differences of opinion, they agreed to rent the house to Rameda since they knew his family.

Rameda moved Arizle into the house in three days. The citadel was immense. It had eight bedrooms, a pool room, living room, dining room, a huge enclosed terrace, an enormous kitchen, a pantry and large servant quarters; however, they only planned to use the first floor. Chico and Antonio went with her. Ricardo stayed in the Tijuca home with Leumas. Rameda took almost nothing from the Tijuca home with them. The castle was furnished and they only needed linens and their personal clothing. Rameda made Arizle's bedroom from the two rooms off the large living room, which were probably originally a library or a den. He did not want her isolated on the second floor. He rented a hospital bed for her and a small cot for him to sleep on.

After Chico and João had moved into their bedrooms, the servants went out with Raul and bought everything they needed for the kitchen. Her meals were taken to her room on a tray and everyone else's meals were served at a twenty-foot Jacaranda table. Chico was very worried because Arizle was not eating. Rameda explained to him that she was not hungry. However, like all chefs, Chico wanted her to eat what he was cooking for her, and he claimed he was using extra affection in performing his work.

Their only amusement was watching old movies. Rameda rented all kinds of old movies for her to watch, projected by a 16 mm movie projector, with sound, that he had bought in Switzerland for her. Ricardo, though younger, enjoyed those movies as much as Arizle. Ricardo spent all day long with them. He had taken a leave of absence from college to be with his mother. The movies kept her mind off her cancer.

She was in pain all the time and she could not find a comfortable position. She saw all the movies with Rudolph Valentino and the other old timers that she liked. She cried with the dramas and laughed with the comedies. The days were going by fast. She tried walking through the garden supported by Rameda, Leumas, Ricardo and Raul. They all wanted her to enjoy the sun and the magnificent view they had. Arizle loved the view, and liked seeing the flowers, but had no energy; her muscles were failing her. She had no strength to stand on her own. Whenever she went into the garden, she would sit on a chair or lie down on the grass.

Rameda had a simple one-room, one-bath and small kitchen hut built for her on the last piece of land he had bought for her. The workers from the meat packing plant built a hut for her in two weeks. They worked night and day to finish the cabin so that she could move into it. She told Rameda and Leumas that she did not want to be wealthy any longer. She wanted Leumas to use his power of attorney and give away all her assets. From that moment on, she wanted to observe vows of poverty. They did not question her request; they followed her wishes, for they understood the discovery she had made about the importance of living and the irony of being able to buy everything but life itself.

They had discovered a homeopathic medication that had relieved her pain. This medication had been a tremendous help to Arizle. She wanted to be alert, and morphine made her sleepy. Dr. Hermogenes was a hero for finding her the drops that had the same analgesic effect of morphine without its side effects. She was taking the drops every four hours. Without pain, she could eat better and walk closely enough to her flowers to enjoy them.

The cottage was ready, and Rameda returned the rented home to the broker, and moved Arizle into her one-bedroom bungalow. She required someone with her all the time now. Rameda was exhausted, and Ricardo was fatigued as well, and they asked her if they could get her a nighttime nurse. Rameda kissed her hand and told her that he wanted to be alert to help her, but he was finding himself so groggy that he was concerned that he would drop her. Arizle agreed with Rameda and Beatriz was hired. He and Leumas interviewed over twenty women. They soon tired of talking to women whom they thought did not have enough human warmth. Beatriz, however, was different. She was very caring and unassuming, and her references were exceptionally good. Ricardo continued to cook for Arizle just as he had done in New York. The meals for everyone else were catered and delivered to the cabin. Chico and João remained in the house that now belonged to Ricardo. Leumas gave Marcos the house in Petrópolis as a gift from her. She had nothing.

November came soon and Arizle was weakening daily. It seemed like there was nothing more for her to lose, but she still lost weight and looked gaunt and ghostly. Her beautiful head of hair had turned completely gray. Her eyes, though enormous in her thin face, had lost their sparkle and they looked glassy. She spent most of her time looking through the picture window by her bed. Rameda had planted geraniums, zinnias, daisies and petunias for her. The flowers were lush and beautiful. Arizle talked to them every day while Rameda watered them early in the morning. Through her window, the sun gave her a great deal of joy in her last weeks. She watched ladybugs inside the flowers, she followed bees removing the nectar from the center of the flowers, and she watched the clouds move and form giant figures before dissipating their various shapes into thin streamers of mist.

One day in mid-November, she asked for paper and a pen and to be propped up, so she could write a letter. Rameda asked her if she was going to write Dr. Arenson. She smiled at him and answered "no" softly. She wrote:

> My dear young man,
> This letter is from a woman who knows she is going to die. I am forty-four years old, have two exceptional sons and a companion who has no equal in the whole world. We were a happy family, wealthy, living in luxury and comfort. Ibrahim, I have been running to doctors, taking X-rays, blood tests, passing stomach tubes and not a single doctor was interested to seriously research my case in depth.
> I would say to them, "My digestion is difficult, I have constipation, my stools are only the diameter of a pencil—these symptoms are not normal."
> The doctors and professors then answered me, "Your gallbladder is lazy; it does not even respond after fifteen to twenty minutes of trying to siphon bile out of it through a tube."
> I would then ask them, "Then the problem is a lack of digestive enzymes, right?" They would not respond to me and would not do anything. They prescribed

tranquilizers for me to deal with my forty-four years and premature menopause.

This medical aloofness and disregard pushed me to see Professor Luiz Feijó. I found that he was interested in researching my case, and he arrived at the conclusion that my problem was in my pancreas. I am lying in my bed, feeling life running way from me, and I plead for someone who is a good human being. There are good doctors and doctors who are good people, but they do not have time to observe and pay attention. I call this human warmth! They need to take more interest in their patients. Oh, God, two years ago I could have been saved!

I read about the Campaign for Poor Mothers. They need education and guidance so those young women do not conceive before they are ready. We need a campaign to develop more love and responsibility in doctors who are professors, surgeons and clinicians. Some surgeons are so pompous and so proud that it is impossible for the patient to talk to them. Others are big gamblers or womanizers, for they make easy money. The more clients they have in one day, the more money they make. Others go searching for awards and public commendations that add value to their names and pounds to their pompous egos.

Take pity, my young man. Take pity on those who so desperately need it. Encourage others to work toward the Campaign of Pity. I know that a few doctors are sincere and committed to their profession, but I have not found them until the final phase of my life.

Earlier in my life, one professor had even told me bluntly, "Do not search for more doctors, for what you have is simple to cure; it is an inflammation of the duodenum." He told me to drink ten glasses of milk per day. That much milk only made me feel more ill. I called him to let him know that I felt worse.

He replied, "Drink more milk."

"Professor," I argued, "I am urinating a brown that looks like Coca-Cola!"

He answered, "This is the result of a lack of liquids. Drink more milk."

Ibrahim, if you publish this letter, he will read it, and he and others like him will learn about their indifference, ignorance and incompetence. They will also learn about their lack of compassion for their fellowman. It will not cost you anything, only the newspaper, *O Globo*—a newspaper that at least owes me that after my death. I have been a loyal customer for twenty years, and have been reading it every morning recently, in search of articles about the Mayo Clinic and their discoveries.

Women, mistresses, mothers, sisters, brides, think! Tomorrow it may be you, and like me you will leave your children, your beloved companion and beloved home. Work, therefore, to change this situation among the older generation and among the young medical students. Raise in them the consciousness that those who search for a doctor are not always hypo-chondriacs. They belong to the legion of those who suffer, and they need to know from what illness they are suffering.

Help the doctors and the patients to find the cause for their illness. I say to God that they did not help me. The con-sciences of every one of them will be their judges. Remind the medical schools to teach human psychology. Tell them not visit a client who cannot eat, and speak about yesterday's dinner engagement. Tell them not to talk about the gorgeous women to the husband of a woman who is dying and looks it. Doctors need to learn bedside manners.

I am not jealous of the beautiful women; I am only envious of the next woman who will kiss my husband's lips when I am gone. We have been suffering tremendously, my husband and I, but we found each other in the end.

I finish this letter wishing you and your wife, Glorinha, blessings of good health. What I most liked especially in your columns was what you did not write; you know what I mean.

Farewell, my captain, we shall meet again some distant day, very distant. Do not forget to help the doctors. Help them gain consciousness of the value of others.

The Human Campaign is a manifestation of God!

Yours truly,
Arizle Pachêco

Ibrahim was a bright reporter whose chronicles and articles were always read by Arizle. He was from Minas Gerais, her state, and he had class. She admired him because he never wrote anything inappropriate. She wrote him several times during her life, praising his discretion and letting him know that he was a young man of intelligence and class.

To her family and friends she wrote:

My friends,
In the light of eternity, I say goodbye to you with nostalgia and love. May my short life serve as an example to you so that you may ponder and become more enlightened. May you overcome small obstacles in your life without hurting each other, always smiling and intensely enjoying each moment. May you also always enjoy your lives with good health, the health that God gives us.

I lived intensely these last days after my last surgery. I was a bird that flew swiftly through space, I saw the mango tree in bloom with small and large mangoes, and I heard the airplane going by and the noise from the trolleys and the people hurrying up to catch it in the morning. My big window to the sun, the one I look through by my bed, shows me life. Life! To be alive! I now have everything. This oneness has brought me a tremendous awareness of what I wanted to be, what I wanted to become. What a sweet sensation I experienced in gaining this awareness!

I never opened my heart totally to you. Your small complaints I heard with smiling eyes. How lucky and happy you are compared to me! I did not share my suffering with you. I was envied. I never thought you needed to suffer with me. My family, my friends... I only shared laughter with you. Friends are the ones with whom we laugh all the time. Like this I wanted you to be and always remain in my memory—smiling people. I learned a lot from my aunt who remains among you. I learned about fashion, about what is refined and chic, about how to entertain people graciously. I read a lot, learning from all those books and magazines in which you sometimes saw me hiding. I always shared with you all that I had learned from them.

Forgive me for the tea parties and the fashion parades to which you were invited. I was not being ostentatious; I was trying to give you an orientation in harmony and color coordination, transmitting the classic way of dressing that is always new and that never goes out of style or looks outdated.

Forgive me if I seemed vain. I needed you and your appreciation, for appreciation failed to reach my heart several times when I searched for it. Your appreciation helped me greatly.

To you Rosina, whom I admired for your zeal, taste and order, I leave these small tokens of my esteem. They will be given to you. To you Duarte, from whom I received a great deal, I leave a hug.

To you, João, for your respectful admiration, I leave you my humble plea that you take care of Rameda in the same manner that you take care of me. I leave you 100,000 American dollars for you to buy a home for your old age.

For you, Chico, my devoted chef, I leave you a hug and 100,000 American dollars for you to purchase a home for your old age. Be good friends and continue to enjoy working for Rameda and Ricardo. If Rameda remarries, take good care of his new wife. Enjoy your lives and be healthy. Promise me that you will?

God keep you all in serenity and keep the family united and safe.

To my father-in-law, a member of our family who hurt Rameda and me deeply, I leave our forgiveness and affectionate kisses. To you Geny, my elementary school colleague, my love and gratitude. To my brother-in-law, Laura's husband, a self-made man of value, my deepest esteem. God bless you for the tears I witnessed in your eyes when I sought you out for your guidance. It has been over fifteen years, but I have not forgotten.

To my brother, I leave a ring for his daughter, my Goddaughter.

To Laura and my sister-in-law, I wish you both health, joy and love.

To Leumas, my best and greatest friend and the only father I ever had, my eternal love and gratitude. Thank you for the pure friendship that you gave me, for the support you showed me in all the moments of my life, for the sacrifice you made on behalf of my happiness, abandoning your own happiness so that I could have mine. Blessed be you, Leumas, by all men! There is no other like you.

To Rameda, my companion of twenty-one years, I get on my knees to thank you for the privilege of having known and loved you. You have been a hard-working man, a friend to your friends, to your employees, and to your relatives. No one knows you as I do. How great you are in your silence! How kind you are to those who treat you with injustice. How many people hurt you and how many hurt me. Our doors have been opened to all. We never hid, pretended or stole from anyone. We did not take from anyone; we gave to everyone. We have never turned against anyone. We were two strong people because your strength was my strength. You are the jewel of your family and they did not know it! Not one of them is worth one of your fingers. I pray to God that God will forgive them. What can I say if everything I had and enjoyed was because you gave it to me? I owe you everything I have and who I am. Your laughter caused my laughter. From you I received love, respect, kindness and goodness. Blessed be you who sow good deeds. You are respected among men!

To you Ricardo, my little treasure, I respect your kindness and loving nature. God protects you. Forgive me for your exhaustion, for the work I created for you when you brought to me the food that you lovingly prepared with your hands. I will take with me the proximity of your heart near mine and the tough of your kind hands holding me securely.

In this house there is a doctor and a priest. They know me and know my life well. They know that others judged me as imprudent, but in their judgement I was not. I was a human being searching for peace. I was a human being on a quest to find love and discover acceptance. I bounced back and forth between the cruelty of lust and the fragility of love. I discovered that love is indeed fragile, but true love is not.

Respect the dead and the silent ones in pain. No one is worse than we are. When our fellowmen respect us, they respect themselves.

Farewell! Peace on earth and among my friends. I loved you deeply. Forgive me for my sins and weaknesses.

Yours,
Arizle

To Marcos, she left a separate note. It was covered with the stains of her tears.

My son,
I suppose you knew that this would happen sooner rather than later, but my death happened much faster than even you and I anticipated. I had always wanted to see you, your children and Alice and God allowed me to realize that dream.

Forgive me if I was not the mother you expected or needed to have. I suffered a great deal; however, Father Valdir says that the responsibility of my actions also lies on other people's shoulders. I forgive all. I take nothing except nostalgia and a longing for all.

I long for your face and your laughter. How I missed you, being far way from me all these years! Love me.

Your mother, who never forgot you,
Arizle

On November 23, Dr. Arenson wrote to Arizle:

My dear Mrs. Pachêco:
I was extremely pleased, but at the same time saddened by your last letter. I was pleased to hear from you, but I was saddened to hear that it was necessary for you to undergo another operative procedure.

I received a letter from your Brazilian doctor, and thanked him for the detailed letter that he had sent me. I wrote immediately to him, stating that I was disappointed that you had developed an obstruction necessitating another operation. I also expressed my opinion that this was not of a too serious consequence and that it was my hope and expectation that the results of the treatment which we had given you here in New York would finally overcome the disease in your abdomen.

I also volunteered that should you have any additional difficulties, I would be willing to come down to Rio de Janeiro and give you some isotope treatments. I think so very much of you and have every hope that you may be completely well one day.

I was somewhat saddened by your fatalistic philosophy, as it was so unlike you to develop this philosophy—namely, one of pessimism. You impressed me so favorably as being an optimistic person, willing to fight and to look forward to the very best that can happen. You tolerated the treatment that we had given you very well, and I was pleased with the immediate response here. In a situation such as you have, there are bound to be ups and downs and one must not be too happy and overjoyed when things are going well, and by the same token one should not be too pessimistic and downhearted when they don't go so very well.

I have great confidence in the ancient proverb to the effect that there is al-

ways hope as long as there is life. We see
so many unusual cases that are markedly
benefited and even cured, that it keeps me
always hopeful. In fact, I had a little girl
in my office about a year ago— she was
twenty-three years old and her entire abdomen was filled with cancer. I gave her
treatment and five months later she developed a large abdominal mass that had me
worried and I was fearful that my treatments had not been successful. Imagine
my pleasant surprise to discover that she
was pregnant. Three weeks ago, she delivered a perfectly normal baby and the
baby was delivered by Cesarean section
and during the operation she was found to
be completely free of any disease. It is
such instances that make us realize that
there is no such thing as a too optimistic
outlook, and I hope your attitude will
change as you condition improves.

Permit me to take this opportunity
to again express my heartfelt appreciation
for your kindness and generosity in sending me a gift that is an heirloom of your
family. It is the latter which has such
tremendous significance that I can't express with words my heartfelt gratitude
and appreciation.

I look forward to you improving, and
I hope you continue to improve steadily
without any further exacerbation of
symptoms and I hope it will not be necessary for me to come to give you any treat-

ments in Brazil, but rather that I shall see
you here next June.

Trusting you are well these days, I
remain most respectfully yours,

Irving M. Arenson, M.D.

On December 27, Rameda wrote Dr. Arenson a thank you letter on her behalf.

My dear Dr. Arenson:

I am very sorry to inform you that
our beloved Arizle passed away last November 23, the very day after you wrote
her your gentle letter.

We did all that we could in Rio to
continue her fight against this treacherous
disease that attacks without mercy, as you
well know in your specialized career. We
were also shocked by the sad event for we,
like you, expected her to recuperate after
the treatments she had received from you.

She always kept a very loving recollection of you, your kindness and affection. She had been confident in her recovering most of the time, until the last day,
but sometimes she felt that something was
wrong with her and showed some doubt
and pessimism would take hold of her
temporarily. In God we trust... we must,
after all, we must find somehow a way to
accept His sentence without blame and
reproach.

Please permit me to use the same
words of your letter, for my knowledge of
English is poor and restricted. Please ac-

cept my heartfelt appreciation for your kindness and generosity in sending to my wife such a nice letter. Your assistance and the caring manner with which you treated her will never be forgotten. Thank you for giving us hope during our sojourn to New York and to the Parke Medical Group.

I take this opportunity to wish you a very good New Year.

I remain, most gratefully yours,
Rameda Pachêco

Arizle's window to the sun had been full of vicissitudes. Maturing and gaining awareness and understanding was painful for her. Learning who she was had been a wandering path of complex moments and difficult decisions. She loved everything and everybody. She was a nurturing human being, whose love for life, for learning, for gathering wisdom, enjoying the sunlight and developing nurturing relationships was unsurpassed by all who knew her. She had wanted to please all, but had discovered the real truth—that one must please oneself first. She learned that she had to have so that she could give. Her life had been challenging, but she felt that she was a part of everything around her before she died. She had been a part of everything around her. She had found true peace and the meaning of true love. She had found her window to the sun.

About the Author

Dr. Lisa Whatley, Ph.D., was born in Rio de Janeiro, Brazil where she spent most of her childhood and teenage years. She then lived in New York City for ten years and has resided in Denver, Colorado for the last 25 years. Dr. Whatley loves life and people. As a counselor, educator, school administrator, employer, and mother she understands keenly the inborn need of every human being to learn, to comprehend the meaning of life, and to cope with its vicissitudes. She attended lower and middle school at a Catholic educational entity and has had the opportunity to observe the struggle that many people go through to reconcile their emotional needs with their religious beliefs. Dr. Whatley, like her heroine, in this book, believes in understanding, forgiving, forgetting and loving without conditions.

Dr. Whatley holds a Ph.D. in education administration from Colorado State University and is the recipient of many education awards. Her first book, <u>Life-Long Learning Through Vocational Education: The Path of the Snake</u> explores her experiences in education from the age of five to the present. It has won an award from the Colorado Independent Publishers Association (CIPA), in 1998, and is available at local bookstores, Amazon.Com on the Internet, or directly from Whatley Publishing, 899 Pearl Street, Unit 4, Denver, Colorado 80203.